What if..?

By Claire Burns

To my cherished family, whose steadfast love and support have been my guiding compass through life's journey.

To all the remarkable women embarking on their quest for purpose and understanding, may your journey be filled with hope, enlightenment and empowerment.

To Dad and Dove, my sincerest apologies for the swearing.

Chapter 1

The phone call

Monday, 1st June

Monday morning, seven forty-five, and Rachel already had a ladder in her tights. Frustratingly, she had had to stand for the whole of her 20-minute tube journey, which was when she spotted the hosiery horror. The train had been stationary for ten minutes, just outside her station and Rachel was now late. Despite the discomfort of new shoes, she disembarked nimbly and sidestepped the slow-walking tourists who foolishly chose to sightsee in London during peak times. She avoided the uniformed children loudly chatting whilst tapping their mobile phones and consuming more than the annual sugar supply of an ordinary person before starting school. These interactions compounded her already foul mood. She hastily scaled the steps and exited Sloane Square station.

"Seriously? Are you kidding!"

The heavens had opened, and it was pelting with rain. Rachel dodged the downpour as much as she could, but the huge drops drenched her at an oddly horizontal angle as she ran to her office. She arrived sopping wet and fuming, taking the lift to the seventh floor.

"Why, oh why, did I wear new shoes today?" she protested as she hobbled into the office.

"Morning, Rach," said Christie as she removed her wet coat and put it on the back of her chair.

"Morning."

Rachel dumped her wet belongings on her desk and grabbed a few things from the drawer. Thankfully, she was prepared for mornings like these; she had a spare pair of fifteen deniers, a comfier pair of shoes, heel plasters, lipstick, and paracetamol.

"God, I've got to dry my hair now," she groaned, dashing past Christie, overlooking her friend's appearance.

To see if she could cheer Rachel up, Christie followed her into the Ladies' to 'conveniently' check her makeup. Rachel turned off the wall-mounted hairdryer in astonishment.

"Blimey! What have you done to your hair?"

"Do you like it?" Christie replied, giving a twirl, happy that Rachel had noticed. "I decided to do something a little wacky."

"Well, I think you've achieved the desired effect!" exclaimed Rachel. "Unbelievable, I didn't think hair could go that colour!"

"It's called vivid vermillion red."

Rachel stood in bewilderment, bare-legged, with a brush in one hand and the hairdryer in the other. Her long brown wavy hair had nearly returned to its pre-downpour style, and the bright red lipstick she'd applied had refreshed her face. Even with her shoes off, she stood tall, possessing an athletic body from years of fitness. Never trying too hard, she appeared professional in her tailored charcoal grey skirt, white shirt and mink-coloured short-sleeved jumper.

"That's remarkable, Christie. It takes real guts to do that. I love it!"

"Thanks," Christie beamed, checking her reflection in the mirror again. "Well, as a celebration for my new hair and possibly a way to improve your shit mood, I made my famous cheese scones last night. Do you want one?"

"Ooh, you star, that is exactly what I need right now."

"You've got your call this morning, haven't you?" Christie asked.

"Yes, Bob said he'd call me at 10 a.m., so I'll have time to eat your gorgeous scones. I still need to get the recipe off you."

"I'm going to get a coffee. Do you want one?" Christie asked as she left the Ladies', assuming the answer was yes.

"Yes, please!" Rachel shouted through the closing door.

She finished drying her hair, applied the heel plasters and put on new tights. She checked her lipstick and took two paracetamol. She wished she hadn't had three large glasses of Merlot last night, although she'd enjoyed it at the time. That was the trouble with Sunday nights; she wanted the weekend to last that little bit longer, but it always played havoc with Monday mornings. She put on her patent shoes, returned to her desk and sat down.

Logging onto her computer, she checked her email: 37

unread messages. Although she'd checked her inbox over the weekend, she'd missed several flagged messages from her colleague Rick in Boston. He must've worked on Sunday. She'd need to attend to those this morning before he got online.

"Voila!" Christie placed a colossal cheese scone wrapped in a napkin and a large cup of coffee on Rachel's desk.

Rachel raised her head, breaking her concentration. "Oh, thanks, you're too kind. That looks yummy."

"You're welcome," Christie smiled.

Rachel took a sip of the sweet black coffee and a nibble of the scone."Oh, God, these are delicious!" Rachel exclaimed. The carbs and paracetamol kicked in, and she felt much better.

For the last nine months, Rachel had worked for Luxur Media in Knightsbridge as a Senior Design Consultant and had always been highly driven. Having joined the agency three years ago from Accenture, she'd asked to move around to get a broad and deep knowledge of media advertising. Working her way up from Marketing Consultant when she joined, to a Digital Marketing position, her accelerated development had caught the management's attention. Studying Business Management at Southampton University, she'd always enjoyed advertising. Her love of art, which she'd gained at an early age, coupled with her strong interest in brand strategy, meant she had her eyes set on another promotion.

"Good weekend?" she asked her friend.

Christie sat across from Rachel and bit into her scone. She waved her hands animatedly and pointed to her mouth, implying that she couldn't talk momentarily as she needed to swallow her food. Rachel giggled, knowing that she'd deliberately asked at that very moment to annoy her. She nodded, returned to her computer, and reviewed her emails again.

"It was quiet," Christie finally responded, licking her lips. "Although I met this really nice guy in the pub on Friday night. Trouble was he was like twenty-two, and I've told myself recently that I shouldn't go for younger men anymore."

"You're not getting morals, are you?" Rachel asked sarcastically.

Christie had just taken a second bite of her scone, so when she laughed, she sprayed small cheesy bits all over the desk. "Oh, bugger!" she said through the crumbs, standing up and wiping the desk.

Rachel laughed as she picked up her napkin and cleaned her desk. "So, what was he like?" she enquired, taking another sip of her coffee.

"He was lovely. He looked a lot like Finn, actually, tall, black hair, blue eyes, and a strong Irish accent."

"It's always the accent, isn't it?" Rachel smiled.

After a pause, giving her time to finish her mouthful, Christie continued. "His name is Aidan, and he's from Dublin. He'd come to London to watch the rugby. He's gorgeous."

"And?"

"He bought me a few drinks, we chatted, I gave him a cuddle, and we said our goodbyes."

Rachel raised an eyebrow.

"Well, I would've invited him back to my place, but he was with friends and going to another pub."

"I knew it! You shameless hussy!" Rachel exclaimed.

"Why do you think I dyed my hair the following day and did some home baking?" Christie laughed.

Rachel chuckled, forgetting her morning misfortunes. At that moment, the phone rang. She picked up the handset, "Rachel Logan speaking...."

"Hi Rachel, it's Bob Coleman from Head Office. Is it convenient to talk?"

Rachel's eyes opened, and she stared at Christie, pointing to the handset, silently communicating that this was the phone call she was expecting, but he was early! Christie mouthed the words *'good luck'* and turned her attention to her computer screen.

"Of course, Bob. How are you?"

"Shit, Rach," Christie gushed, "that's such great news! I'm so happy for you."

Rachel exhaled slowly and kicked off her patent shoes. She glanced at her phone, 9:32 a.m. It was too early to phone Finn, as he would still be in his morning meetings. How would she tell him? *'Hey, Honey, you won't believe this: I'm in the running for the Senior Brand Strategist role.'* Or, *'Honey, we might be moving to Boston!'* No, she needed to say it straight. *'I'm closer than ever to my dream job.'*

"I think I need another coffee."

"Coffee?! You should be getting champagne!" Christie added, clapping.

"Oh, it's far too early for that!" Rachel laughed. Yet, it was certainly something to celebrate. "Would you like one?"

"No, thanks, I'm good."

Rachel walked to the coffee machine and selected the double espresso with one sugar. Listening to the machine grind the beans and squirt the hot water into the mug, she contemplated the phone call. The news hadn't properly hit her yet. Grabbing her coffee, she returned to her desk. She sat in her chair, rotated it slowly to look over Cadogan Hall, and caught her breath.

Two months ago, she had come across the role profile on the HR intranet. It described a position requiring a self-motivated, creative, conscientious, strategic, and problem-solving achiever. And she wanted it. Badly. After weeks of preparation for the presentation, the interview went well, and now she was even closer to the prize. She was shortlisted to the last two for the role, with an interview in a few weeks. Wow! She couldn't wait to tell Finn. The idea of moving to the U.S. would be so exciting for them both. For the last year, they'd talked about stretching their wings and significantly changing their lives. Surely this was it? She'd risen through the ranks within the company, and this was her chance to branch out into a more corporate arena and a more substantial part of the organisation. It was all she'd ever wanted for her career, and she had it firmly in her sights.

"Have you spoken to Finn yet?" Christie asked.

"No, he's still in his morning meetings, and I don't want to interrupt him." She glanced at her watch, then Christie, and beamed and exhaled, "I'm so excited!"

"You should be! You're one step closer, at least. I know you can't call him, but could you text him?"

"Shit! I can text him. What was I thinking?"

Rachel grabbed her phone off the desk just as it buzzed.

> Hey - can you talk?

She froze for a second and re-read the message. It was Ellie. Why did Ellie want to talk now? Was she OK?

"Sorry, Christie. I have to take this." Rachel quickly put on her shoes and walked briskly away, trying to find an empty meeting room. However, they were all taken. She walked to the Ladies', texting Ellie en route.

> What's up?

As she entered the toilets, she texted Finn too.

> Hey babe, let me know when you're free.
> No panic. Got some great news.

Another text came in from Ellie.

> Can you talk now? I could do with a chat.

Rachel couldn't remember what time it was in Greece. What did her friend want? She called Ellie's number as she found herself a cubicle in the toilets for privacy.

"Hey."

"Hey, you. What's up? Are you OK?"

"I…just…needed…" Ellie broke down on the phone, deep sobbing with little time between breaths. "TT, it's happened again."

Inconsolable weeping flowed out of Rachel's phone. She froze. "Ellie? What do you mean? I don't understand." Panic started to set in. Rachel grabbed her face with the hand not holding her phone. The phone buzzed, but she didn't hear it. What could she do to help her best friend?

"Again…it's happened again," Ellie slowly managed to articulate over sobs, cries, breaths and sniffles.

Rachel put the lid down on the toilet seat and sat with a heavy heart. She opened her eyes, stared at the sterile white light that shone down from the ceiling and blinked repeatedly. It suddenly dawned on her. She must hold back the tears. "Oh, I am so, so, so sorry, Ellie."

"I can't believe it. How can it have happened again?" Ellie asked.

"You didn't tell me you were pregnant. What happened?" Rachel asked and then panicked. "Are you OK? Well, of course, you're not OK. But are you OK, if you know what I mean…"

"I know, I didn't tell you. I had my reasons. But I'm O… K…," Ellie said very quietly. There was a long period of silence. Neither wanted to interrupt it, and the silence seemed as important as talking.

"When?" Rachel asked, "Is Gino there?"

"Yes, he's been with me the whole time, thank God," Ellie quietly offered. "It happened three weeks ago. I don't know what I would've done if he'd been away."

"What can I do?" Rachel asked, slowly wiping her tears away. Her stomach started to stir; was it yesterday's Merlot, the overdose of caffeine and heavy carbs this morning, the job news, or this? "Have you told Alice?"

Ellie continued to sob, and Rachel felt the pain transfer through the phone. It was real, and it was profound. "I'm coming to see you." She knew her friend needed her. Why else would she have called?

"What?"

"I need to hug you, to tell you that it's going to be OK. Let me sort out a few logistics, and then I'll be over."

"Are you sure?" Ellie's voice strengthened a little.

"Absolutely."

Rachel's phone buzzed, and she ignored it. Her brain raced as she figured out how to get to Ellie at the next opportunity. She needed to speak to Finn, he'd help her make sense of all this. He'd tell her what was best to do. She also needed to talk to her boss about getting some time off, and then she needed to consider the job offer. Shit! She needed to think about that. "Ellie, can I ring you back? I will find a way to get over to see you soon."

"Thanks, TT," Ellie sniffled, "I just needed to speak to you. I haven't told Alice yet."

"Do you want me to tell her?" Rachel automatically blurted out.

"No, please, I'll call her now," Ellie replied timidly.

"Just let me know if there is anything I can do, honestly. And let me know when you've spoken to Alice. I'll try to organise for us both to come and see you."

"I love you," Ellie sobbed down the phone.

"I love you, too. I'll ring you back as soon as I've spoken to Finn and sorted out work. You won't need to do this on your own."

Rachel took a deep breath and exhaled. Silences with Ellie were never awkward.

"Bye," Ellie said quietly and hung up.

Rachel let her phone fall onto her lap, hung her head and dropped her shoulders. Poor, poor Ellie, that was her second miscarriage in as many years. She hadn't even told Rachel she was pregnant. What on earth must she be feeling? She must be devastated. She wanted to see her friend so much that she would find a way to visit her.

Her phone buzzed again. She picked it up and saw two messages from Finn.

> I will be free in 2 mins x
>
> Am free now x

She called Finn and walked out of the toilet. She quickly checked her makeup in the mirror and wiped away some rogue mascara. "Hey, sorry I didn't get back to you sooner, I was on the phone with Ellie."

"Ellie? I thought you were speaking to Bob. It's 10 o'clock. Actually, I was surprised to get your text. I thought you'd be on the phone with him. What's the great news?"

"Oh God, it's terrible news, Finn, poor Ellie," Rachel stared at herself in the mirror, "she's had another miscarriage." The line went quiet.

"Oh fuck," Finn whispered.

"I need to go to Greece and see her."

"Is Gino with her?"

"Yes, thank God."

"Does she have any other friends to lean on?"

"I didn't ask. I'm still in shock." Rachel wiped her eyes again and turned away from the mirror. "I'm sure there are, but I just need to see her. I need to speak to Alice, too."

"Whatever you need to do, Babes. Perhaps I'll call Gino."

"I think that's a great idea. I'm sure he is reeling, too. I will need to speak to Joanna about getting a few days off. Oh! I got through to the final interview stage."

"What?"

"Yeah, I had my call a bit earlier than planned, and Bob told me I'm through."

"So that's the great news? Well done!" Finn said cheerfully, then realised, "But then you got Ellie's news.

Fuck, what a morning. Are you OK?"

"Not sure right now. Can we chat later? I have a few things to think through. Can I call you at lunchtime?"

"Sure, I can imagine. As I said, whatever you need to do. Well done, though, Babes, I knew you'd get it. Love you."

"Love you too, Honey."

Chapter 2

Feel the pressure

Tuesday, 2nd June

Ellie folded the clean laundry and gazed out the open window at the sparkling sea. The dusk light was catching the pulsing water, making her smile. The smell of the warm air mixed with the fresh linen was comforting. Coming to Greece was the best thing she'd ever done. It had given her time to reflect on her life choices, and this was definitely one of her best. It was a million miles away from where she used to live in the U.K. with her great-aunt. That home resembled Satis House, the home of Miss Haversham in 'Great Expectations'. It was a dusty, aged, and sterile shell occupied by a wealthy, elderly spinster who provided a roof over Ellie's head and food on the table but had no maternal instincts. And that was when she wasn't at boarding school.

The lack of a loving and nurturing home meant that Ellie had brought herself up and learned to fend for herself. At the time, she was grateful for the freedom but craved guidance. Having no close family, she gravitated to Rachel's and the Templetons treated her like their daughter. Ellie and Rachel used to spend the school holidays riding around on their bikes, making perfume from the neighbour's prize-winning roses that stained their wrists and necks and getting tarot readings from Alice's mother. She'd dealt with a lot as a young girl, and Rachel and Alice had always been there for her. She was so happy they were coming over and that she'd have time to share her new life in Greece with them; to show them how far she'd come and how she'd been able to create a beautiful home that was fresh, vibrant, and charming. The past few weeks had been so hard, and it was going to be a relief to cry and emotionally release with them; they were always good at letting her deflate.

"Ellie, where are you?" Gino called from the hallway.

"I'm in the spare room, just putting away some washing."

Gino entered, and Ellie saw that he'd been crying. "What's wrong?" she asked with concern as she dropped the pillowcases she was folding onto the bed. She walked over to him and gave him a tender hug. "Gino?"

Gino sank into her embrace and buried his face in her neck. Ellie held the moment and gently tightened her squeeze, feeling his heart beating and warm breath on her skin. She loved this man immensely. They'd been through so much lately, and she was saddened to see her strong soulmate so upset. Gino gently pulled away from Ellie and wiped his eyes. He pulled her hair back from her shoulders and kissed her sweetly on the neck.

"Ti amo. You're a superstar."

"I love you too," she said, gazing into his red eyes lovingly. "It's all too much, isn't it?"

"It really is," he replied. "I was just preparing dinner, and it blindsided me. It felt like a punch. It knocked me off my feet." He walked over to the open window and leaned against the frame. He visibly exhaled, and Ellie thought he looked tired.

"I know exactly what you mean. It just comes as a wave of emotion and physically impacts you. I thought it was just my body recovering from the pregnancy, but that has passed now, and the pain is still there."

Gino focused on her and smiled. "You're so strong. I don't know how you do it. Where does it come from? I know you went through a lot growing up, but this strength you show is something else."

"Hmm," Ellie swallowed, "I've had to deal with a lot of death in my lifetime. But this is different. This has blame. I'm having to deal with whether I caused the deaths of our babies. There was nothing I could do to save my parents. That was just a terrible accident."

"Oh, mia cara," Gino whispered as he moved quickly towards Ellie and hugged her gently, "Please do not think that. It was not your fault. It wasn't meant to be, no?"

"I know that now, but it's taking me time to come to terms with that. That's why I fell apart yesterday and had to speak to Rachel. It's going to be good to talk to the girls. I think it will help a lot." She focused on Gino, then opened her eyes wide. "Oh, sorry, I didn't mean it like that. You know that you're my everything. It's just that I can dump on Rachel, which I don't want to do to you. You've enough to be going through. I can use Rachel for that." Ellie twisted her hair between her fingers, "Oh God, that's not what I mean; I won't use Rachel. I want to talk to her and Alice and use them as a sounding board to clarify my thoughts." Her eyes started to fill with tears, and Gino offered another reassuring hug. She accepted it quickly, and they held their embrace.

"It's alright," he said, "I know what you mean. I get it."

She wiped her eyes and pursed her lips. "I think spending some time with Rachel and Alice will be good. It will be a nice distraction and allow us to vent completely about our feelings."

He started towards the bedroom door. "Let's discuss it over dinner. I think it'll be good, too."

"Let me finish here, wash my hands and then I'll be down."

"OK, I'll serve up. Should be ready in 5."

Gino left and Ellie went back to folding the laundry. She had lost her parents when she was seven and hadn't recalled their horrific, fatal car crash for years. She'd dealt with that long ago and laid it firmly to rest. Her Italian therapist had helped her overcome the fear of death, teaching her to accept that death happens to everyone, including herself. Managing to conquer the thought that what had happened to her parents wasn't her fault, she'd applied her learnings to how she felt about her baby. Her beautiful baby wasn't meant to be on this earth; she was playing amongst the stars with her big brother. Void of tears, she stared out the window and let her eyes survey the sky. Sunset was fast approaching, and the stars were awakening.

"Sleep sound, my lovelies, shine brightly and know you're both in my heart."

Bloated on lamb moussaka and Mediterranean salad, Ellie sat back in her wicker seat on the veranda and sipped a glass of cold white wine.

"When do Rachel and Alice arrive?" asked Gino.

"Thursday. I think about lunchtime," she replied.

"Are you sure you're up for doing this?"

"Do you know what? I am." Ellie took another sip of her wine. "It hit me yesterday that I needed to speak to Rachel. I needed to feel her energy, and Rach, being Rach, put a plan in place. She will help me find comfort; that is what she does. Alice will ground me. They give me so much strength. I think it will be good to talk everything through with them. We share so much history. There is so much I don't need to explain or tip-toe around. It wasn't the same with your family."

Gino sat back in his seat and exhaled. Ellie watched him and frowned a little. "Are you OK with them coming?" she asked. "I wouldn't have agreed to it if you weren't." She sat forward in her seat and placed her wine glass on the table.

"No, it's fine," he said. "You're right. When my family was here, it felt awkward. I felt claustrophobic. They were trying to help but didn't. It felt too soon after…" he looked across at Ellie and swallowed, the emotion clear on his face. "I think seeing them will be good for you and us. Perhaps I could organise a short charter for a few days so you can spend some exclusive time together out on the water."

"But what about you?"

"I've got some work to do, which may mean I'm away, so it would help me that someone is looking after you." They looked at each other and smiled. "I only found out today, and I wasn't going to go. But because Rachel and Alice are here to be with you, I accepted. It will only be for Friday night and Saturday." He ran his hand through his hair and scratched his chin. "There will be a stage where I must work out the new normal. I'm here for you, you know that, but I need to work out where my head is at. How do we progress from this? What do I do about the future? I know these are massive questions, but it's been so turned on its head now that I need to think about my direction."

She looked across at him and sighed. Since they'd married four years ago, he'd always said he would support her financially and that she'd have nothing to worry about. He would take all the responsibility of earning money so they could buy and renovate this beautiful villa. Choosing to pause her career in interior design to have children was what they'd always discussed, but it had been a few years since she'd last worked, and she wondered what the future would hold. He'd been such a rock for her after they'd moved to Greece. She wanted to support him, but they hadn't gotten to that part yet.

"I don't want this to burden you," Gino continued, "We always agreed you could take the time to do what you wanted, and I stick by that. I'm just not so sure about me. Where is my business going? Where do I take its direction? Am I now allowed to put more time and effort into my work now that I don't need to be here with you and...the baby?" Gino gulped, visibly affected.

Ellie reached over to him and clasped his hand. "It's OK."

"See? It's these crazy moments where it just floors you, no?" he clamped his hands over his face and exhaled.

Ellie chose not to say anything. She knew how he felt and understood his pain. They would need to think about their future soon. What would it hold? But they were not ready yet.

"Ever since we lost the baby," he said, "I've been trying to understand why. Why did it happen to us? Why did it happen - twice, for God's sake? I missed our first baby so much, and now another. Am I a bad person? Did I bring this on myself? What could I have done better? Should I have adamantly told you not to do the villa and take it on myself? Is this some strange karma for working too hard? Should we have come to Greece in the first place?"

"What?" exclaimed Ellie. "You're not a bad person, Gino. Not at all. This is not your fault. You've done nothing wrong. It was my medical problems; this is not on you. And what do you mean? Don't you want to be in Greece?"

"No, no, no. That's not what I'm saying. I love it here, and I love that you love it here. I'm just starting to realise the effect of the whole situation. After the event, no? It just hit me this evening, and I'm reeling in the aftermath."

"Do you want me to cancel Rachel and Alice? I don't mind. I didn't realise you were going through these types of work dilemmas. I'm so sorry. I should've been more perceptive." Her eyes welled up with tears, and she wiped them away.

"Oh, mia amore, it's OK," he grabbed her hand this time, "We're both here for each other. We get each other. We always have. But I think we're coping with things at different times, and I'm only now allowing myself to look beyond the immediate sadness and think about the future and what I need to do." He pensively looked out to sea, staring at the moonlight dancing on the undulating water. The gentle rhythm increased his contemplative mood.

"Are you happy here, Gino?"

"Sorry?" he turned his head gently and returned his focus to Ellie.

"Are you happy to be here in Greece? Or would you like to be back home in Sicily?"

"No, I love it here. However, I do miss my parents. But they'd never leave the island, and I'd outgrown it. My business means I can be here, and managing the properties is much easier if I can visit the mainland. But I need to think if this is the best direction for me now."

"I think it'll be good for you to speak to Finn. It's a shame that he isn't coming over, too. Perhaps you could call him when Rachel is here? To talk about the work-life balance. He's spent the last few years working remotely and finds it easy and flexible. That's why they've aimed to go to Boston."

"But that is a bit radical, no?" he asked, "She doesn't have any family over there, nor does Finn."

"Yes, but you know what Rach is like. She's shooting for the big job and the big bucks. It's an opportunity to show her family that she's made it. I can't believe how competitive the Templeton family are. James is making big profits in London, and Tom has just sold his business. Rachel feels the pressure to succeed."

"I hope Finn is happy with her corporate hunger," Gino added. "He has such high expectations of Rachel. He's always seen her as a winner and someone with a clear path to success. He's so lucky to have a job that allows him to work where he chooses, but Boston is far away. I must drop him a note."

"The Logan family is so different from the Templeton family. I think that is why Rachel was attracted to Finn in the first place. He's a gentle, compassionate soul who strongly supports her but lets her be the powerful woman she is. He also doesn't do conflict, which Rachel loves. Especially after years of arguing with her mother through her late teens."

"She's such a headstrong woman; whatever she chooses, I hope Finn isn't disappointed," Gino said. "He emailed me some time back to tell me about his career direction and that he was talking about diversifying when they were in the U.S., so perhaps all is good."

"Rach is certainly steering this decision," Ellie added as

she took another sip of her wine.

"It would be nice to have them both here, no? It has been a long time since the four of us last got together. I will say that to Finn. I'll organise a charter for you and the girls. Rachel will love that. I don't want you to spend time alone just yet. Is that OK?"

"Oh, Honey, you're the best. That would be great. I appreciate your understanding."

He stood up and started stacking the plates and clearing the table. Ellie finished her glass of wine and stood up, too. "Let's get an early night," she said as she smiled at Gino.

"That would be lovely. How about a little snuggle, too?" Gino replied with a wink. He leant over to her and gave her a tantalising, slow kiss.

Chapter 3

Don't deal with this on your own

Thursday, 4th June

Rachel paid the driver, grabbed her small suitcase and handbag from the seat next to her and jumped out of the taxi. Alice exited the taxi from the other side with her luggage. They headed towards the beautiful steps of the Mediterranean villa. Ellie stood in the doorway barefooted in a long, flowing white skirt with a white shawl around her slim shoulders and her long, wavy hair tied up in a messy ponytail. She'd been crying. Rachel and Alice ran towards her, dropping all their belongings on the step and moved to hug Ellie.

"God, Ellie, I'm so, so sorry," Rachel spluttered as she

maintained the three-way, heartfelt embrace. It was gentle and sincere and much needed.

Rachel had tears streaming down her face before she'd even left the taxi, and the vision of her friend looking so frail at the entrance to this spectacular building moved her immensely. She'd desperately wanted to appear strong and had been going through a speech for the whole journey from the airport to Ellie's villa. She'd asked Alice how she should start the conversation. *'It's going to be OK, Ellie... You and Gino have years to have a family... You're such a strong woman. You can get through this... There are many options available to you both.'* Alice advised that it was best to let Ellie talk and listen without judgment, pointing out that they'd all been best friends from a young age, their relationship was naturally intuitive, and they would work it out.

The three women remained in their embrace and didn't pull away. Although Ellie was not crying yet, Rachel could feel her body slowly relax in her arms and knew that their show of affection would soon cause the tears to fall. Ellie pulled away and adjusted her shawl and hair, which had slipped from its ponytail.

"Thanks so much for coming. Are you sure you were both able to get away?"

"It's a welcome break, sister," Alice added, "And a pleasure to be here. This place is gorgeous."

Ellie reached down to pick up the discarded luggage.

"Hey, stop that!" Rachel corrected, wiping away her tears as she pushed Ellie's hand away. "You aren't picking up anything heavy, OK? You need rest, and Nurse Rachel will see to it, alright?"

"Nurse Rachel?" Alice laughed as she picked up her suitcase.

"Yeah, Nurse Rachel?" Ellie chuckled. "You can't stand the sight of blood; you're rubbish with needles, and blue is so not your colour. You aren't going to be of any use at all!"

"Well, I can get you things?"

Rachel grinned as she reached down to pick up her handbag. The contents had fallen out when she dropped it earlier, and her phone, lipstick, paracetamol, passport, pens, tissues, wallet and keys were strewn across the porch. She quickly swept them into her bag and picked up her suitcase. She stood bolt upright and saw Gino appear from over Ellie's shoulder. He seemed weary and sad.

"Rachel, il mio Bell'amico. Thank you for being here. My lovely Alice, welcome."

He sincerely and softly embraced Alice and then Rachel for what felt like a long time. Ellie placed her hand tenderly on the two of them. Rachel recognised that she needed to hold it together.

"So, where's my room?" Rachel pulled away and blinked away the tears.

"Shit, TT, manners!" Alice added.

"Crap, TT, you don't change, do you?" Ellie wiped her face and smiled as she led them into the villa. "This way."

Gino listened to the women's familiar loquacious tones and was so happy they were together in their villa. It had been such a terrible period for his beautiful wife, and it would be lovely for her to spend time with her friends. He'd tried his best to console her, but she'd been so devastated that he believed she would only find reassurance from this enduring and loyal sisterhood.

His parents and two brothers had come to visit as soon as they'd heard the devastating news. Gina and Ellie had only told them and a few local friends. Their visit was meant to be comforting, but the villa felt crowded, and he couldn't relax. His brothers helped him with his work so he could focus on Ellie, and they organised food to be delivered to the villa for everyone instead of cooking, which felt awkward. Their well-intended support was infiltrating their grief. Ellie had returned from the hospital a vacant woman, and his parents, especially his mother, did not know how to help her. Ellie stayed in bed and didn't spend any time with them. After a few days, they agreed that he should spend time with Ellie, expressed their condolences, and left. Dealing with his own grief had been secondary to comforting Ellie, and hopefully, Rachel and Alice would provide a distraction so that Gino could come to terms with the loss of his daughter. As he thought about this, he started to cry. It was perfect that they were here; he had to focus on getting his strength back.

Rachel followed Ellie and Alice and surveyed all aspects of the stunning villa. It was so beautiful.

"This is your room, Alice. Towels are in the bathroom."

"Thanks, Ellie. I need to go pee."

"This way for you, TT."

They walked into a stunning room at the back of the villa. The view of the sea through the massive open window was magnificent, and it took Rachel's breath away. Gino joined them and brought in two glasses of ice-cold water. She turned, took one, nodded, and smiled, and he put the other one on the side.

"Mille grazie."

Taking a long sip, she recalled her planned conversation in the taxi. How would she start the conversation with Ellie? Nervous, she defaulted to small talk.

"Did you decorate this place or was it like this when you arrived?" she asked as she inspected the bedroom.

Gino left the room quietly as Alice entered and picked up the glass of water from the side.

Ellie stared out of the window. "No, we've done this," she said and then went quiet. She stared at Rachel and Alice. They held each other's gaze in silence.

Ellie sighed as she and Alice sat on the bed.

"What happened?" Rachel asked gently as she sat on the bed.

"I woke up in the middle of the night with terrible cramps and had to run to the toilet. I knew what it was, and there was so much blood. I've never seen so much. I yelled to Gino, and he came running in. Gino and I both knew that we'd lost her. We didn't need a doctor to tell us. We were on borrowed time. We knew. He called for an ambulance, and the rest was a blur." She paused, and Rachel and Alice remained quiet. "I went to the hospital and went into labour. I had to deliver the baby."

Rachel gulped and had to look away so Ellie couldn't see her tears.

"Fuck," Alice whispered.

Ellie didn't look at them but stood up and walked over to the window. She folded her arms into her chest and breathed out hard. "Gino's folks are telling me that I need to move on with my life and that I'll have another baby someday. That is so unfair. I want that baby! They don't understand." She burst into tears and covered her face with her hands.

Alice stood up and rushed towards her, grabbing and hugging her, trying not to be physically inconsiderate as she didn't know if she was still fragile. "Fucking ignore them! Don't listen to what anyone else is saying. It's your life and your body. You feel exactly the way you want when you want. I can't even imagine how hard this has been for you."

"Do you know what the worst thing is?" Ellie said, trying to stay strong.

Rachel and Alice remained quiet as they understood the rhetoric. They knew Ellie needed to verbalise her thoughts and let out what was in her heart.

"That I don't have her in my arms. I had her in my womb for twenty-one weeks. I felt every move she made. I could feel her growing inside me. But now I've nothing. I've nothing in my womb and nothing in my arms. I've no birthdays to celebrate, no cuddles to be had, no toys to play with, no bedtime books to read." Her body slumped as if it had consumed all of its energy and was too exhausted for tears to fall. "After losing my first baby, I thought I'd never be happy again. That experience was just so hard to overcome, but I did. We did. We managed to work through that, and I got pregnant again. We were so happy. But look at what's happened. She's gone, too." She started to cry again with deep-rooted agony.

Rachel's tears flowed, too. She stared at Alice for help. They both knew how hard Ellie's first miscarriage had been, but they had no idea how to deal with this. How on earth can you cope with two miscarriages in the space of as many years? Alice went to the bathroom and returned with plenty of toilet roll.

Ellie had been ten weeks pregnant when she lost her first baby, yet she didn't tell Rachel and Alice until months later. Both friends were devastated that she hadn't. It still haunted Rachel that her best friend had taken on the weight of such an emotional experience and not shared it. Why would you keep that heartache secret? Rachel tried to understand the loss that someone has when such a horrific event happens, so she researched miscarriages and stillbirths, giving her the knowledge that people never get over losing a baby. It's your child. You made it. At the time, all Rachel could offer Ellie was an understanding ear, a limitless number of hugs, and the promise that she would support her through her sadness. She would not let her shut down. But how would her friend cope? Losing an unborn child is agonising. She vowed to always be there for her friend, hoping the event would never happen again. Yet here it was.

"I'm so sorry to be such a mess," Ellie said, blowing her nose with the tissue Alice handed to her.

"Shit, Ellie, not at all," Alice responded, "That's why we're here."

"Exactly," added Rachel.

"Actually, I've had so much from Gino's family lately. Could we not talk about this now?"

"Of course," Rachel said. "We're here for a few days, so we can talk about it whenever you want."

"Thank you."

"When did they leave?"

"Two days ago."

"Ellie, you should have said," Alice apologised.

"Honestly, it's not a problem,"

"Oh goodness, I didn't know. I'm sorry you have more guests," Rachel added.

"That is what we call in the industry a TT railroad," Alice chuckled.

"What do you mean?" asked Rachel indignantly.

"When she's got a plan, it's a plan, right?" Ellie giggled and high-fived Alice.

"Listen, I came here because I wanted to see you and tell you I love you and that you don't need to deal with this on your own."

"Well, you can do the laundry then," Alice laughed as she walked around the bedroom.

Ellie smiled and adjusted her hair; having friends with her was fabulous. They always made her feel whole. The mood could change in a heartbeat.

"This place is stunning, Ellie. I can see why you love it so much," said Alice.

"When Gino and I first came over from Sicily, we wanted to make the house as personal as possible but were bowled over by the Greek styling, so we decided to embrace that. We went for the stereotypical Mediterranean theme. We haven't shipped all the furniture yet, but I think it'll be complete once it's all here and will properly feel like home."

Rachel surveyed the room, which was decorated in a deep terracotta with aquamarine blue detail and a cool grey flagstone floor. The huge bed, placed centrally in the space, was very feminine, with oceans of white lace and pillows. The windows were curtain-less, just blue shutters outside that framed the view and dozens of half-burnt candles that lay along the windowsill. An evocative salty smell wafted up from the sea, mixed with a fragrance that Rachel could not quite place. She noticed a wicker table and drawers in the corner of the room, so she opened her suitcase and started to unpack.

"I think you've captured it," Alice said.

"You mean you've decorated all this in the last few months?" Rachel asked incredulously.

"Yeah. I wanted to get it just right. You know what I'm like," Ellie sighed and contemplated the view through the window. "I wanted this to be the main bedroom because of the fabulous view and the olive trees. The aroma captured me the first time I visited Greece; this room always smells of them."

That was the smell that Rachel could not place. Having nature outside your window was much better than pollution, noise and traffic; she could get used to this.

"But in the end, we chose the larger one towards the front of the villa, next to your room, Alice. Gino loves waking up to the sunrise that comes in through that window."

Alice noticed that Ellie's concentration was drifting and that she was thoughtlessly playing with the tassels on the delicate bedding. "How are you holding up?" she asked, joining her on the bed. "I can only imagine how tough this has been, but don't you think you've been overdoing it? I mean, this is a hell of a lot of work you've done." Alice reached her hand up to Ellie's face, delicately taking one of her long, brown curls, which had fallen out of her ponytail, and put it behind her ear. "You know that you shouldn't have been decorating. You should've been resting."

Slowly, Ellie started to cry again. Alice and Rachel stared at each other. They knew they couldn't keep having Ellie break down in tears; they needed to dilute the emotion.

"Ellie, you've got snot running out of your nose," Rachel smirked.

Ellie's reaction was to burst out laughing as she ran to the en-suite, where she washed her face and blew her nose. Alice and Rachel looked at each other and gestured to say they needed to lift the mood. There was a clattering from the en-suite, and Alice called out,

"You alright in there?"

"Yeah, I'm fine," sniffled Ellie as she walked out with a hand towel. "I think I need to get you a new towel, TT. I've got this one covered in bogies!"

Alice laughed and stared at Rachel.

"Absolutely, I don't want second-rate treatment here," Rachel laughed. "If I'd wanted green towels, I would've asked for them!"

They all smiled at each other, and Ellie knowingly grabbed their hands. "Thank you," she sighed and squeezed their hands harder. "Thank you for coming and for being here. It means a lot. If not just to have the piss taken out of me."

"Well, I'm here to serve!" said Rachel as she returned the hand squeeze, performed a mock curtsy, and pointed to Alice. "And she's here to be generally offensive."

"Fuck off, TT."

"See? Honestly, I can't take her anywhere."

"You fancy a drink?" Ellie asked as she threw the hand towel over her shoulder.

"I thought you'd never ask! You're a terrible host, you know," replied Rachel, leaving her unpacked suitcase and following them out of the room.

After a night of crying, chatting, and laughing with Ellie, Gino and Alice, Rachel lay in bed listening to the sea gently massaging the white sandy beach below her window. The rhythm was relaxing, and its power propelled the aroma of the olive trees and the combination of salt, seaweed and shellfish into her room. She understood why Ellie loved this place so much.

The evening had shown her how important it was to connect with the people she loved. Even through sadness, Ellie and Gino had started to rebuild their lives, and through hopes and dreams, they would find their direction again. Rachel and Alice spent most of the night just listening until the wine started to flow, and then they returned to their usual boisterous selves. Gino laughed at them as they joked around and, at the end of the evening, told them that he'd organised a charter for them to sail tomorrow. It was an opportunity for the women to get away for two nights. Rachel was ecstatic! Jumping up and down and hugging Gino, she couldn't believe he'd organised it. She and Alice could take Ellie away and take her mind off her grief. She thought this trip would be sad, but now she felt optimistic. She called Finn.

"Hey, Babes," said Finn, instantly picking up, "How are you?"

"Hi, Honey," Rachel loved Finn's soft Irish tones. "I'm good. It's been quite a day. Ellie and Gino are sad, but there is hope. We've had a lovely evening. I'm so glad Alice and I came out."

"How's Ellie holding up?"

"Devastated, obviously. Thankfully, she's physically OK, which is wonderful, but it will take time to heal mentally."

"And Gino?"

"He's trying desperately to support Ellie but needs to grieve for himself." Rachel started to cry. "Sorry, it's a bit emotional."

"I can only imagine. Is there anything I can do?"

"Letting me come away was the best thing you could've done. Thank you. Really."

"Jeez, it's not me letting you. I know you needed to do this. I'm having a chat with Gino tomorrow, actually, he wanted to discuss a few things with me. Hopefully, I can give him some moral support, too."

"You'll be amazed at how strong he is. Although, I'm not sure how much masking is going on there. I'm sure you'll get some truths out of him. Oh! You're not going to believe what he has managed to organise!"

"What?"

"We're picking up a charter in the morning to sail around for a few days. How amazing is that?"

"Wow!"

"I know! Honestly, Gino is such a star. He is heading off on business tomorrow, so he wanted us to take Ellie away and distract her. It's going to be some really special 'us' time."

"What a result! I'm jealous."

"I can't believe it. It is going to be amazing." She got up from the bed and walked to the window. Contemplating the evening, she watched the moonlight quivering on the sea. "One thing I did want to ask you, though,"

"Yes?"

"I need to talk about work."

"Joanna was fine with you taking a few days off, though, wasn't she?"

"Yes, she was fine. They gave me compassionate leave for a few days. But I'm thinking about Boston, Finn. I asked Bob when he thinks the final interview will take place, and he was going to email me in the next day or so as he has some annual leave coming up."

"Are you ready for it?"

"I am, but Ellie's news has genuinely knocked me for six. It has put a completely different lens on everything. It's made me think about mortality. What if I lost you, my parents, or my brothers? How would I cope with that?"

"Rach, you don't need to think about that now. Just be there for Ellie. Emotions will be running high, you know that. If you have a few days before the interview, we can talk when you get back," Finn reassured her, "Your mother rang today.

Has she been in touch?"

"Yes, I missed a call from her. I'll call her in the morning. You're right. I'm completely emotionally exhausted. Certainly not ready to deal with my mother right now."

"Well, get some rest, Babes, and hopefully, I'll speak to you in the morning. If not, have an amazing time on the charter. Send me pics."

"I'm not sure what time we're leaving. Gino said we needed to be up by 7 a.m. I'll try to call, and if not, I'll text."

"No worries. Love you."

"Love you too, Honey. Night."

Chapter 4

Nothing's gonna stop us now

Friday, 5th June

Waking early, the three women enjoyed a delicious breakfast made for them by Gino. Sitting at the table on the verandah, he told them their charter was to be picked up at 10 a.m., and he'd ordered a taxi. The sun shone brightly in the clear blue sky, and Rachel couldn't believe the view. The villa and verandah were high up on the hill and had uninterrupted sea views; you could see for miles. Dressed in cut-off shorts and a vest top, she watched the boats sailing out to sea and smiled. This whole experience was so different from where she had been on Monday.

"I've organised for provisions to be put on the boat, so

you should be good to go," Gino announced. "Georgios will help you with any questions. The charter is due back into the marina by noon on Sunday."

"We'll need to be back a bit earlier than that, Gino, as our flight is at 3 p.m.," Rachel replied.

"No worries, just mention that to Georgios."

"Thanks, Honey, you've outdone yourself again," Ellie smiled at Gino and hugged him.

"Taxi's here!" Alice yelled from the front of the villa, where she stood having a cigarette.

"Thank you so much, Gino," Rachel said, smiling.

"You are very welcome, mia amico. Now go and have some fun, no?"

Stepping onto the Sun Odyssey 50, Rachel beamed. It was a stunning yacht. She kicked off her flip-flops and wriggled her feet on the immaculate teak deck. A large spacious cockpit with twin steering wheels at the helm, tidy lines expertly stored, and a generous cockpit table that would house their gin and tonics perfectly lay ahead of her. She walked down below and discovered a living space with a galley kitchen, a comfortable saloon and three cabins, each with its own en-suite. The interior was finished in wood with cream leather cushions and dark brown suede fabric.

"Fuck me!" Alice said as she walked barefoot down the ladder. "This is ridiculous!"

"It's beautiful, is what it is," Rachel added.

"Bagsy the left front cabin."

"You mean the port side one?" Rachel corrected.

"Whatever."

"I think we should let Ellie have the Master Cabin."

"Of course," Alice replied as she entered the galley kitchen. "I'm going to see what supplies we have. Gino is so amazing."

Rachel went up the ladder to look for Ellie and found her talking to Georgios. Looking around the cockpit to familiarise herself with the equipment, she walked out to the bow of the boat to check the anchor line. The conditions were perfect. The water was still, and the wind was slowly starting to blow. It should be good by the afternoon.

"Is this to your satisfaction, Captain?" Ellie said as she approached Rachel.

"Oh, my goodness, Ellie, it's absolutely gorgeous!" Rachel exclaimed, hugging Ellie. "Vastly different from the old boats Tom and I used to sail out of Southampton. It must be brand new."

"It is. Since we only have it for a few days, Georgios managed to get one from the new fleet, as the season has only just started. He also said that he's put a few little surprises in our provisions."

"How did Gino organise this?" Rachel asked.

"He does property deals with the Marina's Management team, and he and Georgios go scuba diving together."

"He's the best; we're going to have a blast on this beauty."

"This boat is insane!" Alice said excitedly as she joined them at the bow. "Oh wow! Look at that view!"

She walked forward, and Rachel knew exactly what she was going to do. Rachel tapped Ellie on the arm, pointed, smirked, and nodded.

"I'm the queen of the world!" Alice shouted, with her arms outstretched.

Ellie and Rachel laughed. Rachel reached for her phone.

"Let's get a selfie. We need to take loads to remember this trip. It's going to be awesome."

Hugging each other, Rachel took a picture of the three women, beaming and looking happy.

"OK, let's get this party started. I'm going to get us underway. Alice, can you help me with the lines?"

Rachel sailed out of the marina and headed to a nearby cove. She understood that this trip was more about having time with each other than the opportunity to stretch the sea legs of this magnificent yacht. She would have to speak to Gino about having another chance to do that. Some time with Finn on a yacht like this would be amazing. With the sails in and the charts checked, she chose a suitable spot and dropped the anchor. It was idyllic, with aquamarine waters and not a soul about. As Rachel checked the anchor, Alice brought up some nibbles and white wine from below deck.

"I could get used to this," she remarked, "Do you need any help, TT?"

"No, I'm all good, thanks."

Ellie put her sunglasses on the cockpit table and poured three large glasses of wine.

"I've always liked being called TT," Rachel said as she sat down at the cockpit table, "not only because it pissed my Mum off, but because it was so unique. I knew it stood for Templeton, but who gave me the nickname?"

"It was Talulla; she always changed everyone's name," Alice replied, "I think it was because she didn't like her own name."

"I'm not surprised. Who calls their child Talulla?" Rachel asked.

"Her brother was called Caspar," said Ellie.

"She tried calling me Wonderland," Alice added, "but it never stuck."

"I wonder why!" Rachel laughed. "What do you think happened to her? She was an odd one."

"She used to call me Smelly," Ellie added.

"Really?" said Rachel. "I don't remember that."

"Oh, I love that!" Alice laughed, "Smelly Ellie! I'm going to call you that from now on."

"No, you're not!" Ellie snapped as they all laughed.

"To Smelly and her future ahead," Rachel said, raising her glass and chinking it against theirs.

"Thanks for this, thanks for coming and thanks for both being so lovely," Ellie said.

"Not at all; this is what friends do," replied Rachel. "You'd do the same if I ever needed you both."

"Indeed," agreed Alice, "it's what we do."

Ellie suddenly started talking. "The doctors said that they thought my body had trouble sustaining a pregnancy, which is why it rejected my first baby."

Alice stared at Rachel, and they both remembered why they'd come. Ellie must be ready to speak, so they said nothing and sipped their wine in sync.

"So, when they said that I might have trouble conceiving again, I was devastated. I wouldn't let them take this opportunity away from Gino and me. We went to see so many doctors in England and Italy, and they told us that we were both fertile and that I may be suffering from polycystic ovarian syndrome. I had very few periods when I was younger, which I never thought was a problem. I just thought I was lucky not having to deal with period pains, pads and mood swings! Can you believe that? I started to think that all the horse-riding and sport I used to do as a child messed up my insides."

She started to cry a little. Rachel thought about saying something and looked at Alice, who shook her head. They sipped their wine again.

"We asked whether I could get pregnant, and after a few consultations, I had a load of tests done. Thankfully, I didn't have any cysts, but they discovered a 'mild congenital abnormality of the uterus', which I was born with. It doesn't cause any problems until pregnancy is attempted. It means that the uterus may not grow normally to hold and retain a pregnancy, and the foetus can naturally abort over time."

"If you knew this, Ellie, why did you try again?" Rachel asked. She knew that this was probably the most challenging question she could ask, but it just came out of her mouth. Ellie sighed, and Rachel wondered if she could take it back.

"Because I thought they might be mistaken, and what if I could conceive? What if I could have a healthy baby, and the first time was just an unfortunate accident? Could they be wrong?" Ellie focused on Rachel and awkwardly grimaced. "I just had to try."

Rachel smiled back and understood Ellie's motivation. Growing up in a boarding school with no family, she'd never been one to take anyone's word for it; she always had to try it herself. She was resilience personified and ridiculously stubborn.

"And what about Gino?" Alice asked.

"He was apprehensive at first but understood how I felt. He was so sweet. He kept saying that he would support me as long I wasn't putting myself in harm's way. We were both devastated after losing our first baby. He desperately wanted to become a dad, and coming from a large extended family, he wanted a baby of his own. We started trying a week after we'd seen the doctors." She paused and gazed out across the water. Rachel and Alice remained quiet. "It took me a further two months to get back to a regular menstrual cycle, and I was pregnant again within the year. I was over the moon."

"That means you were pregnant when I last saw you?"

"Yes."

"But you didn't say anything!"

"How could I, Rach?" Ellie stared at Rachel and blinked repeatedly. They held their gaze for a few seconds. No remorse. "Yes, I was pregnant, but we didn't know how it would work out, and I was scared. I didn't want to tell anyone just in case it went wrong again. In case I cursed it. Of course, I wanted to tell you both, but I promised Gino I wouldn't. I think he thought that if I did, I would convince myself it would succeed."

"Gino knows you well, doesn't he?"

"Too well. It scares me sometimes. Anyway, I kept thinking that if I took care of myself and hoped the pregnancy would go well, it would. So, when I reached ten weeks, I took some time to do nothing. I completely chilled out and spent as much time as I could relaxing, and before I knew it, I was at twelve weeks and still pregnant!" She glowed as she remembered the understandable joy she'd felt then. Her smile quickly faded as she became conscious of reality. "Whenever we visited our doctor, he was always sceptical and told us that we were still in risky territory at twelve weeks. I had none of it and told him to stop being so pessimistic!" Ellie dropped her shoulders, "I should've listened to him."

"Don't beat yourself up. It won't help," said Alice.

"I know, but I remember how great it felt to have a baby

growing inside me. I so wanted to tell you both."

Rachel nodded and couldn't believe how much love she felt for Ellie. This poor woman must've been through so much, but her fire was still alive. The embers were glowing warm, and the strength was still there. Even as she explained her painful last months, her spirit was still strong.

"As the weeks passed, I grew more and more optimistic. Gino kept trying to keep me level-headed, but I was too excited. I knew that if I could get to twenty-six weeks, the baby would be alright, and I would be able to deliver her. It would be risky, but she could survive. I felt strong, and I felt confident. Doing work in the villa was fine; it kept me distracted. I didn't do any labour-intensive work; we got guys in to do that. I just supervised. It was exciting to think it would be where we would raise our baby." Her eyes welled up with tears again, and her mouth quivered. "I made it to twenty-one weeks," Ellie exhaled, "…but I lost her. I only had four, maybe five weeks to go. But I lost her."

Staring at the sea again, Ellie looked away, seemingly out of tears. Rachel knew this was hard for her and felt they'd probably spoken enough today. They had plenty of time to share and talk this over. She looked at Alice, who practical as ever, had placed a packet of pocket tissues on the cockpit table. As the tears returned, Rachel handed her one. They sat in silence. As a gesture of strength, Ellie pulled her hair back from her face and remade her ponytail; she stared at Rachel and Alice and smiled. Rachel suddenly felt she needed to relieve the tension.

"I'm going to put on some tunes and grab more wine."

She left the cockpit and went below deck to put some music on. At the bottom of the ladder, she exhaled. She knew this trip would be an emotional rollercoaster and needed to keep it together. Reaching for her phone, she opened Spotify. What would brighten the mood? Searching through her playlists, she found one called 'Nostalgia', which she'd made months ago to capture her university days. She selected it and smiled. Walking across the galley, she reached into the fridge for more wine while 'Nothing's Gonna Stop Us Now' blared from the speaker. She took the opportunity to use the bathroom and freshen up while she was below deck, wanting to return to deck in a positive mood. Climbing up the ladder to the sunny cockpit, she glanced knowingly at Ellie, who had put her sunglasses back on. Ellie smiled and nodded to the well-known beat. Alice had jumped up and was dancing, shouting,

"Great choice, TT!"

Rachel put the wine on the cockpit table and sat beside Ellie. As they watched Alice goofing around, she grabbed Ellie's hand and squeezed it.

"All that I need is you!" Alice sang at the top of her voice as she swayed her hips.

"All that I ever neeeeeeeeeeeed," Rachel responded.

"And all that I want to do!" Ellie joined in.

"Is hold you forever and ever and ever!" They sang in unison. All three threw themselves into the dance, the sadness forgotten.

That evening, the three friends lay on the deck of the boat staring up at the stars, listening to the sea lapping gently against the hull. Rachel looked across the water and tried to take in every sensation: the sounds, the smells, the temperature, the sights, the tastes, the memories, the moment.

"This is so perfect," she said quietly.

"I love it here," Ellie responded.

"I can see why," Alice added. "You're going to get through this, Ellie."

They reached for each other's hands and held them, feeling the connection of their loyal friendship.

"I know," Ellie said softly. "If you have people around you who love you, who are optimistic, and who trust in your ability to succeed, you will. I read that somewhere, and it really resonated with me."

Rachel wished she could express her hope for Ellie, for she knew her friend would be happy in time. Ellie was too good a person for glorious things not to happen to her. The healing process would take time, but they were here for each other right now.

The silence was golden.

Chapter 5

Wanting something more

Sunday, 7th June

Heathrow Airport was surprisingly quiet for a Sunday night. It was populated only by tired, tanned holidaymakers returning from the sunshine, bored security guards, and adolescent cleaners polishing the floors with rotating machines whilst listening to music through tiny headphones. Greek inefficiencies meant the flight from Kefalonia was delayed by four hours, and Rachel had a splitting headache. Alice was bitching that she wished they hadn't taken the air hostess's offer to put their luggage in the hold. Standing together in silence, they claimed their baggage from the squeaky carousel and walked towards the International

Arrivals exit.

"I'm going to grab a taxi," Rachel said tiredly.

"I need to go and find a train," Alice replied, "Fuck knows what time I'll get home. I need to find some strong coffee."

"You going to be alright?"

"Naturally," she replied wryly, "I'll text you when I get home."

"Please do, whatever time that is."

"Thanks for a fab time, TT. It was an excellent shout. I'm so glad we went."

"It was, wasn't it?" Rachel approached Alice and hugged her friend. "Love you."

"Love you, too," Alice replied, returning the embrace.

Rachel pulled away slowly and picked up her bag. Smiling at Alice, she walked away and headed towards the taxi rank. Reaching for her phone, she texted Finn.

> Just got my bag, going to try and find a cab. See you soon xx

She hailed a taxi outside the airport and gave the hairy, silent driver her Hammersmith address. It would take about 30 minutes to get home, so she settled in to check her emails. Unfortunately, her phone showed only 2% battery. With a sigh, she slipped it back into her handbag. Resigned to the digital blackout, she gazed out the taxi window, watching the countless vehicles pulsating along the M4. She noticed the speeding lorries hauling freight to distant destinations, minivans carrying tired children as their parents returned from family trips, and dirty taxis like hers, dropping people back into their lives. The past few days had made Rachel so reflective; her time with Ellie and Alice had been wonderful. They had shared laughs, tears, memories, and aspirations, but now she felt apprehensive. Or was she just tired? What was she going to do about her job? What had been such a priority for her in the last couple of months had utterly lost its focus; why was that? Her headache thumped hard in her temples. She reached into her bag and grabbed some paracetamol, the last two tablets. She swigged them down with some flat sparkling water and saw a message on her phone.

> Hello sweetie, let me know when you are safely home. Mum xx

Rachel knew her mother wanted more detail, but she didn't have the energy.

> Hi Mum, safely home and in a taxi but have no battery.
> Will call in the morning. Rachel x

She put her phone back in her bag and closed her eyes. Why was she feeling so uneasy? How had just a few days changed her thinking about what months and months of planning had decided? She needed Finn's input because this wasn't just about her. But she was so tired. Could she manage it this evening? The taxi pulled up to her address, and the driver mumbled,

"That's 38 quid, mate."

She checked that her phone had enough battery and paid the driver with Apple Pay, then grabbed her things and got out of the taxi. Finn was waiting at the front door with a glorious smile, and Rachel exhaled.

"Hey, you, how good it is to be home!" she smiled. "The trip back was so long!"

They embraced tightly, and Finn kissed her gently on the lips. Rachel relaxed as Finn took her bag. She followed him into the hallway and threw her handbag on the console table. She automatically put her phone onto the wireless charger housed there. She could smell a mild citrus fragrance and saw that Finn had lit some candles. She checked her reflection in the hallway mirror and wiped her eyes. She looked terrible.

"Wine or peppermint tea? I wasn't sure what mood you'd be in."

"I'll take a tea, please. I had a headache, but thankfully, the paracetamol kicked in. I'm not sure how long I'll be up for, though, I'm shattered."

She kicked off her shoes and walked into the living room. She wiggled her toes into the lusciously thick cream carpet and surveyed the room. It was so different from Ellie's villa and the boat. There was a sumptuous brown leather sofa with glass side tables, each with ornate lamps and many photos displayed in coordinated coloured frames. The oak coffee table had caramel-coloured candles and coasters perfectly laid out. Abstract artwork hung on the walls depicting seascapes, all chosen by Rachel to capture her feelings for the sea and her love of the ocean. But she became aware that it didn't come close. It was nothing like that window at Ellie's, an open space that brought nature into her senses and made her feel alive and part of the landscape and nothing like the open sea, with its limitless horizon.

Finn returned with two cups of tea. He gently kissed Rachel on the forehead, gave her a drink, and sat beside her.

"How was it?" he softly asked.

"Thanks, Hun," she responded, taking a sip, "It was good; sad yet invigorating." She placed her cup on the nearby glass side table. "We spent hours and hours chatting. We let Ellie talk and share her grief, discussing everything we've shared over the years. But it was sad; watching how upset she and Gino were was hard to see. I hope that Alice and I brought them some optimism and hope." She reached over to the glass table again to pick up her drink. There, she saw a framed photo of Ellie, Gino, Finn, and herself smiling in Italy a few years ago. "It was so the right thing to do. I'm glad we went over. I needed it as much as they did."

"So, what are their plans now?" Finn asked.

"I'm not sure, to be honest. It's still so raw." Rachel replied, "I think they need time, time to heal and recover from the whole ordeal. I saw Ellie's strength, though, that fight that she's always had, that hasn't disappeared. And they're in the best place. It is pure heaven. Honestly, the place is gorgeous. You have to see it. You'd love it. Getting a few days on a boat was divine, too. I had a blast. It's the perfect place for her to be right now. It's just like what we used to dream about. The Mamma Mia! place."

"That sounds great. I wouldn't mind going for a sail right now, actually," he said as he sipped his tea. "It's been a hell of a week at work. Some sun on my back and wind in my sails would be just what the doctor ordered."

Rachel sat upright. "Well, why don't we go?"

"What?!"

"Why don't we go and spend some time with them? We've some holidays coming up soon, and we could go and have some R and R with them both."

"Really? But what about your interview? Haven't you got to get that sorted? And isn't it a bit soon after their loss to be taking more house guests? I'd feel like we were intruding."

"I think they're fine taking visitors. It was great that Alice and I were there; you could see that it distracted them from everything. Well, we could do that. The interview is on Wednesday next week, and I don't have much to prepare for it, just a few hours of work. I'm only flying out on Tuesday morning, so all is good. But I'm not bothered about it, to be honest."

"Not bothered? What do you mean?"

"It's so strange, Hun. I've lost interest in the job now."

"What?!" Finn forcibly put his cup on the coffee table and turned to her. "How can you say that? This is all you've been talking about for the last six months. What about Boston?"

"I know this may sound a little drastic, but I've even wondered whether I want to be interviewed. Because if I get the job, I'm not sure I want to go to Boston anymore."

He stared at her for a long time. The pause was long and unfamiliar. And she started to feel uncomfortable.

"I'm sorry," she whispered. Staring at Finn, she felt she needed to break the tense silence, as she could feel her headache returning. But she wasn't sure what to say.

"I'm just surprised, Rach. This is all you've ever wanted since I met you: the corporate job, the travel opportunities, the generous salary, the recognition of your expertise. And you're now so close to getting it, and you 'can't be bothered'?"

They sat silently for a few moments as his comments sank in.

"I know," she whispered, looking down at her hands, "It's troubling me why I feel like this. I'm surprised, too, Hun. Maybe I'm just sad and tired because I've been running this over and over and over in my head, and I can't quite work out why I'm thinking like this. It's absurd. It goes against all I've ever aimed for. All I've told you. But the more I dwell on it, the more I think about it, the more I realise that all I really want is a change." She paused, not to get a reaction from Finn but to let the words sink into her mind. It was the first time she'd articulated her thoughts coherently, explaining why she'd been striving for the job. "I've spent so long pushing myself to achieve in my career without ever asking why. My parents, you know what they're like, always pushed me to work harder, to try harder, and to achieve more, but I never asked myself why. The thought was to get the corporate job and be able to say 'I've done it'. But then what?" She took another sip of her tea and looked at him. He sat quietly. "Now I want something more substantial than just a job change, and I'm not sure about Boston."

They stared intensely at each other; the emotions on both their faces deep and confused. Neither heard the several sirens in the distance, attending a far-off incident. This time, Finn broke the silence.

"Look, you've just come back from seeing Ellie. You're tired and emotional. You're not thinking straight. This was way more than just a job change. We'll be moving trans-Atlantic, for fuck's sake. You've convinced me for ages that you wanted to do this and that I needed to support you. Thankfully, I can work wherever I want, but this will be a massive change for us. Surely you know this? It isn't just a job; it's a life change. I'm sorry, Rach, it isn't just you deciding on this either, it's going to impact us both. How in the hell have you just changed your mind?"

"I know, and of course, I know it'll impact you, and we need to talk it through. But it just doesn't feel attractive to me anymore."

Finn exhaled and put his head in his hands.

"Why don't we go and see Ellie and Gino and have some time to think about things?" she suggested.

"Seriously? You want to go away now?" he said, raising his voice. "You've just dropped a massive bombshell here, and you want to go on fucking holiday!"

He stood up and left the living room, seeking wine. Rachel knew she'd upset him but felt that she was finally being honest with herself. He returned, the wine glass full, and he'd also brought the bottle. He placed it on the coffee table.

"I spent a lot of time at Ellie's thinking about what the future holds for us. Where will we be in ten years? The three of us spoke about our aspirations for the future. I listened to Ellie recount the loss of her baby and her parents when she was younger, and it made me think, what would I do if something devastating happened to me? Do I have the inner strength to cope? Does going to Boston and having a corporate job fulfil my potential? Will that drastic change in my life make a difference to me? Improve my soul?"

"Sorry, Rach, I'm struggling with this. This job is all you've ever wanted to do. You told me this was your dream job. How are you having these thoughts now? Had you not considered this when thinking about your options?" He walked over to the window and stared at the world outside. He gulped down his wine and visibly dropped his shoulders. "How have you suddenly made yet another life-changing decision here, Rach? And how have you decided all this so quickly without even talking to me?"

"I haven't made the decision, Finn, really, I haven't. I'm just thinking. It's just I don't know anymore," she said, gazing lovingly at him. She could see he was distraught but had his back to her, so he missed it. This was never her intention; she didn't want to upset him. "Obviously, I appreciate that this is not only my decision. I'm just telling you what I've been thinking over the last few days." She stood up and walked over to Finn at the window. She put her arms around his waist and gently hugged him. "And remember, I don't have the job yet, so this could all be irrelevant if I don't get it."

His body relaxed slightly. After a slight pause, he released her embrace.

"That's the point, Rach. It has only been a few days. You've changed your mind in the last few days. You've derailed a decision that has taken us months to arrive at and will impact us both. Is this just a reaction to Ellie's news? Because, to be honest, Rach, I think it's an overreaction. This job has been your trajectory for months, years, even. How can it be overturned in just a few days?"

"Honestly?" Rachel apologised as tears started to well up in her eyes. "I don't know, I really don't know. Ellie's predicament triggered something in me and made me look into my heart. What is life about? What if I choose a career path that leaves me feeling unfulfilled? What if I want a family? What if something happens to you or my family? How much resolve and strength do I have to cope with it? Is life just about a career?"

He walked away from the window and towards the sofa, to refill his empty glass. "Jeez, you have been thinking! Those are some pretty big questions, Rach. And I hope you included a 'We' in that 'I' thinking?"

She wiped her eyes. "I know! The BIG questions..." she paused and glanced at him, "What do you think about spending some time with Ellie and Gino? I could do with some 'you and me' time. We've been so consumed by work recently that I don't feel we've had any quality time together."

"What about the interview?"

"I'll do it. I won't close any doors prematurely. I won't say anything to Bob or even Christie. If we can get some time in Greece, it'll give me some head space. Work won't even know."

"What about Ellie? Do you think she would be up for it?"

"I'll text her in the morning." She finished her tea, placed the cup on the coffee table, and then stood up and stretched her body. It had been a very long day, and she didn't have the capacity to continue thinking. "I'm sorry, Honey, I don't want to argue with you. I'm going to have to go to bed. I'm shattered, and I've got to go into the office early in the morning."

Finn knew when to continue a conversation and when to leave it. If there was any chance of conflict or argument, it was best to have both fighters ready. Rachel was clearly tired and emotional. Years of experience in a large Catholic family had shown him when it was best to 'let it lie'.

Rachel left the living room, walked towards the hall and took her phone off charge. En route to the bedroom, she passed the doorway and said, "Just think, in a couple of weeks, we could be sailing in the Aegean, with the wind in our faces and the sun on our backs. Away from the mundane day-to-day interruptions and worries."

Her phone buzzed.

> Hi sweetie, when you ring me tomorrow, could you do it after 10 am, as I need to drop Dad off at the golf course. Thanks.
> Mum x

"See what I mean?!" She showed him her phone and grimaced. "Can't we just sail into the sunset and never return?"

Finn walked over to her and hugged her.

"Hmmm, although I've no idea how we'd fund it. I'll lock up. You go upstairs."

Chapter 6

Uncertain smile

Monday, 8th June

Ravenscourt Park was beautiful at 6 am, with light trickling through the leaves of the magnolia trees as the early morning dawn arrived. Finn always liked to run at this time in the morning, as he could guarantee he wouldn't see too many people. Having moved to London from Ireland several years ago, he still struggled with living in a large city. He missed the open, lush green fields and crystal-clear loughs of Donegal. London just had too many people in it. Not only did he like to run at this time as the air was fresh, but he also found it helpful to clear his head for the day ahead. With all that went on last night with Rachel, today was most definitely a day that he needed to clear his head. Having completed 10 km already, he decided to do some short, sharp bursts and checked his watch to see how his heart rate was doing. It immediately buzzed.

> Hey Finn, are you running?

It was his brother, Ryan; he must be bored. Finn reduced his pace and concentrated on the watch face. Another message appeared.

> Are you free for a chat?

Finn's watch suddenly came alive with Ryan's name; he lifted his phone from his pocket and answered it reluctantly. "Jeez, I'm running, Ry," he panted, "is it important?"

"No, I just fancied a chat."

Silence. Finn stopped and caught his breath. "So that's my run finished then." Silence. He slowed down to a walking pace. "Go on then. What's up?"

"I just finished morning prayers and have some time before breakfast. I thought I'd check in and see how you're doing."

"Ha, you nosey bugger, you just want some gossip!" Finn laughed, his breathing restored to a more normal level, and his heart rate was now 120 bpm. Years of fitness meant he recovered quickly. He walked over to a park bench and started to stretch his legs.

Ryan was the parish priest of The Church of the Sacred Heart in Mountcharles, Donegal, having chosen never to leave the town where they grew up. He was a quiet man who liked the calm reverence of a simple life but enjoyed living vicariously through his younger brother, whether Finn wanted him to or not. With three sisters and a cheerful female housekeeper, he liked to delve into Finn's more masculine view of the world.

"It's been a quiet week in my congregation, actually, so I wanted a little idle talk. How's work? Have you completed the project you were working on when we last spoke?"

"Yup, my design submission is being processed by the procurement department in the New York office. I should find out when the head honcho returns from his holiday in a few weeks. If I get it, it should be about six months of work, which would be great."

"That's great news. Well done."

Ryan rustled something on the end of the phone. Finn smiled as he thought about Ryan's world. It was so utterly different to his. Finn spent his days designing websites and mobile applications, and Ryan listened to older people's problems. Finn waited to hear Ryan's news.

"I watched Breakfast TV yesterday, and it's just so boring. It's all about celebrity stuff at the moment. Celebrities do anything to get on our TVs, whether it's cooking, dancing, fashion or cars. I don't know why they bother."

"Father Logan has been watching Strictly Come Dancing?" Finn asked incredulously, "What would our Ma say?"

"Ma would turn in her grave!" laughed Ryan, "But Mrs O'Sullivan introduced me to it, so I can always blame her."

Finn laughed, too. This unexpected call was a welcome release. "And you interrupted my run to tell me you've been watching Celebrity Masterchef? It must've been a really slow week in the confessional." He continued to walk around, ensuring that the lactic acid did not build up in his legs. As he was only about a 20-minute walk from home, he decided to return to the flat at a calmer pace and talk to his brother. "So, Ry, how are things with you? Surely, it can't be so dire that you must trawl through the TV schedule to find out what's happening in the world. Donegal is in the 21st century, you know?"

"Haha, brother," Ryan laughed, "I knew Rachel was going for that job interview, and I just wanted to see how it went. Celebrities can wait for my dear sister-in-law."

Finn suddenly realised that his and Rachel's thoughts and plans were not confined to their world; they affected others who had their own opinions. He decided to download, "How much time do you have?"

"What do you mean?" Ryan enquired.

"Well, you feckin' called me, and actually, I have loads I want to sort out. So, since you interrupted my run, I reckon you've got to give me at least 15 minutes. Can you do that?"

"Wow, so this wasn't a chance call I made this morning; you do need a chat?"

Finn exhaled and paused. "If you can, Ry, I don't know what to do."

"Oh, my goodness, Finn, are you OK? Hang on, let me turn off the TV."

Finn sighed and stopped walking. Ryan returned to the phone.

"Go ahead."

"Rachel has reached the final stage of the interview, and it's looking very positive. The job is based in Boston and could be an awesome opportunity."

"Well, that's fantastic news! I'm so pleased for you both."

"But Rachel also got some bad news from her best friend Ellie, who has recently suffered her second miscarriage. It's such sad news and has had a profound effect on her, to the point where she is completely disinterested in the potential new job. She only told me this last night."

The sun had risen higher in the sky, and the world was beginning to wake and take shape. Finn paused and perused Ravenscourt Park as other runners started their morning exercise, and the dog walkers repeatedly threw multi-coloured squeaky balls to over-eager dogs. Ryan remained quiet, understanding the power of peaceful silence. Years in confession taught him that people could often sort out their problems if they were just given the opportunity to articulate them.

"Obviously, I want to support her, but I don't get how quick this change of heart has been. This job is all she's wanted for so long." Finn sighed again and started walking, having stretched his legs out.

"And what about you?" Ryan interjected as he sensed his brother's turmoil. The question was no different from what he would ask the members of his congregation.

"What do you mean?"

"How has this news impacted you?"

"Well, I'm with Rachel on the terrible Ellie news..."

"That is tragic news, to be sure. But I mean, the job; are you happy that she doesn't want to go to Boston?"

"Well, when we started discussing this last year, I was sceptical about going to the U.S., but the more I thought about it, the more I think it's a great chance for us both. I have to say, deep down, I was concerned about the cultural differences, although there is a high Irish population, so that'll be nice. My job is completely transportable, so that was never a concern, and I'm doing more work with U.S. companies. So, it would be good to be on U.S. time. What if it is the best thing that could happen to us?"

"Now that Rachel may cancel the move, how do you feel?"

Finn sighed. He hadn't thought about how much this was troubling him. "The thing is, Rachel has introduced another issue. She wants to visit Greece in a few weeks and spend time with Ellie. She mentioned going sailing and getting away from it all. I fear that this is more than just a career decision, it feels like a complete lifestyle change, and I can't be an obstacle to that."

"I think a break for you both would be a fantastic idea, and I'm sure you'd benefit from a change of scenery."

"Yes, I know," Finn agreed, "I don't think I've relaxed since Ma died, and Rachel and I haven't had any quality time lately. Life has just been driving me at 100 miles an hour. Perhaps Rachel is right, and maybe we just need a break."

Finn left the park and made his way toward his flat. He took the quiet back roads, without traffic noise, to continue speaking to his brother. "Boston is a long way away, though. I wouldn't see you, Caitlin, Fiona or Sinead that much. How are they doing?"

"Caitlin is super busy in Dublin and loving her new job. Fiona is knee-deep in nappies, but I'm worried about Sinead. She's not doing great, to be honest," Ryan paused. "She's struggled since Ma's death and continues to put on this ridiculous brave face. She came over to see me a few weeks ago and was a real mess. I know she is hurting inside. Do you think you could get some time with her?"

"Definitely. I've been meaning to ring her for a while. I'll do it this week. Perhaps we could catch up for a drink?"

"Thanks, Finn. I think she'd certainly appreciate that. Hang on..." Ryan rustled the phone again and murmured something Finn could not hear. "Sorry about that. Mrs O'Sullivan just walked in and asked if I'd like a cup of tea.

Seriously, that woman should have shares in Tetley's."

"You two sound like the stereotypical Father Ted household!" Finn laughed.

"Haha, you have no idea!" Ryan laughed. "So, are you going to Greece then?"

"Rachel has to check with Ellie, but I think it might be too much for her. We won't have her do anything while we're there. And I must say that when Rachel mentioned getting a yacht and sailing around the Mediterranean for a few days, I did get pretty excited. It'll be a nice change to cold, blustery manoeuvres around the Isle of Wight. Can you imagine the secluded white sandy beaches, the lack of tides, and the sun beating down on our backs - what's not to like?!"

"Careful, Bro. You might be making a decision right there."

Finn laughed and stopped walking. This had been such a tonic. He always enjoyed speaking to his brother. Ryan somehow always managed to bring positivity and calm into his life. Finn understood why Ryan was such a brilliant priest and how he could fully support and nurture people just by his gentle encouragement and calm demeanour.

"I might be, but that doesn't solve the long-term decisions. How should I approach Rachel's lack of interest in this job?"

"Is she happy?"

"Happy about the job or happy about not wanting the job?"

"Either. Do you feel that she is happy?"

"Shit, I really don't know. But, as I told her last night, this isn't just her decision; she has to consider me." Finn exhaled, "That isn't unfair of me, is it?"

"Oh goodness me, no! It would be best to think as a

team, but that's not always easy. I'm not sure it's about fairness, though; it's about being the best version of yourself. What about your purpose? I know that sounds a little clichéd because some argue that our purpose is to survive. Others say our purpose is to love others, to seek true happiness, or to follow God's will. I would advise talking openly and finding your purpose together. If you're unsure of any of this, then you need to tell her. Moving to Boston is a huge thing. I know you told her you don't have an issue with changing your job, as you'll be doing the same thing over there, making the change less for you. But have you considered that it might be scary for Rachel? Perhaps she is overwhelmed."

"Oh." Finn paused, stopped walking again and leaned against a railing. "Wow, I didn't think of it like that. Since I thought this job was all she ever wanted to do, I just thought she was ready. And that the only issue was getting the job. Shit, I didn't even think of it that way." Confused and astonished that he hadn't seen this coming, he was desperate to get home and hug Rachel. She'd gone through so much over the last week, and he shouldn't have shouted at her last night.

"I'm not one to be able to say I understand the female mind, but through years of having to hear Mrs O'Sullivan harping on about her daughters and her granddaughters as she serves me copious amounts of tea, I've got a feeling that women honestly struggle with allowing themselves to feel deserving of an achievement. Even if it's something they've been planning for their entire life, there's a possibility she sees it as a burden to overcome. She's so close to the prize that it feels unbelievable."

Finn frowned and tried to think if this was plausible. Surely Ryan couldn't be right? Rachel, an A-grade student throughout school, captain of the school's hockey and netball teams, then a first-class degree and a Certified Yacht-Master, was there nothing his superstar wife couldn't do? She had spent her whole life being a high achiever. Surely, she wasn't nervous about going for her dream job. They'd spoken about how it would help financially; she'd become the breadwinner, and they both agreed that they were equal in their marriage. Did this worry her?

"I don't think that's the case, Ryan, but I appreciate your observation. I'm nearly at the flat now, so I'll mention it over breakfast."

"Please do. And remember what I said: you need to be there for each other. I'm off to get some more toast, and no doubt Mrs O'Sullivan will be brewing my third cup of tea. Honestly, this is why I didn't get married!" Ryan laughed. "Seriously, though, Finn, please call me whenever you need me. And if you can catch up with Sinead, I'd really appreciate it."

"Yeah, I will." Finn nodded, realising that Ryan couldn't see him, "Thanks for the chat."

"No problem, Bro, it is always good to talk. God bless."

"Bye."

Finn ended the call and reached for his door key. As he entered the flat, he heard the ear-piercing smoke alarm and could smell burnt toast.

"Shit!" Rachel was standing on the kitchen chair, wafting the fumes away from the smoke alarm with a tea towel. Finn smiled and thought how much he loved this woman. He reached up and pressed the button to turn off the annoying shrillness.

"Oh, thank you!" she said, stepping down from the chair. "I'm so sorry, Honey. I was trying to make you breakfast, but I was on my phone and got distracted, and I burnt the toast."

He grabbed her by the waist and hugged her.

"What was that for?" she asked.

"Just because I love you," Finn responded, gently kissing her on her lips.

"Oh, Honey, you're all salty!" Rachel laughed as she pushed him away, "and now you're covered in lipstick!" She wiped Finn's lips with a tissue.

"That'll be my run," he said as he wiped his face. "I'm sorry if I was a bit harsh last night. I hadn't realised how stressed I was with work, and I know you've been going through a lot lately. Can we chat over breakfast?"

Rachel's phone buzzed. "Sorry, I'm heading to the office in about 10 minutes. Christie has already emailed me this , and we have a few things to review before our morning catch-up." She inspected her phone and saw a text from Ellie.

> Totally up for that. Gino and I would love to see you both. E xxx

"Oh, fantastic!" Rachel exclaimed, showing her phone to Finn, "Ellie agreed."

"What do you mean?"

"So, I texted Ellie this morning to see if they'd be up for us going over in a few weeks. And she has just got back to me, saying yes," Rachel beamed at Finn. "Isn't that great news?"

"Boy, you don't hang around, do you?" he said as he slugged a glass of water.

"Nope," she smiled even more. She reached over to her prepared travel mug and sipped her coffee. Discarding the burnt toast into the food recycling bin, she asked, "Can we chat over dinner tonight? I want to plan what we must do in the next few weeks. What time will you be home tonight?"

"Normal time. Shall we get a takeaway, so we don't need to cook?"

"Perfect!" Rachel gathered her phone and handbag. "This is SO exciting. I can't wait to tell Christie." She walked towards the front door, gathering up her handbag.

"What are you going to say to Bob about the interview?" Finn shouted from the sink, where he was getting another glass of water.

She stopped, turned around, and stared at Finn blankly. "Shit, I'd forgotten about that."

Chapter 7

Tell it to me straight

Saturday, 20th June

It was early afternoon, 2:04 to be exact, and Rachel sat at the bar sipping a gargantuan glass of Merlot. Discussing fabric choices for her mother's Parker Knoll dining room chairs was not what she'd wanted to do this morning. Thankfully, she'd managed to cut short the mother-daughter shopping trip as she mentioned that she was catching up with Alice while she was in Southampton. Returning home was becoming less frequent these days, so when Alice suggested a local coffee bar, Rachel insisted she would probably need a drink, so they should try a bar instead.

They decided to go to Los Marinos. Rachel had always

loved this place as it reminded her of former beer-filled evenings spent discussing optimal racing lines and weather with old sailing friends. Situated in Ocean Village, overlooking the yachts and power cruisers, the bar was always full of a great mix of people, and back then, Rachel could always rely on the fact that she would bump into someone she knew. Unfortunately, that was a long time ago, and as she drank her wine, she saw countless unfamiliar faces, which made her sadly realise that this place was now firmly seated in her past. For God's sake, the barman couldn't be more than eighteen! Surely, she never looked that young when she was drinking here.

Earlier, when she'd walked into the bar, she had expected to be greeted by the familiar fragrance of roast dinner, stale cigarette smoke and spilt lager. But, instead, a strange smell met her, one she could only place as a peculiar variation of vanilla. She turned around on her barstool and observed the shadowy spotlighting and marine memorabilia that had been recently installed. It completely changed the look and feel of the place. She hated it when bars felt the need to staple fabricated props and false artefacts to walls in an effort to make them feel nostalgic. It would be a complete miracle if any of these flimsy objects would survive the sea, let alone aid a sailor or hard-working fisherman. Precariously perched on an eye-level shelf, Rachel spotted an oil lamp burning; that must be the source of the aroma. Why on earth does a bar need to invest in aromatherapy? Rachel smirked at her cynicism and decided to enjoy her surroundings and not judge them. The old charm she fell in love with all those years ago was still ghostly evident; besides, she'd never known a place to serve such huge drinks.

Alice had just nipped to the loo, a welcome break on Rachel's eardrums. After politely chewing the fat for the last forty minutes and recounting their incredible trip to Greece,

Rachel jumped straight into her news. She mentioned that she wasn't sure about Boston, had postponed the interview, and wanted to escape to Greece. Alice had not stopped asking questions. The mere mention that she was thinking about not taking the corporate job in the U.S. had Alice quizzing her. Having spent time with Alice recently, she wasn't expecting this interrogation. Rachel feared it would be a long afternoon and took another long sip of her Merlot.

Alice headed to the Ladies and felt her phone buzz in the pocket of her jeans.

> Hey you, how's it going?

Alice knew it was her Mum and ducked out the door to call her. "Hey Mum, how's things?"

"Just wanted to check on you, Darling, and see how it's going with Rach. Is she behaving?"

"She's getting pissed, is what she's doing." Alice reached into her hoody pouch and pulled out her cigarettes. She expertly lit one whilst talking. "She's not going to take the job in the U.S. and is talking about heading to Greece to see Ellie."

"But haven't you both just visited, Ellie?"

"Yes!" Alice answered, "But Rach wants to return with Finn and go on a sailing trip."

"That'll be nice for Ellie. It'll be good for her to have the people who love her around. It sounds like Greece has planted a seed of intrigue for Rachel."

"Yeah, sure, but for fuck's sake, dropping the corporate job. What's she thinking?"

"Have you told her this?" her Mum asked.

Alice peered through the window into the bar to see if Rachel had noticed she'd been longer than expected. Rachel was staring around the room. She took another puff of her Silk Cut. "She wouldn't listen, Mum. You know what she's like."

"Have you told her your news?"

"No, I haven't managed to get that into the conversation yet. Too much of Rachel's ego is on display right now. I may move on to the wine soon."

"Listen, Darling, don't get annoyed with Rachel. She's a Leo and will always be a bit charismatic. That's why we love her so much. You always hated the idea of a corporate job, why are you so annoyed?"

"I'm just a bit angry that she won't see it through," Alice sighed and took another puff of her shrinking cigarette. "Rach was the one to get the top job. That was the deal. That's what we wrote in the yearbook. That's what everyone spoke of at school. Rachel Templeton would be the high achiever, and that was that."

"Are you jealous? Because school was a long time ago. Things have moved on, and people have grown up. She's married now; you need to move on."

Alice finished her cigarette and exhaled deeply. "Yeah, I know, Mum, many years ago. But I get a bit twitchy when things don't go as they should. Look, I'm going to have to go. Speak later."

Rachel raised her head and saw Alice returning from the Ladies. She had such a unique style, with her long red hair messily pinned up and her platform Buffalo boots, ripped jeans, and a North Face hoody, Rachel loved everything about Alice, she was the salt of the earth. Alice was the best regardless of Rachel's mood or temper, but she wasn't sure she could answer the questions today.

Alice sat back in her seat, sipped her Diet Coke and went straight into the questions again, "But you've always wanted a strategic role, TT. I remember you talking about it when you finished Uni. Why are you going to give it up now? You've worked so hard."

Rachel sighed. There she goes again, straight for the jugular. She shifted position on the high bar stool and adjusted her short skirt, wishing she'd worn trousers instead. "I know, I know. It's just that things feel stale now, especially after what happened to Ellie. You saw how much strength she's had to muster to get up in the morning. It's just that the high-flying corporate job doesn't feel attractive to me anymore."

Rachel took another sip of her wine and swept her hair out of her eyes. It felt strange to be impatient with Alice; they were generally so well aligned. Rachel knew she had good intentions and always had her back. But Rachel had made up her mind and was getting a little tired of Alice asking her to justify her decision. She was getting enough hassle from her family.

"I know how we feel about Ellie. It was truly terrible news. And I'm so glad we were able to share some of the pain with her. But how does her situation affect you?"

Alice, Rachel and Ellie had been friends since primary school, and although they'd gone their separate ways in their mid-twenties, they were still very close. They told each other the things that would test most friendships. Growing up, Alice would encourage Ellie to escape from her great-aunt's house and visit Rachel, where they would go to a nearby wood and talk about school, sneak cigarettes and eat Alice's Mum's freshly baked biscuits —three individual little girls who adored each other's differences.

At seventeen, Ellie headed off to Europe to pursue a fashion career. She travelled between Milan and Paris, became proficient in several languages, and sent Alice and Rachel postcards telling them about catwalk gossip and designer tantrums. After high school, Alice headed away, too. Working a few waitressing jobs whilst travelling the world, she went awry for a few years. The three of them lost contact for a while until Alice returned. She seemed more mature and experienced, and with a flourish of tattoos to document her trip; they didn't talk too much about her time away. Rachel went to university straight after school, graduating with a first-class degree, and immediately moved onto the ladder of achievement. On returning to the UK, Alice went to university to study Psychology and volunteered at a local homeless shelter—three individual, strong women who embraced each other's differences.

When Alice and Rachel pursued different careers, they lost contact for a while. Rachel moved to London, and Alice stayed in Southampton. At that time, Ellie and Rachel had become very close. Alice admired Rachel for her intelligent ambition and confident poise. She'd be jealous if they didn't have so much history. Rachel loved Alice's honesty, tenacity and empathy. The unspoken truth between them was that Rachel was always destined for success; she got the best grades at school, dated the most fancied boys, captained all the school teams, and now worked for a top Marketing company in London. Alice had had none of that. But Alice was solid and proud of her grit and determination, even if she had a few secrets.

"Ellie's news hit me hard," Rachel took another, more modest, sip of her drink. "I had no idea what impact it would have on me, and it has messed with my previous thinking. That's what's happened. It was so great for us to spend time with her. But it was tough."

"Yeah, it was," Alice said as she placed her hand on Rachel's, hoping to reassure her.

"I loved being on the boat with you both," said Rachel, taking another sip of her drink, disturbing Alice's hand. It wasn't intentional, and Alice didn't pick up on it. "It was so tranquil. Gino is amazing. I don't know how he does it."

"He works too hard."

"Yeah, I think that's his way of dealing with it."

Rachel thought about Gino's strength and profound ability to overcome tragedy for a second time. She gazed around the room coolly as if her concentration was lost elsewhere. A couple walked in, hand-in-hand, and erupted into laughter as they embraced a group who had already taken residence in the far corner of the bar. An individual from the group handed the couple a glass of champagne each, and they all happily toasted each other in a public celebration. Poignantly, this reminded Rachel that she should've been celebrating with Ellie and Gino when she was in Greece, not grieving.

"But it must be hard without any family around," Rachel said, turning back to the bar and focusing on Alice. "His folks have only visited them a few times since they moved to Greece from Sicily. Shit, it was something I should've done ages ago; at a time that wasn't steeped in grief. Gino and Ellie are so strong."

"They've had to be."

"That's for sure."

They sat silently for a few minutes, proof of a good friendship when the quietness was comfortable.

"Back to you, then. Why this sudden decision?" Alice questioned again, crossing her legs and making herself comfortable on the unnecessarily high bar stool.

"Sorry?" Rachel responded, still thinking of Ellie.

"To drop the corporate job and head off around the world with a knapsack on your back? Are you jealous that I did that? You're getting a bit old for that shit, TT."

Rachel laughed a little and gawped at Alice. It was so good to have another ear to listen to her thinking. Poor Finn was getting the brunt of it these days, and her mother was so annoying when she shared her thoughts.

"It's just a week's holiday! It might seem sudden, Alice. But I think this has been niggling me for a while now. Ellie's situation was just the trigger." Rachel straightened her back, adjusted herself in her seat again and took another sip of her wine. "I've come to a point in my life where I'm fed up with conforming. I feel like a product of middle-class normality. Admittedly, marrying Finn was a little off the standard-conforming path. Nevertheless, I'm married. Everything has followed a route. A route that I feel I haven't steered myself. And now I have my mother asking when I will make her a grandmother!"

"What's wrong with that? You're happy, aren't you?" Alice asked with a bit of disdain.

"Oh yes, don't get me wrong, I'm thrilled. Finn was the best thing that ever happened to me, and I'm super grateful for my education and job, but something's missing."

Rachel tried to set a gaze on Alice, to make her understand, some telepathy perhaps. She wasn't sure if she succeeded as the Merlot had definitely gone to her head. Alice was an intelligent woman, and her intellectual capacity always overawed Rachel. They always joked that Alice should have been a lawyer because of her knack for extracting the truth from people. Alice pointed out that growing up with a mother who was both an Animal Rights activist and a Fortune Teller had already provided her with all the communication skills she could handle.

"Finn and I've been married for five years now, and as my mother pointed out - only this morning - she'd had Tom, James and me by my age. Can you believe that? She didn't say this as a question. Oh no! That would've been too easy. She merely put it out there. Implied it. She's uncannily clever at saying nothing specific but with the deepest hidden meaning." Rachel noticed that she was getting quite animated and pulled a stray hair back behind her ear. "I asked her what she meant, as to whether she was actually trying to make a point, but she just started talking about Dad's golf tournament as if she'd said nothing. I was so annoyed."

"Come on, TT, you know what she's like. Your Mum's always been like that and has never meant any harm."

"I know, but she gets me every time. Why can't she just get off my back?" Rachel slammed her wine glass on the bar, and the barman glanced over. She didn't notice and continued to fume. "She's spent my whole life telling me how great I am and that I could succeed at anything I try, and then any time I crack under pressure, she wonders why! Is it any wonder? God, I'll never get that woman."

"Fuck, TT, you can be so rude. Why would you have an issue with someone telling you you're amazing?"

"It's the way she says it," Rachel replied, "And now she's telling me I shouldn't give up on the job and continue pursuing it. You know Tracy Edwards?"

Alice stared at her, shook her head and stared further.

Rachel was not making any sense.

"The woman who set up and skippered the first all-female crew in the Whitbread Round the World Yacht Race?" Alice continued to stare vacantly. "That woman is such an inspiration to me," Rachel continued. "She never took shit from anyone. She sought her own destiny and pushed against all who questioned her. She once said, *'We all have these reserves that I don't think we use anymore...keep looking for those parts of yourself that you have ignored.'*" Rachel was in full flow now and realised she was so glad Alice was here. Only her long-time friend would be willing to hear her rant this way.

"Hey, that's a separate issue, TT. That sounds like imposter syndrome to me. This decision isn't about your Mum, and I don't think you want to go down that road. Or do you have a problem with your Mum?"

"Will you stop being Dr Freud!" Rachel snapped. "I know you're good at this shit, but I don't need it, OK?"

"Whoa! I'm only trying to help here, TT. Don't fucking bite my head off, alright?" Alice gulped her flat, ice-diluted Diet Coke and sighed. She scanned the bar, deciding whether she should get a stronger drink. She caught the barman's attention and nodded. "Large rum and Diet Coke, please."

They sat in silence for a few minutes. Rachel continued to pore over the activity around the bar in a vain attempt to calm herself down. This was not how she expected her day to be going. "Look, I'm sorry, Alice. I didn't mean to have a go at you." She reached over, placed her hand on Alice's and squeezed it. She stared Alice in the eyes and smiled gently. "Honestly. It's just that I've so much going on in my head right now. A morning with my mother has not put me in the best of moods. I'm sorry, you know what I'm like when I'm with her. She isn't the problem, but I do think it's a little about what she represents in my life."

"Look, no offence taken, but stop being hot-headed. I'm only here to help, OK? Dealing with your mother is an issue you need to address. There seems so much anger in there; you need to resolve it."

"Yeah, I know," Rachel whispered, not wanting to deal with it at all.

Rachel finished her drink, surprised at how long it had lasted. She started fiddling with the beer mats on the bar, a trait she'd picked up at university, and Finn hated it. He always complained as she proceeded to rip the mats into tiny pieces, and generally, by the end of their evening, a small mound of Heineken-branded sawdust would be left on their table. It made Rachel smile, and she felt a calmness come over her.

"Ellie was so optimistic; I couldn't believe it. Optimism! How could that be? You saw that, right? She's the strongest person I know, and I'm in awe of her. And she's always been like that, dealing with such hardship from an early age. Dealing with her folks' accident and then growing up with no family and being put in a boarding school at seven must've been so hard. I didn't see it at the time. I was just always happy to see her home during the holidays. I want to be able to have that kind of strength. A strength that's borne out of life experiences and not taught in a lecture theatre or pointed out at a job appraisal. When she headed off around Europe on her own, she was just so brave. I couldn't have done that then. Not only that, she became friends with the top names in fashion, learned several languages, and set up her own business by age twenty. That's fucking incredible. She exudes strength. How did she do that?"

"You know, I know all this, right?"

"Her strength comes from her resilience," disregarding

Alice's comment, Rachel continued, her words flowing into what was now becoming a speech, "from introspection, from delving deep within oneself. I believe this profound wisdom often emerges from grief and contemplating mortality. Ellie has endured more than I can fathom, but what she is processing is soul-enriching. It's like soul food, and I want to be at that table."

"We all grew up, TT," Alice said, a little jealous of Rachel's comments. She felt left out of this reflection. Rachel deliberated her empty glass and signalled to the barman for another glass. Alice was immersed in thoughts and decided not to point out that Rachel probably didn't need another drink.

"Her lifestyle is very different to yours, though," Alice rationalised. "She's in another country and on her own most of the time. I know that she's always managed to excel in those types of situations. She was seeking soul-enriching experiences when she went to Greece, but now she is nursing an immense loss and needs to devote all of her time to healing. Everything she has had to address in her life to date will play a huge part in doing that."

"Yes, thankfully, because of Gino's job, she has no financial worries, at least. And because she has spent so much time away from the UK, she knows how best to use her surroundings to support her. I know what I said about Gino's parents, but not having any family around must be so hard. She has always had to deal with things alone."

"Yeah, but sorry, TT, the soul food you speak of comes from a deep level of psychological healing. And Ellie has done a lot of that. In my opinion, anyway. Your situation is nothing like Ellie's, so I don't think you can use her as an example. You need to sort out your 'mother issues' for a start. You're running away from—what did you call it? Middle-class normality. You need to make a lifestyle choice, not think you need to find soul food. You need to heal."

Rachel looked up from her second glass of wine and stared at Alice. Boom! There it was. They studied each other in silence. Rachel could always rely on her old friend to tell it to her straight. Rachel envied Alice's clarity of thought; even though it often hurt a nerve, there was never any animosity. Pursuing a psychology degree meant that Alice was an expert at being coherent and removing ambiguity.

"Look, I'm sorry," said an unperturbed Alice, "but only slightly. I think that what you want is different. You've everything, TT. You always have had. You maintained that the corporate job would be the icing on the cake."

"You see, that's just the bloody point!" Rachel raised both hands in the air, "I've had everything, and of course, I'm immensely grateful for that, but just because I've always done well, it doesn't mean I feel like I've achieved it. Yes, that's the imposter syndrome you speak of. Shit, Alice, you know what? I don't know the real me. That's the problem here, nothing else. This whole thing has just sparked something in me. I want to know I can survive in the big, wide world, without relying on my degree or my job position. I know that sounds like something out of a cheesy movie, but I need to do it before I turn into my mother."

"Your mother? You clearly do have a problem with her, then. Although honestly, I don't think you could turn into her in a million years!" Alice laughed, "For a start, Finn wouldn't let you!"

"That's true. Finn would die if I became my mother," Rachel laughed, too.

"You could always try religion," Alice casually interjected.

Rachel glanced at her, smiled, and raised her eyebrows. "Don't even get me started! Only the other day, Ryan explained the importance of spiritual journeys and reconciliation. You know I'm not against religion in any way, but I think that what I'm searching for cannot be found in the covers of a book or an old church."

"What then?" asked Alice, sipping her drink.

"Sailing in Greece on our own yacht."

Alice coughed, and Rachel laughed.

"Shit, I didn't see that coming!" Alice wiped her chin with her sleeve, "Seriously? When? How? Honestly, TT, you're a car crash!"

"Haha." Rachel shifted excitedly on her barstool. "Not sure quite how we'd do it. But think about it, Alice. Just think how amazing it would be. The freedom, the great outdoors, the ocean, no plan. The open water has endless possibilities, just like when we were with Ellie. But for a longer time."

Looking at Rachel, Alice played thoughtfully with a curl of her hair that had fallen in front of her face. "I agree. That would be incredible. What does Finn think about the idea?"

"He couldn't be happier," lied Rachel as she smiled and altered her posture again. "I was so surprised that he didn't need more convincing. As soon as I mentioned it, he was sold. But then you know Finn, he's game for anything."

Rachel didn't want to tell Alice that she hadn't actually told Finn the whole story, that they'd only discussed going over to see Ellie and do some sailing for a week and nothing more permanent. He certainly liked the idea of being away, and Rachel was convinced that once they were there, he would fall in love with her idea; fall in love with her idea of making long-term changes to their lifestyle. Because it would be an excellent opportunity for them both, he'd love that they could live on their boat and go wherever the weather took them. He could work whilst they did. They could have it all. Why explain something that will be inevitable to Alice?

Alice finished her rum and Diet Coke and ordered another. She waited for the glass to arrive so that she could raise it. Was this the time to tell Rachel her news? Once the spicy sweetness of her rum hit her palate, it could be. "Well, I suppose we should be celebrating then? TT, you're a mad woman, but I wish you the best," Alice held her glass high. "Besides, whatever you do, you'll succeed anyway. So, why would this be any different?"

Right, Alice decided to tell her now.

"Also, I wanted to let you know that I'm now a fully qualified psychotherapist and have started a new practice in Southampton as a founding partner. I've business cards and everything. I think, therefore, we need a celebratory hug." Had she said that right? She was so nervous about telling Rachel the news. What would her response be? Would she approve? Would she be proud of her?

"What?" Rachel yelled as she fell off the barstool, not maintaining any dignity in her short skirt. "Why have you only told me now?!" After realising that she'd probably had too much wine already, she hugged Alice tightly. "Were you testing out your qualifications on me?" Rachel laughed.

"Well, you didn't give me any air time, did you?" Alice smirked, "And it was good to see how you developed your argument."

"Alice, you're good. Congratulations, Honey. That's so amazing. Well done. I'm so happy for you. Now, do you fancy properly celebrating?"

"Well, I was supposed to go to the gym this afternoon, but hey! What the hell!" Alice raised her glass. "Here's to old friends… and their crazy dreams."

"And to your success, darling. You're the best."

Rachel beamed and toasted her glass; maybe this would be a good afternoon after all.

Chapter 8

Sorry, I've had a better offer

Sunday, 21st June

Sunday evening, Rachel returned from her weekend in Southampton. She burst through the front door, wanting to exclaim that they should sail off into the sunset tomorrow. Finn sat in the living room watching Top Gear, sipping tea. He raised his head and smiled; he hadn't heard her come in. "Good weekend?"

Rachel walked over to him and gave him a big kiss. "Great, thanks!" She flopped on the sofa beside him, "Although I'm shattered…sorry that I've been away so much lately."

Finn turned the TV down and glanced over at her. "No

worries, it was quite nice, actually. I did some work, had a run, and caught up with Jonathan for a few beers last night."

"Hopefully, you got some rest time, though. You work too hard these days." She reached into her jacket pocket and placed her phone and car keys on the coffee table. "Mum was a pain in the arse, getting me to traipse around fabric shops to look at colours for her old dining room chairs. Thankfully, I caught up with Alice, and we got a bit pished. She's set up a psychotherapist practice and is winning at life now. How was Jonathan?"

"Really good. He invited us to dinner on Thursday. The whole team will be there. I accepted. I hope that's OK?"

"Oh, that would be great! It'll be so good to catch up. I haven't seen them all in ages."

"Yeah, I told him about the job, and he was pretty excited about it. He used to work in Boston, you know, and said that we'd love it there."

"Oh... Did you tell him that I'm not going to do the interview?"

"What?!" Finn turned and glared at Rachel. "When did you decide this?"

"When we spoke earlier this week," she answered, surprised at his outburst. "After I'd booked our flights last Wednesday...I told you I would speak to Bob, but he's been on holiday. He's back tomorrow. I emailed him yesterday to say that I don't want to go ahead with the final interview."

"Fuck, Rachel, I don't recall having that conversation." He turned off the TV as Jeremy Clarkson's monotonous tones distracted him. He slammed the remote control down on the coffee table. "Was it one of your Rachel conversations? Where you say it out loud and believe that I've heard you. Because I don't remember, and I definitely would've remembered that."

"Honey, I thought you were fine with me doing this. After the thing with Ellie, I no longer have it in me." She looked at him and saw that he was fuming.

"Did you not think it would be worth discussing this with me? When you returned from Ellie's, you mentioned some thinking, but it was not a concrete decision. Yet here you are, back from being with Alice, and it's all confirmed. This decision involves me, too, remember? Shit, since you came back from Greece, you've been a right fucking pain."

"What?" Rachel's eyes immediately filled with tears. "That's a shit thing to say."

He turned towards her to see her better and sat upright on the sofa. "OK…so…look, we've repeatedly spoken about this. But can I be very clear so you can hear it from my perspective?" He adjusted himself in his seat. "You've spent the last six months working your butt off trying to get noticed at work, and then you get an opportunity to try for a new role in the U.S., and you want it, really want it. And when you want something, Rachel, very little can sway you. This was the career path you'd always wanted. This was the direction you had to take. You didn't consider what it meant for me, but I knew what it meant for you. I thought about what work I'd be doing while in Boston. What our life would be like. I thought a lot about its impact on me, but I also thought about how best I could support you. You convinced me it'd be an excellent move for us. We talked about selling the flat, moving abroad, and starting a new life together…"

"You insisted that your work wouldn't be affected by location," she interrupted.

"That's true, but the time difference could impact some of my deliverables, but I was happy to work with it. I'm doing more work in the U.S., so it may work out eventually. I even considered it an opportunity to rethink my job and look at other options once I was there. Talking to Jonathan about possible contacts I could catch up with when we got there excited me." He wiped his chin. Tiny drops of saliva had landed there as he made his points vehemently. He was furious. "But let's go back a bit, shall we? You then focus on getting the interview, doing nothing else for weeks, and you reach the last stage. In true Rachel fashion, you got it. Sure, you did. I was ecstatic for you!" Finn raised his hands, "Of course I was. Why wouldn't I be? It was what you wanted. At that stage, I suddenly knew that this was it. It wasn't a pipe dream anymore. We would be moving to Boston. It was quite a shock, to be honest, and I had to come to terms with that. Whilst you were with Ellie, I thought a lot about it, Rach, and I started to get ridiculously excited."

"I didn't have the job yet," Rachel whispered.

Finn paused and glared at her. "Yes, but it's you, Rach. That's simply a formality. Bob said you were the favourite, and HR was doing due diligence. So, in my mind, that was it. We were starting a new chapter. Moving abroad is a massive thing, Rach. It shouldn't be considered lightly. And now you've made a complete U-turn. How are you surprised that I am pissed off?" He stared at her. "Do you know how long I spent thinking about going away and how much I would miss my family? Miss my friends. I thought we'd talked about this. I thought you understood all of the thoughts I've been having. Have you forgotten all that?"

"Of course not," Rachel whispered as she wiped her eyes. "Why didn't you say?"

Finn's mouth was dry; he reached for his cup and finished his tea. "I've been saying things, but you've not heard them. You've been so focused on you. Which is OK, but what about me? I discussed this with Ryan the other day, and as I heard my voice, I realised that Boston could be a great new opportunity for us. I convinced myself that it would be good for me. And now you want to take that away, with little discussion," he exhaled. "I'm just so fucking shocked. Thank God we haven't put the flat on the market." He stood up, grabbed his cup, and left the living room.

Rachel burst into tears and grabbed a tissue from her handbag to blow her nose and wipe her eyes. She'd been so excited about sailing into the sunset that she'd forgotten reality for a while. But why had Finn not known her change of heart? Had she genuinely not told him? She was sure she had. She stared at the art hanging on the wall, one she had stared at thousands of times. It was an abstract design of swirls of teal, azure, cobalt, and aquamarine. It had constantly reminded her of the sea; that was why she had bought it. Right now, though, it represented chaos and confusion. How had she gotten this so wrong? Why was Finn talking to Ryan? What had he said? Had she honestly ignored what Finn wanted? How could she have been so cruel?

Finn returned and sat beside her on the sofa, placed his head in his hands, and sighed.

"I'm so sorry, Finn. I was sure I'd told you," Rachel sniffed as she wiped her nose. "As you know, this stuff with Ellie has really knocked me for six. It triggered thoughts in me that I hadn't had before."

"Look, can you stop putting this on Ellie, for fuck's sake?" Finn shouted, "This is completely different."

He stood up and started pacing. Rachel was astounded by his reaction.

"I know it's different, but the thoughts it stirred in me are genuine. When I saw how she has dealt with real-life problems, it showed me how unprepared I am. What if that happened to me? What if I lost you? Or Mum? Or Dad? How would I cope? I'm just so unprepared. You've always been my strength when it comes to things like that. The strength that you showed when you lost your Mum was truly amazing. How much you thought about your sisters and how you were there for Ryan was wonderful. You're such a strong man." She wiped her eyes again and stared at him. Finn stared towards the blank TV, not holding her gaze. "Since we met, you've always been such a rock, and honestly, I use you so much as my strength. You know what? I want to be strong for me. I'm fed up with having this predefined map that my life is following. I want to change it. I want to sail into uncharted waters and get some true experience that can't be taught or gained from a job promotion."

"But you were the one that wanted the job," Finn interjected.

"I know! And that's the bloody point: I don't want it anymore. I've changed my mind. And I'm so sorry that I haven't explained this better. Since seeing Ellie, I've concluded that my boring middle-class life is not enough for me, and I want to try something else. When I investigated a move to Boston, I saw that as a chance to change. But looking at it now, the change isn't big enough. I want something drastic."

"Moving to Boston wouldn't be drastic enough?" he asked, astonished.

Rachel exhaled, realising that she was not explaining herself well; no wonder Finn hadn't seen this coming. "For sure, it'd be drastic, but it would be safe too. You said it yourself: I was the favourite, which was the path I was taking. And I'm getting sick of everyone thinking it's a given. The route my mother presumed I would follow. The big corporate job. Tick. And then what? Working extra hard to get recognition in the industry. Tick. And then what? What if something happened to my folks? I'd be so far away. What if something happened to you?"

"Well, I'd be with you." Finn's voice softened.

"I know, but I've used you like a rock for so long. I need to do this for me."

"So, what did the job mean for you?"

"It was going to be an awesome achievement, and I'm so happy I tried for it. But I'm searching for inner strength now, not achievements. I want to learn the real stuff that can't be gained in a boardroom. I need to learn resolve, resilience, and courage, all the things that I see in Ellie."

"Seriously, you don't think you have that?" he asked incredulously. "How the hell do you think you got your job in the first place? You've demonstrated those things since I met you. You're an incredible woman, and I'm so surprised you don't think you have those."

She stared at him, feeling vulnerable. "But I don't feel it. I've searched deep in my heart, and as I look back on where I've got to at this stage of my life, there is nothing I've got that I'm immensely proud of, other than you, and I can't take credit for that." Finn grinned a little and took another sip of his tea. "I think it'll be perfect for us to get some time in Greece to re-evaluate things. I told Alice yesterday that we would buy a yacht and sail into the sunset together."

"What?" Finn exclaimed, his mood altered again. "Shit, Rachel, you are full of this, aren't you?"

"What do you mean?" she frowned at him, deeply confused.

"So, you don't want to move to Boston, yet you want to move to Greece. God!" Finn sighed, "You're making some pretty big decisions here and not including me at all."

"I need a break, we both do, which is why we'll see Ellie in a couple of weeks, but this goes beyond that, Finn."

He sipped his tea again, still not looking at her. "So, what are you going to do tomorrow?"

Rachel frowned and took a second to realise what Finn meant. "You mean the interview?"

"Yes, of course, I mean the interview."

"I'm going to speak to Bob and decline it formally."

Finn decided to finish his tea, put his cup on the coffee table and straightened up in silence. "OK, look, I'm exhausted and going to bed. Let's talk in the morning."

Rachel stood up and moved in his direction. Finn ignored her and walked out of the living room. Rachel watched him leave and stared back at the art on the wall; it didn't look anything like the sea anymore. It looked like a storm. "Night," Rachel whispered.

Riding the District line the next day, Rachel stared at the dirty window, seeing only her warped reflection against the darkness outside. The carriage was three-quarters full of half-asleep commuters, and the air reeked of dust and diesel. Recalling last night's argument, she felt sick. She hated fighting with Finn but wasn't sure what to say today, so she'd left the flat before he woke. How could she have read him so wrong? She thought he would be excited to go to Greece; she felt he understood why she wanted to decline the interview. But there must have been a miscommunication, and she couldn't work out when the confusion occurred. She swallowed and sighed. Was this all her fault? She was so consumed by the thought of escaping to Greece that she hadn't thought about what he wanted. On reflection, she'd been making all these decisions independently. God, she was so selfish! How had she not considered her husband? Is this actually what she wanted? She'd been listening to her mother too much.

"You've got some serious growing up to do, Rach," she whispered to herself.

She arrived at the office early to prepare for her call to Bob but wouldn't speak to him until later. Having grabbed a strong, black takeaway coffee on the way in from the tube station, she sipped it while staring out the window. Even though it was very early, the streets below were becoming busy. Deep down in her heart, she felt that going for the interview would be wrong; that was what she told him via email the day before. He'd responded immediately and been very positive about her decision but wanted to know more about why she'd declined.

On her journey in, she thought about logging on early and dropping Bob an email explaining her thoughts before she spoke to him. But what should she say? *'Bob, sorry, I've had a better offer?'* No, that won't work. It wasn't a counter-offer she was after. She just didn't want the job. However, was it presumptuous to think that she had the job? Should she explain that she wouldn't go for the interview because she was utterly disillusioned about work and perhaps wanted to quit altogether? No, she couldn't do that either. That wouldn't be fair on Finn. She would definitely need to talk to him before doing something as extreme and immature as that. But was it true? Did she want to give it all up? So many questions… She sat back in her chair and sipped her coffee. No one was in the office yet, and it was probably best to wait to speak to Bob in a few hours.

Rachel turned on her computer and logged into the system. There was a green light against Bob's profile. He was online. Rachel shuddered. It was 3 a.m. in the U.S. What on earth was he doing?

Good morning, Rachel. You're online early.

Shit! She didn't think that he could also see if SHE was online. She'd better respond. Was this it? Was this the last chance to get her dream job? What would happen then? What would Bob think of her? Would he think her indecisive? Should she do it now? Was she willing to give it all up? What would happen to her career? Did she genuinely want to escape her middle-class life? Shit, this was it! All the thinking, conversations, meanderings, arguments, and chats of recent weeks had come to this moment. And she wasn't ready! Panic set in. Rachel inhaled deeply and reminded herself that they were due to chat later today and that she'd be ready then.

> Good morning Bob.
> Yes, I'm in early. Quite a few things to sort out today, and I wanted to get ahead of myself.

No response.

Rachel watched the screen expectantly. His profile light remained green, and Rachel's eyes blurred over as she stared so intently at it. Was that the correct response? She took another sip of her coffee and took a deep breath. There was still no response. Should she say something else? She turned her chair to stare out of the window again. Suddenly, her computer beeped.

> Me too. I've been talking to Singapore and got a bit carried away!

This is it, Rachel. Now's your chance; there is no time like the present.

> Do you have some time now?
>
> I have a few things that I'd like to discuss with you before our call today.
>
> Sure. Can you give me ten minutes?
>
> Sure. I will call you at 8 am GMT. Thank you.
>
> Great, speak then.

Rachel stood up and walked over to the Ladies'. She entered the same cubicle where she'd heard the news from Ellie a few weeks back. This was where she started her change of course. God, was that only three weeks ago?! When she chose to rethink her destination. Where she entertained the idea of going into uncharted waters, was she still excited by this? All the scenarios she'd mulled over in her mind would change today. What if it was wrong? She had a pee and then washed her hands. She stared intently at herself in the mirror and took a deep breath. OK, Rach, you've ten minutes to decide your destiny. Are you in or out?

Chapter 9

That was way too close

Friday, 26th June

It was Friday evening, and Rachel was exhausted. Finn was away with work, and having been out with Jonathan and their friends the night before for a few too many school-night drinks, she wanted nothing more than to get home, immerse her feet in a bubbly foot spa, pour herself a smooth and fruity glass of wine and turn on the TV. It had been a tough week at work. She'd had to appease colleagues quizzing her on why she'd declined the interview, more comments about how she 'was made for the job', and questions about what she would do next. Despite that, she'd agreed to meet with her younger brother, James, after work and drive south to see their older brother, Tom. They'd had the visit in the diary for months. He had had a delivery of a new Aston Martin Vanquish only three weeks earlier and hadn't had the chance to take it on a long journey, so rather than take the train, he suggested driving to Tom's. His immature insistence made Rachel think it was merely an excuse to show off to his brother and sister, but then he was a show-off. She'd thought it would be a stupid idea to get out of central London at this time of day on a Friday, let alone go down to Southampton. But James had harped on about his incredible new car and announced they'd not need to worry since he would beat the traffic. Rachel was not convinced.

Rachel wasn't into cars at all. She didn't know many women who were; it must be one of those 'guy things'. James had swamped her with statistics that were utterly irrelevant to her, saying, *"...it has a top range of one hundred and ninety miles per hour, a nought to sixty of five-point one seconds, a six-litre engine with four hundred and sixty brake horsepower...."* All these figures went straight over Rachel's head, although she was aware that 007 drove an Aston Martin, so James at least had the correct name. She was interested, though, in how much it cost, and when her brother smiled and said, *"A shit load"*, she concluded that men never grow up and spend too much money, time, and effort on their toys.

James worked in Canary Wharf as a risk assessor for Morgan Stanley and, in Rachel's opinion, worked too hard. He pointed out that he needed to work hard to pay for his expensive toys. Since this was the case, Rachel agreed to go to his building to save time. She was there by six o'clock. It was a fabulous twelfth-floor office, and before the receptionist could even greet Rachel, she heard a familiar voice,

"Over here, Rach!"

Leaning out of a doorway, James appeared, smirking and waving flamboyantly. Rachel immediately blushed, thanked the receptionist, and approached the zealous holler. Because of the nature of the open-plan arrangement, Rachel did not have a direct route from the reception to James's office, so she had to weave between desks, computers, conference tables, and mock walls. She tried desperately to remain composed as she walked past James's work colleagues, who'd also heard the outburst and were now looking to see who it was directed at. Rachel knew that James was renowned for his many female friends, so this was an opportunity for them to take a peek. By the time she reached his office, she was furious.

"Thank you very much, dickhead!" She spat at him as she walked into his office and shut the door, "That hasn't helped my mood at all!" She fell into a leather chair in the corner of the office and kicked off her high heels. "God, I've had a shit day!"

"What? I don't even get a hug from my old sis?" James moved over to her chair with his arms outstretched. "Come here and give me a hug, you old tart."

Her younger brother's humour never ceased to make Rachel smile, and her earlier embarrassment was short-lived. Rachel stood up and grinned. "OK, but lose the silly voice, alright?" They embraced, and James started to tickle her playfully. "Stop it!" she laughed, trying to wriggle out of his arms and walk away. She sat back down in the chair.

"Good, at least you're in a better mood now!" James cheered, returning to his desk. "I'll be about fifteen minutes. Sorry. I thought I'd be done by now, but something cropped up. Is that OK?"

"You bet, I could do with sitting down for a bit and doing nothing for a while. What time is Tom expecting us?"

"I said about nine o'clock, but you know what Tom is like, anytime would be good for him. At least if we get there at that time, Beth and Joseph will be in bed."

"Aah, you're such a pig. You really don't like children at all, do you?" Rachel removed her jacket, laid it on the chair, and neatly put her shoes next to her overnight bag and briefcase.

"I love my niece and nephew because I can give them back. Those two adore me. They call me Magnificent Uncle James."

Talking easily as he jotted notes down, James didn't even look up. Rachel studied him. She'd always marvelled at his multitasking ability, but being one of the brightest corporate brokers in London meant you had to be a bit special. Still, she only ever saw him as her little brother. "It's only because you buy them expensive presents, you know," she replied, "But how do you know they call you that?"

"Lucy told me," he looked up this time. "She said that Beth wants to run away with 'macnivsent' Uncle J. She has told all of her primary school friends that her uncle lives in a big castle in the sky where he plays with cars and toys all day."

"You love that, don't you?" Rachel smiled.

"Unconditional love from a young female?" James smirked, "Who wouldn't?"

Rachel laughed, "Where does she get the idea of a castle?"

"God, you know what? I have no idea!" James returned to his paperwork. "It must be Harry Potter."

"How do you know that Harry lives in a castle?" Rachel asked.

"Shit, does he? How would I know that?Ω "

She stood up and walked around the office in her stocking feet. She picked up a picture frame from James' desk with a photo of James, Rachel, Thomas and her parents. Rachel had long, curly, auburn hair. "Good God, James! When was this photo taken?" she exclaimed, turning the photo around to show him. "I can't be more than seven! Look at Tom's super baggy trousers! And Mum's shoes!!"

James raised his head, stared at the photo, and laughed. "It's great, isn't it? I found it about a month ago. It was taken in 2002 at a piano festival that Tom won. Can't you see the trophy he's holding?"

"Oh shit…I remember that day. Wasn't there a boy called Paul Richardson who burst into tears when he started playing his recital and then ended up kicking the piano? It was awful, the poor kid!"

"I can't say I remember," James laughed, "But I'd have loved to have seen that, though. It sounds hilarious!"

"Poor boy was so sad," Rachel said, putting the photo back on the desk. "You wouldn't remember it; you slept through the whole thing." She walked over to the small fridge in the office, "May I have a drink?"

"Of course, help yourself."

"Ooh, I might have a beer," mumbled Rachel as she investigated the fridge contents, "Although that will probably mean that I'll need the loo en route. And if I have a glass of wine, I'll probably fall asleep in the car. So perhaps I should have a G&T as that is nice and refreshing, but then the safer option is no alcohol, so maybe I should have an orange juice…"

"Rach!" exclaimed James.

"What?" she asked, startled, looking up from the fridge,

unaware she was verbalising her thoughts.

"Anything will do. We'll be leaving in ten minutes anyway. Can you please pass me some water?"

"Sorry," she responded, throwing James a bottle of Evian. "I think I'll join you. Sorry, it's just been a completely shit day."

They left the office at half-past six and were through central London by seven-thirty. James had decided to avoid the M25 and nip through the back streets of Fulham and Richmond so he could get to the M3 quicker. He'd driven very fast, and Rachel, although she knew and trusted James's driving, had pointed out on several occasions, "That was way too close, J!" James was enjoying himself and in awe of his car, so disregarded her with a laugh and a boyish smirk. Once on the motorway, Rachel started talking about her plans. It was all she thought about. Christie was fed up hearing about her new dream, its sunshine, sailing, and seafood ingredients.

James zipped past a BMW, "God, man. There is no need to go that slow!" He drew his hand through his hair and hit the horn. "Yes, dickhead, I was behind you!"

"Calm down, J. I want to see Tom in one piece, OK?" Rachel hesitantly pointed out as she grabbed the car door handle for security.

"Sorry, Sis. I'm just a bit excited. It's great, isn't it? I am SO thrilled I bought it," James gushed enthusiastically.

"I agree, this car is lovely. But it would be just as nice to go less than ninety miles an hour."

"Ahh, stop being boring," he moaned as he slowed down and exhaled. "I'm just trying to beat the traffic."

Rachel took her hand off the door, stretched her arms, and

yawned.

"See, now, you wouldn't be yawning if I were driving fast." James hit the accelerator, and the car roared with power. It moved with incredible elegance, and Rachel admitted to herself that she was enjoying the ride. She watched her little brother and smiled.

"So, back to this bonkers trip of yours. What about the logistics, Rach? And what the hell does Finn think?"

"You know, Finn, he's always been a free spirit. He thinks it's a terrific idea to take some time off." She didn't want to tell James about her and Finn's arguments. They'd nearly resolved their differences, but she didn't want to show any chinks in her armour. "You'll love this… I asked him whilst he was cooking. He was cutting up raw chicken, and I sidled up to him and said, Finn, do you fancy giving up everything and sailing around the Greek Islands with nothing but me and a bottle of suntan lotion?"

James laughed as he overtook an Eddie Stobart lorry, "Ha! You're lucky the guy didn't chop his fingers off!"

Well, that had been a little embellishment, Rachel thought, but James liked it. "I know!" laughed Rachel,

"Straight away?"

"Absolutely! At the time, I think he thought I was joking," continued Rachel, slightly frowning as she stared at the traffic, "But once I'd convinced him, he thought it was a crazy and wild thing to do, yet completely the sort of thing we would both do. God, I love him for that. Whatever happens, I can always rely on Finn to surprise me. I had no idea he would be so easy to persuade!" Rachel gulped. Why was she lying?

James had reached the M3 and was able to make up some time. The traffic was heavy but not congested, but that would soon change once they reached the M25 junction.

"Rach, the thing is, have you properly thought this through? What happens to your flat? What about your jobs? What will you do for money?" he asked concernedly. "Is it wise at this stage in your career? Weren't you going for a role in America?"

"So many questions, J!" Rachel replied, exasperated. "Why must everyone keep asking me whether this is a wise decision?"

James was always interested in the money aspect, which pissed Rachel off. "I'm asking because I'm concerned about you. I want to know if you know what you're getting yourself into. You've been pushing your career for years," he observed a long line of red brake lights and slammed his brakes on. "Oh great!" he spat as he slammed his hand on the steering wheel. "We aren't going to get to Tom's before ten at this rate!"

"I'm fed up with people saying that they know what is best for me," continued Rachel, "that I have the perfect little life, and I should be happy. Why would I want to give it all up? Don't I realise how lucky I am?"

"Who says this?"

"Oh…you know…everyone…" Rachel replied. She needed him and Tom to understand her decision and approve of it.

"I'm not saying that. And I'm sure that Tom won't either."

She prodded his left shoulder, "Shit, I thought you, of all people, would understand! Everyone else telling you how to run your life."

"Look, Rach, I'm not going to be the one to say this isn't a good idea. I think it's a fucking great idea and a great opportunity for you and Finn to try something new." He nipped up the inside lane and waved at the cars and lorries that beeped him. "All I'm trying to say is if it is a good idea to give up so much?"

"Have you been talking to Mother?" she exhaled loudly.

James laughed loudly, overtook the coaches, and accelerated up the hard shoulder. They'd reached the M25 intersection, and he wanted to bypass everyone joining it. "She did ring me last night."

"I thought as much!" she scowled, "Why does she have to be so bloody nosey? I'm twenty-nine, for fuck's sake. Can't she just piss off? And why in the hell is this decision seen as giving up so much? How about the possibility that this could be giving me so much more?"

"Hey! Whose rattled your cage?"

"Sorry, J. It's Mother. She questions everything I say. This is my life! She can be so selfish sometimes. Why can't she leave me alone!?"

"Because she's your Mum, and she loves you." He said gently.

"It's because she's jealous," Rachel muttered.

"Wow! Where in the hell did that come from? Come on, that's a little below the belt, Rach. I thought you and Mum were on good terms at the moment?"

She gazed out the passenger window at the passing cars and went silent. James thought it best not to disturb her thoughts. Instead, he sat deep into the sumptuous leather driving seat and beamed. God, this was a great car, indeed. At last! It was the car he'd always dreamed of owning. Rachel wasn't the only one who had dreams.

On the previous Monday, Rachel had decided to hedge her bets with Bob Coleman and tell him that she had family issues to deal with, which was why she'd declined the interview. It wasn't the brave 'I'm off to find myself' speech, and she felt a little disappointed with herself. Bob was very supportive and added that new exciting positions were being discussed in next year's roadmap and that he'd be more than happy to interview her then if something appropriate arose. Their conversation was positive and hopeful for the future, and Rachel was grateful that she had not burnt any bridges. She knew Finn would be more pleased with this outcome but felt deflated. She'd kept it safe. This troubled her. But this was the right thing to do, right?

Still smarting from last night's argument, Rachel was unsure whether to tell Finn about this outcome. They hadn't sorted their differences out, and she felt uneasy. Instead, she called her father.

"Hello Rachel, what a lovely surprise!" her father answered warmly.

"Hey, Dad, have you got a minute?"

"For you, Sweetie, always. Let me get my cuppa and go into the garden; otherwise, your mother will keep asking me to do things." Rachel thought about how much everyone made accommodations for her mother. "Right, I'm all yours. Shoot."

She told him she'd just turned down the Senior Brand Strategist interview in Boston and contemplated taking some time off work, heading to Greece with Finn, and escaping life on a yacht. She added that she knew her mother would be disappointed and wanted to tell him first.

"Your mother won't be disappointed if she knows you're happy. Honestly, I know she is hard on you, but that's because her mother was hard on her, and that is all she knows. Is there any way I can help? I'm a bit long in the tooth, so I may have some experience to dispense you.

Although, honestly, you'll not find the answers you seek until you've done it yourself. I think going off to Greece is a fantastic idea."

Rachel took in the view outside her window, surveyed the empty office, and blinked away a pending tear. "Thanks, Dad. You're the best." She paused, "Give Mum my love, and I'll call you tomorrow."

"Any time, Sweetie. Take care."

James was gaining ground, so he decided to call his brother.

"Tom? James."

"Yo, what's up, little brother?" replied an enthusiastic voice from the hands-free. "How are you guys doing?"

"Great, thanks. This car is a fucking dream to drive. I'm making good time. No one else can catch me," James laughed.

"Watch, you don't get done by any speed cameras. There are quite a few on the M3, and they're not obvious if you're speeding."

Hearing Tom's voice broke Rachel's sullen mood. There was no need to fester bad feelings about her mother. She did love the woman deeply, but it was just that she had a clever way of undermining Rachel's confidence and controlling her thinking. How in the hell did she manage it? But that was for another day. Rachel didn't get the chance to see her brothers very often, and she was determined to enjoy the weekend with them. She couldn't wait to see Tom.

"… yes, she is. But she's in a dreadful mood. Tell Lucy to crack open a bottle of red. I think it'll be the only thing to redeem her! Tom, you're going to love this car. Can I take you out for a spin when we get to yours?"

Rachel always loved James's vibrancy. It was going to be a great weekend. For the last few days, her plans for Greece, the job, and arguments with Finn had been chasing around her head, and she could do with Tom's level-headed calmness and James's positive vibes.

"We should get to Tom's by nine-thirty," interrupted James as he hung up the phone, "if we don't get any more traffic."

"Huh?"

"Tom's? We'll be there by nine-thirty," he repeated. "You OK, Rach?"

"Sure, sorry, I'm just a bit tired," replied Rachel. "I can't wait to see Tom and Lucy. It's been way too long."

"You're right. I don't think I've seen them both since Christmas."

"We really should make more of an effort, you know," pondered Rachel, "It isn't as if we live that far away."

"Yeah, I know," he sighed. "But we're always all so busy."

"Well," she smiled, becoming more positive, "You'll both have to come out and see me on my yacht!"

He glanced over, "Do you know what? I might take you up on that!"

Chapter 10

You just know, don't you?

Saturday, 27th June

Rachel awoke with a pounding headache. The sun shone brightly through the gap in the striped curtains, so she kept her eyes closed. She blindly reached for the glass of water next to her bed and sat up to take a large gulp. Beth and Joseph sat quietly on the end of her bed, giggling.

"You snore, Auntie Rachel." Beth piped up, and Joseph giggled.

"What are you two doing here?" she asked, somewhat shocked as she abruptly opened her eyes and took another gulp of water. She rubbed her eyes and remembered how much wine she'd consumed last night.

"Daddy said you need to come down for breakfast," Beth instructed. "Macnivsent Uncle J has already been to the gym with Daddy, and Mummy is making pancakes with crispy bacon and scrambled eggs." She jumped off the bed and grabbed Joseph. "You have five minutes."

They left the room with Joseph still giggling. That isn't even time for a shower, Rachel thought.

"Urrrrrggggghhhhh!" she shouted into her pillow. Today was going to be a tough one.

As she brushed her teeth, she thought back to the previous evening. Spending time with her brothers and Lucy had been lovely. They ate home-cooked lasagna, Italian salad, garlic-coated ciabatta and finished with boozy Tiramisu. All washed down with Chianti and Malbec. They all chatted about their work and how James had excessive energy and an insatiable hunger to succeed. He told them about his plans to be a partner at his firm in the next three years and how much he loved the pressure. Tom explained his relief after selling his mobile app development company. Lucy commented that the stress levels in their house had returned to a manageable level (with two small children anyway!) and that the past year had been very difficult for them both.

When Rachel spoke about her work and having turned down a great job opportunity, her siblings grilled her about her career direction and future. That was why she drank so much wine. They relentlessly asked all the questions Alice and her mother had already raised. She recalled fervently asking James, 'What is the cost of inertia? What am I not learning to do whilst I spend so much time doing the stuff I have always done?' to which he promptly burst out in fits of laughter. That was far too late in the evening and not as eloquently formulated as she'd have liked. She smirked in the mirror and rinsed her teeth, splashing cold water on her face. In this morning's relative sobriety and staring at the bags under her eyes in the bathroom mirror, she questioned why she was not more confident in her convictions. What was she waiting for? Why was it so hard to commit? Whose permission was she seeking? Had she convinced them of her wishes? Why did she need their approval, anyway? Why couldn't she just make the decision and get on with planning it? All these questions worsened the pounding in her head, and she reached for her trusty paracetamol and finished her glass of water. She grabbed a flannel and wiped away the crusty mascara and eyeliner she had forgotten to take off last night.

"Breakfast!" Beth yelled up the stairs. "Come before it's gone!"

Rachel dried her face, efficiently applied moisturiser, tidied her hair into a bun, and exhaled. Grabbing her yoga pants and an oversized sweatshirt, she quickly dressed. She looked terrible, but she was with family, so they wouldn't mind. She headed down the stairs barefoot into a strong fragrance of bacon and pancakes, deciding only to take coffee; it was too early to stomach the greasy calories.

"And there she is!" exclaimed James, "The woman of the moment. How is the head this morning, Sis?" He stood by the coffee machine pouring an Americano, looking annoyingly fresh and vital. "Want one?" he asked as he raised the cup towards her.

Rachel nodded and headed to the table, where she nimbly squeezed into a seat at the end, far away from the feast Beth and Joseph were consuming. They dug into Nutella-doused pancakes with remnants left around their lips and all over their fingers. It further confirmed to Rachel that she didn't want anything to eat. Lucy made more pancakes, and Tom got something from the fridge. James handed Rachel a coffee, and Tom gave her a glass of orange juice.

She mouthed 'thank you'. They sat at the table on either side of her, staring at her and chimed in unison,

"What is the cost of inertia?" Then, both broke into belly laughter.

"Behave, you two," Lucy smiled as she added more pancakes to the pile before the children. Beth looked up, thinking she'd been told off, but saw that it was for her Daddy, so she grabbed a fresh pancake. Rachel thirstily gulped the cold orange juice and instantly regretted it, having only just brushed her teeth. It smarted and made her feel queasy. She sipped the hot, strong, sweet coffee and felt slightly better.

"What does in-err-sha mean?" asked Beth. Joseph giggled whilst licking his dirty fingers.

"I think it's a place in Scotland, Beth." James cheekily responded, and Tom laughed again.

"Would you like some pancakes, Rach?" asked Lucy, laughing.

"No thanks. I think I will stick with the coffee for the time being."

"Ooh, that bad?" Lucy asked as she put some pancakes on her plate.

"So I hear you've been out this morning?" Rachel asked.

"Yes, Auntie Rachel, Daddy and Macnivsent Uncle J went to the gym this morning whilst you were snoring, and Joseph and I watched Peppa Pig. Mummy has done all this cooking, and you've done nothing."

Rachel looked up from her coffee cup and stared blankly at Beth. Joseph giggled. Tom and Lucy didn't say anything, trying their best not to show how much they were laughing. Tom's shoulders were bouncing up and down. The silence continued for a little too long, and Tom couldn't hold it any longer. "Oh, Beth, that was perfect! Well remembered!" He went over to her chair and high-fived her. "You're the best."

James and Lucy were laughing, Beth was unashamedly proud, and Joseph continued to giggle.

"I suppose I asked for that, didn't I?" smirked Rachel as she took another sip of her coffee.

Finn had finished his early morning run in good time, and as he checked his lap time, there was a buzz on his watch. He suddenly remembered that he hadn't called Sinead. She'd been away in Japan on business, and they'd been unable to catch up properly. Ryan had been messaging him repeatedly to see if they'd managed to meet, and Finn had been avoiding his texts; that buzz was another of those messages. Finn decided to call her immediately. The phone rang for five rings.

"Hey, Finster, what's the craic?" answered a throaty voice. A chronic smoker, Sinead was starting to sound like Miley Cyrus.

"Alright, Boyo," greeted Finn. He missed his little sister so much; he never called anyone else that. They always started their conversations with stereotypical greetings, which had been an inside joke since leaving Ireland.

"What about ye?" Sinead audibly smiled. "This is silly o'clock, you know."

Finn thought it might be too early, especially for a Saturday, but continued anyway, "Sorry, I just had to call you before I forgot. You were going to call me when you returned from Tokyo."

"I only got back yesterday, so I've been trying to get over my jet lag. I was going to call later today."

Finn could hear her lighting a cigarette. "Are you free for

dinner tonight? Rach is away, and I haven't seen you in ages. I thought it might be nice to grab some food, have a few beers, and a good ole chinwag."

"That'd be grand. How about seven o'clock at Bill's?"

"Perfect. See you then."

Rachel reached across the table to add another spoonful of sugar to her steaming coffee. Tom and James talked about golf, and Lucy took Beth and Joseph to wash their faces and hands. "Why do you think Mum has such a problem with me?" Rachel mumbled, more of a rhetorical question that she wasn't expecting her brothers to hear. They stopped chatting.

"What do you mean?" Tom stared across the table at her. James looked over, too.

"She has such an issue with me doing anything not on her plan. She gave me such an earful when I said I wasn't doing the interview."

"That's because that's all you've been talking about for the last few months," James interjected. "She is allowed to be viciously curious."

"Yes! Yes! See, you get it, that's what I mean." Rachel sat up in her seat. "You're right, J. Telling me it's weak to quit. She's been vicious to me…telling me I must see it through. Like I'm a disappointment to her if I don't."

"Is that how you feel?" asked Tom. "A disappointment?"

Rachel stopped and stared at him. Her eyes immediately filled with tears. They both studied Rachel in silence. James got up from his seat, moved to the chair beside her, and grabbed her hand. "I've been thinking about what you said last night and trying to understand why you're going so off course. Tom and I discussed this morning how much you've achieved over the years, and it seems that you're so close to the prize yet you want to throw it all away."

She sharply took her hand away from James. "You sound like Mum." She wiped her eyes. Her head started to pound again. She looked at her older brother, "Is that what you think, Tom? Am I a disappointment?"

"That is not what I said, Rach." Tom responded, "I asked whether YOU thought you were a disappointment to Mum. I think you're amazing. You know that. You're such a strong person, and I admire your confidence and attitude. But I'm hearing a confused soul here. You spent so much of last night trying to get our blessing on your decision. Why is that? It was not like you at all. And why are you fighting with Mum? Dad called me the other day to see if I could talk to you about why you've such a problem with her."

Lucy walked into the kitchen, holding a dirty hand towel. She sat at the end of the table and looked at Tom.

Rachel sighed, "Of course, she would make it about her."

"Oh, come on," Tom tutted, "You're as bad as her. You have to get over how she reacts to you. What she thinks shouldn't impact what decision you make. What about Finn? You're making this all about you."

"And what is so wrong with that? This is my life, you know."

"You normally do things safely, Rach. This doesn't feel like you. You're usually measured and considered. How can you be throwing this all away?" James asked. She glared at him. Her head hurt.

"Rach, can I interject?" Lucy asked.

"Of course," Rachel replied, happy for the non-family opinion.

"I struggled with your speech last night. I'm sorry, is that a bad thing to say?"

"It was a bit of a speech, wasn't it?" Rachel agreed with a grimace, "Go ahead."

Lucy blushed a little and pushed a hand through her hair. Looking at Tom for approval, she put the dirty tea towel on the table. "It's probably because I reacted to it," Lucy explained, "I don't think I could throw it all away, mostly because I'd be too scared that I'd not be able to get it back."

Rachel stared at Lucy in silence. Lucy blushed again.

"Sorry."

"No, don't apologise, Lucy. That is a valid point of view. And I appreciate your honesty. But I'm not thinking of what I will lose; it is more about what I could gain."

James stood up, grabbed Rachel's empty coffee mug, and approached the coffee machine. He refilled their mugs and returned to the table. Tom and Rachel remained in silence and watched him.

"Look," Rachel sighed. "Last night, we talked about the incredible successes that you two are, about how everything is going your way. You both know your direction, and you both have such drive. I just think that I don't anymore."

"But you had the dream job in Boston, Rach? I don't understand. You have drive; Boston was your direction. What's changed?" James asked.

Rachel raised her left index finger to her nose and then pointed it at James. "I got the interview. I didn't get the job. Please don't make that assumption." She stirred a spoonful of sugar into her second cup of coffee.

"Stop being arrogant, Rach. We're trying to help you here," James responded. "You talk about Tom and my successes, but it's not all roses. It's been hard work, many difficult times, challenging decisions, and times when we've doubted ourselves. But you're on the same trajectory. You're a success story, too. We've all worked hard to get to where we are, always encouraged by Mum and Dad, and we're all a little surprised at this change of heart."

Rachel put down her teaspoon on the table and exhaled. "Seeing how fragile and vulnerable Ellie was made me think. It hit me hard, and it hit me quickly. Catching up with her and seeing her pain and how she has had to dig so deep to overcome her sadness was inspiring. I was in awe of her strength. A strength I want and am aware I don't have."

"So, was that all the speak around inertia?" James asked.

"Well, I clearly didn't explain myself very well last night, did I?" Rachel grimaced slightly and looked sheepishly at James. "What I was trying to say is that I am sailing down this career route with a strong wind powered by expectation and legacy, but what am I missing out on? What am I not learning or experiencing because I'm so busy doing the things I've always done? What is the cost of inertia?"

"I'm sorry to tell you this, Sis, but it's called growing up," Tom interrupted, "I fully support you wanting to make choices. I do. We all do. You and Finn don't have children yet; you're both doing well in your work, so why wouldn't you want to look at options? When I said I see a confused soul, I meant you're fighting the decision. You need to maturely weigh the pros and cons of not taking the interview, which has been your direction for so long. It would help if you discussed what could come next amicably with Finn; it's his life, too. And it would help if you stopped fighting with Mum and anyone else who is questioning you. We're all here for you because we love you and will always love you."

Rachel's eyes welled up with tears again, and she stood up and walked over to hug Tom. He stood and greeted her with open arms.

"Why are you always so damn good at articulating shit?" she asked as she held his embrace. "You just know, don't you?"

"I've struggled with a few things in my lifetime and had to look after you two. So, yes, I know a few things."

Rachel pulled away and wiped her eyes. James stood up from the table, walked around, and made them hug again.

"What he said..." he added, and they all laughed.

Chapter 11

What about me?

Saturday, 27th June

"Fuck's sake! This halloumi shawarma is the best I've ever tasted!" Sinead exclaimed as she wolfed down her dinner. "I always get so ravenous when I've been travelling. This is amazing!"

Finn watched his younger sister hungrily eat her dinner whilst he sipped his beer and smiled. They'd met at seven o'clock and hadn't stopped talking. By eight o'clock, they'd realised they probably needed food to mop up the beer and gin they were drinking. It had been such a long time since they'd last caught up, and he was grateful that Ryan had urged him to get in touch. Finn reflected on how crazy it was that they were both living in London and caught up so rarely.

Bill's restaurant was excellent. It was uniquely designed with colourful velvet-upholstered chairs and tall ficus and bamboo plants in large, shiny ceramic pots. A large golden chandelier was hanging in the middle of the ceiling, and tall mirrors reflected the candles lit on every table. He and Rachel discovered it last year, and it had become a firm favourite.

"Do you want any of my fries?" Sinead asked.

"No, I'm good. My burger was more than enough."

Sinead finished her shawarma, licked her fingers and wiped her lips with the linen napkin. "Hmmm, hmmm, hmmm. That was delicious!" She put down the napkin, lifted her handbag, and took out her phone, a packet of Marlboro and a Zippo lighter. "I'm going for a smoke," she said as she rose from the table and headed outside.

"Do you want another G&T?" Finn asked.

"To be sure."

Finn's phone buzzed, and he lifted it off the table. He hoped it was Rachel and wondered how she was getting on in Southampton. She'd texted this morning saying she had the worst hangover ever and had been having home-truth conversations with her brothers. Finn wondered if this weekend would help her to realise what she wanted to do. He couldn't seem to make any difference to her thoughts these days. The phone buzzed again.

> You two look FIERCE! I miss you guys
> Glad you've managed to catch up

It made Finn smile. He'd sent a picture of himself and Sinead offering a *'cheers'* to Ryan, and this was his response.

Finn finished his beer.

Six months ago they'd lost their mother, suddenly struck down with terminal liver cancer, and it had hit them all hard. Ryan turned to prayer, Caitlin and Finn turned to work, Fiona turned to her children, and Sinead turned away from everyone. Mary had been a fiery woman who brought up her five children single-handedly, having lost her husband to an unexpected stroke when they were young. She'd taught them to be strong individuals, and Sinead was the epitome of an independent woman.

Finn attempted to flag a waiter and saw a slim brunette who was surprisingly attentive and came over directly. "Another gin and tonic and beer, a Peroni, please?" he asked as he made eye contact.

"Certainly," she responded, blushing slightly. Finn didn't notice.

He peered out to the front of the restaurant and saw Sinead smoking, staring at him, and smiling. She waved enthusiastically. She seemed much slimmer than the last time they'd met. He had to find out how she was doing. He'd been so wrapped up in his world lately that he hadn't looked out for his little sister. It made him feel sad, but at least they had this evening. Sinead walked into the restaurant smiling.

"Oh gawd, she is SO into you!" she exclaimed as she sat down.

Finn frowned and scrutinised his sister. "What do you mean?"

"That waitress. Did you not see the way she stared at you?" Sinead exclaimed. "Hey, watch! Here she comes…"

The waitress walked over and placed the gin and tonic in front of Sinead, knowing their order.

"Thanks!" she overzealously proclaimed as she beamed and stared at the waitress.

Finn glared at her as she smirked. The waitress blushed further, handing Finn his beer. "And the beer for the gentleman," she spoke with an Australian accent.

"Thanks," Finn caught the waitress's eye and smiled. He could see she was flirting a little, making him feel surprisingly good.

"No problem," she replied and walked away.

"See. ?!" Sinead exclaimed, eyes wide open, once the waitress was out of earshot. "You still got it, Bro!"

"What, this old thing?" Finn smirked and cocked his head to the side as he sipped his new cold beer. "Anyway, enough about me. How's things with you? I've heard about how busy you are at work and how you can't stand your flatmate. But what's going on with you?" Sinead looked at him, and he held her gaze. "Sincerely."

She moved uneasily in her seat and took a long sip of her new drink. "Ach, you know how it is. Work is crazy, and I work way too hard for what I get paid. Marla is just fucking weird. And, well, it's been…difficult." She awkwardly glanced over to the window and took a deep breath. Finn waited to hear more. "I miss Ma so completely. It's all-consuming. It hits at ridiculous times. I was in a critical work meeting a few months back, and our CEO mentioned something completely benign that sent me over the edge. I had to leave the boardroom. I went and cried uncontrollably in the toilet. I can't even remember what he fucking said, but it floored me. Most days, I'm fine, but then I think I want to ring Ma to chat with her and tell her about my day. But I can't."

She started to cry and reached into her handbag for a tissue. She wiped under her eyes so as not to mess up her makeup and took another sip of her drink. Finn remained quiet. "I never knew what a great friend she was and how much time I spent bending her ears and telling her about my life. Whether that was bitching about work, sharing goat's cheese recipes or moaning about Marla. The crazy thing was that Ma couldn't stand goat's cheese and never understood how much I could eat. She used to give me so much advice, though, and I truly miss it. Did you know she used to text me every morning and give me little pep talks about how I should deal with stuff? Did she do the same to you?"

Finn shook his head and remained silent. They both took a sip of their drinks in perfect synchronicity.

"She kept telling me that Marla was helping me pay my mortgage and that things could be a lot worse...like having a lustful man, a smelly student, or a cat woman! She used to say the funniest things. Every Tuesday, she sent me a Reader's Digest joke, often mistyping words that meant the joke didn't make fucking sense. They were so corny but always funny, and I used to start my Tuesday that way." Sinead reached into her handbag again. "Tuesdays are shit now. I need another smoke."

She stood up without any permission from Finn and headed for the restaurant door. Finn sighed and stared up at the ceiling. He knew that Sinead had been close to his mother but had no idea about the nuances of their relationship. After Mary had died, why had he not been there for his little sister? Why had she not reached out to him? Why had Ryan not told him anything? He missed his mother, too, but in a very different way to the one Sinead described. He missed her motherly attention, but they didn't have a close relationship that involved daily interactions. They barely spoke every month. Since Finn had left Ireland, he distanced himself from his childhood ways and spent his energy trying hard to fit in with the London scene and Rachel's life.

Learning to sail in Southampton and meeting new friends was important to him, and he only rarely caught up with his family. Missing a male father figure in his life made him get very close to Rachel's father, Frank, and her brothers. He chose a life vastly different from Ryan's and reflected that probably would have upset his brother hugely. But Ryan dealt with this stuff every day. Surely he knew that he loved him and no harm was done? Grief is complicated to understand and manifests itself in many ways. No wonder Ellie's news had impacted Rachel. He must speak to Ryan tomorrow and apologise for being such an arse. How did Rachel think that he was there for his siblings? He was rubbish; he didn't offer any solace or support at all. He'd been a vacant mess. He must've lied to her; he couldn't remember.

"Sorry about that. I just needed a break," Sinead returned to the table and put her cigarettes and lighter in her bag. "What about you? How've you been?"

Finn sat in his seat and zoned into Sinead eyes, suddenly unprepared to say anything. He was feeling guilty for being a shit brother. "I need a piss," he announced, cutting their gaze, and walked off to find the Gents. Sinead turned away, unaware, and flagged the waitress.

Ryan had a strong faith and an incredibly close relationship with his mother. As the eldest of five children, he assumed the role of 'Man of the house' at an early age and coped well under what Sinead called *'unfair pressure'*. Mary was overjoyed when Ryan was ordained, citing, *'God has got a good one there, Ryan, your Da would be so proud.'*

After Finn and Sinead had left Ireland to settle in London, Ryan had been there for his mother, helping her with craft classes, gardening, shopping at Lidl ("*the deals are amazing!*") and bingo evenings. He was truly devastated when she got sick. Whenever he attended a doctor or hospital appointment, his faith quivered a little as he watched his mother, the formidable woman, deteriorate into a fragile shadow of her former self. But he was reignited because she never lost her fire and continued to be there for him during her terrible illness.

Ryan recounted later that although she became physically weak and bed-bound, she still had a fierce tongue on her. He was comforted that he could give her the last rites just before she died in his arms. Sadly, Finn and Sinead had not gotten to Ireland in time, arriving shortly after Mary had passed. Being a priest, there was never any blame directed towards his siblings for not being there, but on challenging days, he wished they had been more in tune with her and his needs.

Finn returned from the toilet to see Sinead chatting to the waitress. She was exuberant and friendly, and he wondered how many drinks they'd already had. Two tequila shots were waiting on the table, hence the smiley waitress.

"And this is my brother, Finn," Sinead waved her right hand in his direction, "He works in IT and does stuff I don't understand."

Finn smiled at the waitress and extended his hand. "Good to meet you."

The waitress blushed and shook his hand in return. "Hi, I'm Amy."

Finn looked at her and smiled. All she could think was that

she felt like she'd just said that famous line from Dirty Dancing ('*I carried a watermelon*') and was cringing on the inside.

"Hello, Amy." He took his seat, and Amy departed quickly.

"Ryan texted me earlier saying that he missed us. Shall we send him another pic?"

"I wish he was here. I really miss him."

"Well, why don't we ask him?" Finn asked, realising that the beer had started to go to his head. He took a silly selfie of the two of them and sent a message to Ryan.

> Miss you bro, when can you come to the big smoke and spend time with us?
>
> We're having a blast and we want you here!

He placed his phone on the table and all of a sudden appreciated how good it was to see his sister and how much he missed his brother. Sibling understanding was so primaeval, and he genuinely missed the genetic connection. He must thank Ryan for getting him to contact his little sis.

"When are you guys off to Greece?" Sinead asked.

"Next weekend."

"Oh, that'll be so much fun. The weather will be glorious. Are you looking forward to it?" asked Sinead as she raised her shoulders excitedly and beamed.

"Honestly?" Finn questioned, "I'm not sure."

She paused, stared at him more intently and raised her eyebrows.

"Rachel and I've been fighting so much lately, which you know is just not us, and I'm worried about what the trip represents to her."

"Really? So this is more than just a holiday, then? She's doing the interview, right?"

Finn exhaled. "So, she's not doing the interview but hasn't closed the door; keeping options open with the boss guy in Boston. But I don't know what that means in London. It feels like limbo. Oh, fuck, I don't know. I think this trip is just a chance for Rachel to get answers. I want to get some sun on my back, and it will be lovely to see Ellie and Gino. But I don't know what the next stage is. It's currently all in Rachel's court, and I feel helpless. Having rethought the potential move to the States and wanting to step off the career train, she wants to head off into the sunset on a yacht and find herself. I'm just amazed at how selfish she is being. I'm not even sure where I fit in the picture anymore. I just want to stop bloody arguing!" He exhaled again as he was finally able to articulate his feelings.

"Feck, Finn, that sounds fucked up." Sinead took another large sip of her drink and adjusted her hair. She reached into her handbag for her cigarettes.

"You smoke too much!"

Unfazed by his comment, she looked across the table momentarily and then burst out laughing. "Yeah, right, fucker," as she walked out of the restaurant to have another cigarette.

Finn smiled and thought it was a complete breath of fresh air to be spoken to this way. He'd been walking on eggshells for the last few weeks dealing with Rachel's insecurities, decisions, and turmoil, and he'd forgotten about himself. His sister could always bring him around. He cared deeply for Rachel and would do anything for her, but she'd undoubtedly tested his resolve recently. It had been all about her, and the last few weeks had been truly awful. Had she even thought about him? But then, had he told her that? No, they'd just argued. Constantly. He didn't understand what was happening in her head, but he knew she was being selfish. It suddenly occurred to him that he didn't want to give it all up and go to Greece and sail into the sunset. He wanted to go to Boston, and he wanted the corporate life. He wanted her to see her promise through and commit to what they'd planned.

"You alright, Bro?" Sinead interrupted his thoughts.

Finn shook his head slightly to regain focus. Was that a rational thought? Or just the beer talking? "Sure, yeah. I just had some clarity of thought. Thanks, Sis; you're the best."

"Shit, I didn't do anything." she laughed.

Finn's phone buzzed, expecting a response from the photo he sent Ryan; he picked it up.

> Hello sweetie, I miss you so much. I hope you're having fun.
> Rach xxx

He returned his phone to the table, turning it over so he couldn't see the screen without responding to the message.

"Do you fancy a dessert or a brandy?"

Chapter 12

Searching for serenity

Sunday, 28th June

Rachel loved being in Southampton and was so glad Tom still lived there. Being a keen sailor, he'd always known he would end up living by the sea. When their parents had moved to Kent after all the children had left the roost and Tom had finished university and a stint in London, Tom vowed to return. Tom and Rachel had spent so much time on the water in their younger years that the harbour was their second home. Rachel shared his love, and this place was soothing and safe. She had great memories of sailing out of Hamble Marina at dawn with her brother and heading towards the Isle of Wight on a cool breeze. The feeling of freedom as you prepared your boat for open water was unlike any other. Tidying your lines, untying fenders and placing them in the lockers, and checking your charts with the promise of a new adventure. Being here was so nostalgic, and it made her feel happy.

Feeling so much better this morning after not drinking any wine last night, Rachel had walked down to the coast before anyone awoke in Tom's house, even sneaking past Beth and Joseph, who were engrossed in another episode of Peppa Pig. She'd grabbed a coffee to spend some time with her thoughts. Tom was so lucky to be this close to the sea; she was envious. She inhaled the salty air; it was a different aroma from the one she experienced when she was with Ellie, but it was equally comforting. She and Finn would be heading to Greece in six days, and she wanted to know where her head was. She was desperate to stop arguing with him but also wanted to remove any uncertainty from her mind. Have I considered all the options and weighed up the pros and cons? If so, why can I not make up my mind? What is stopping me from making a decision? What was the reason? Why am I arguing with the people I love? She exhaled and took a sip of her coffee. She wanted to speak to Ellie but knew it was too early, and it would be rude to call now. She took her phone out of her pocket and called her Dad, knowing he would be up.

"Morning, monkey, you're up early!" Frank answered the phone joyfully.

"Hey, Dad."

"Is everything alright?" Frank asked with concern whilst clattering some equipment.

"Yes, I'm fine. I just wanted to have a chat. What on earth are you doing?" More loud clattering came down the line.

"I'm...." Frank's voice became inaudible, and it sounded

like he had dropped his phone. "Hang on!"

Rachel smiled as she thought about how sweet her father was. He was probably packing his golf clubs to leave the house before her mother woke. The phone line clattered.

"Are you there?" he asked, somewhat flustered.

"Yes, Dad, I'm here."

"Sorry, I dropped the phone while taking my golf clubs out of the bucket. I'm cleaning them before I go to the club. They were pretty muddy from my last round on Thursday."

"No worries, Dad. Is it OK to talk? I can call later," she asked, staring at a sailing boat that had just completed a smooth tack and was heading west towards Cowes. She was a little envious.

"I always have time for you, Rach. Now, what's on your mind?"

"Aww, Dad, thanks. It's just that I'm so confused at the moment, and I don't know what to do. I'm constantly arguing with Finn. I've not had any good words with Mum lately, and I feel everyone is against me."

"Oh." Frank paused, and Rachel could hear a door close.

"Dad?"

"Sorry, Sweetie, I've just gone into the kitchen. I didn't realise this would be a cup of tea conversation."

Rachel laughed. "Sorry, that was a bit of a download. Are you sure you have the time?"

"As I said, I always have time for you, Sweetie. I have a round of golf booked for 9 a.m., so I've plenty of time. But I will need a cuppa. Let me make one."

Without waiting for a response, she heard him place his phone on the side and clatter around, grabbing a cup and opening cupboards, preparing a hot drink. The kettle drowned out the noise for a time whilst it boiled. Rachel sipped her coffee and waited for her father to return to the phone.

"Do you know that George Harrison song, 'Got my mind set on you?'"

"What?" Rachel laughed.

"That song…*I got my mind saaaaiiiiirrrtt on you*," Frank continued, singing the song badly.

"Yeah, I know that song. Never really liked it myself."

"Did you know that is about him buying an old, renovated classic car?"

"Really? No, I didn't know that."

"I heard it on the radio the other day, and it was a bit of trivia that Ken Bruce told me. Knowing that fact made me think about the song completely differently. Anyway, where were we?" Frank made a few more sounds, and Rachel could hear he'd sat down somewhere, so she assumed he was ready to give her some time. She sighed and gazed up into the sky.

"Dad, what do I do? Do you remember me saying I would head to Greece and run away? I don't know whether that is what I want to do." Water welled up in her eyes, and she swallowed hard.

"Oh, Sweetie, I've never known you like this before. Your mother and I only said yesterday about how uncharacteristic this is of you. You're generally so upbeat and focused. I thought you'd decided; you were so convincing the last time we spoke. What are you struggling with?" He took a sip of his tea and paused, "For me, it seems that everything is taller these days…well, I suppose it's just that I feel smaller in so many ways. Anyway, that's probably not very helpful and not what you wanted to hear." He took another sip of his tea.

She smiled; she loved her father's mindless meanderings. "You see, Dad, I think that's the whole issue. Everyone's been telling me that I should keep doing what I was doing and that this is not what I'd planned. And I'm pretty annoyed at their responses, to be honest. Mum has been on my case since I told her I wouldn't do the interview. She keeps texting me snide messages, which is not helping me."

"You know your mother loves you, Rach. She is just trying to help you find answers, and I'm sure they're not snide; you're just reading them that way."

"Dad, she's not helping me at all, and Tom and James are the same. Telling me I'm 'off plan' and that they're surprised I'm being so frivolous. Can you believe that? Frivolous!!! Like I've decided to invent a water-soluble umbrella or something."

"Do you care what everyone thinks?" he asked.

"Of course I do," she snapped back. "Sorry, Dad, I didn't mean to say it like that. But it's important to me that my family and friends support what I do."

"Why?"

"Oh, Dad, come on. Please stop with the questions. Could you help me find answers? Not make me more confused." Rachel sipped her coffee and realised she was being very impatient with her father.

"Can I be frank?" he asked, and she grinned as this was a running joke in her family. When she was young and living at home, her Dad would say this whenever tensions ran high, which always dissipated the mood.

"Yes, Dad, I want you to be," Rachel responded genuinely.

"You've spent your whole life being the golden child.

Succeeding at everything you put your mind to, studying hard, and achieving whatever you tried. Your mother and I were always so proud of you. I remember when you got your sailing qualifications and overcame real challenges on your nautical adventures. I often wondered where you found your courage and discipline, but I knew you were fiercely determined. And that is what we all see, the people who love and know you; we see how much you've worked to be at this stage in your life. Your mother doesn't want you to throw that away."

"Dad, I'll never be good enough for Mum, and I certainly wasn't the golden child! That had to be James. She's forever telling me how much I need to work. She was the one who pushed me - actually, guilted me - into achieving so much. I had to prove it to her."

"And she was so proud of every single thing you achieved, from your Brownie badges to your University degree. She glowed with pride at every parent's evening and every hockey match. You didn't see that. She was over the moon when you got your job in London. And it would help if you didn't compare yourself to James. You are our only girl. There is something to be said about that. You always saw it from your perspective. Your mother wanted you to believe in yourself and work hard to get whatever you wanted. She never had that support when growing up and was determined to give you as much encouragement as possible. Your mother knew that women need to try so much harder than men to succeed, and she wanted to instil integrity and a professional work ethic in you. As you got older, she trusted your instincts and judgement to make mature decisions, applauded everything you did, and cried at anything that didn't go your way."

"Really??!" Rachel asked, very surprised. "She never told me that."

"Well, she wouldn't now, would she? You know what she's like. But I can tell you she felt the angst of every one of your decisions and simply wanted the best for you. And, obviously, I do, too." He paused and took another sip of tea.

Rachel surveyed the Solent and saw more sailing boats joining the outgoing tide and heading in different directions. A comforting warmth spread over her body as she recalled what an early morning sail felt like. Even though it had only been a couple of weeks ago, she was desperate to go sailing again.

"Dad, I just want to do something different and get off the juggernaut that has been my life to date, which is why I came up with the idea of escaping to Greece."

"Are you proud of yourself?"

"Sorry?"

"Are you proud of yourself? It's a simple question you should ask yourself when having these thoughts. Also, ask yourself, 'Am I happy?'"

"But these are more questions, Dad. I know what I want to do."

"I thought you said you didn't know."

Rachel sat up on the metal bench she had perched on that overlooked the sea. *'Do I know what I want?'* She asked herself. *'Did I know all along?'*

"Rachel?" Frank asked, "Are you still there?"

"Yes, sorry, Dad, I may have just had an epiphany."

"Didn't you go to school with a girl called that?"

Rachel laughed out loud. "Persephone, her name was Persephone, Dad. You're so funny. That is so strange how I've just realised what I want to do."

"Wow, really?" Frank laughed, "Blimey, I'm good!"

Rachel laughed. "Dad, you're the best."

"So what do you want to do?"

Rachel scanned the endless horizon of the sea and thought, *'What if I just got into that boat out there and sailed off into the Atlantic? Kept going and never came back. Take in the sea air and be at one with nature. What if I do that?'*

"I want to take some time off to sail around Greece, just as I said. That's what I want to do," she replied with solid conviction. Boom, there it was.

She blinked a few times and took a deep breath. Her father remained quiet. She felt an enormous weight lift from her shoulders. The decision had been made. The thoughts had solidified.

"Awesome, Rach, that is such a fantastic idea. Back to your original wish. Well done you. With Finn, I presume?"

"Absolutely! And I want him to be happy. I've hated fighting with him recently, and I don't want to ask him to do something he doesn't want to do, but we'll need to work that out. But I think that I know what I want. And I know he'll be happy."

Rachel started fidgeting with her hair and placed her lukewarm coffee in its cup on the bench. She stood up and started pacing the pavement. "Obviously, I need to decide a time frame…which brings other questions. I need to think about work and how I fund it." Rachel paused and stared up into the sky; her father remained silent. "Jeez, I'm scared now."

"Don't be," Frank offered reassuringly. "There is a point in your life where you need to make decisions for yourself. It's called being a grown-up, and we all have to do it at some stage. Perhaps as an adult, Rach, this is your tipping point. Choosing a path that is yours, not something that your husband, Mum or Dad, or boss takes you down. That is perhaps why you've struggled recently to find your answers. Until now, you've followed the path laid out for you by someone else. Whether your 'new' decisions are good or bad for you, you must be accountable. And if you're being true to yourself, no one should derail your thinking. The funny thing is that whenever I took the approach I've just explained, I quickly realised that although I have strong opinions, I'm easily swayed. I started to learn about myself and how I deal with things. And I'm OK with that. But knowing that fact has kept me on your mother's good side and allowed me to keep my integrity. The moral of the story is that you need to stay true to yourself. Clearly, you need to consider others that your decisions would impact, like Finn, and very often, a compromise is the ultimate decision. But life is too short, and you must be happy with your choices."

He paused, and Rachel waited; this was good advice. "Also, there is no point in fighting with something you can't control. Why should you take on board what James says? He's so career-focused, and your thinking jars with his life decisions. But those are his decisions. He will then subsequently tell you that he disagrees with you. And Tom will want to help you not make the errors that he made because he is your caring older brother. But no one can tell you what you need but you. And you need to listen to your heart and not always your head." Frank paused, took a final sip of his tea, and placed his cup down with a clatter. Rachel is silent. "Are you there?" Frank asked.

"Yes, Dad," Rachel whispered quietly, "Those are such amazing words. Thank you."

"Aww, Sweetie, you're very welcome. I've picked up a few things in my lifetime, and if I can pass on any of my learnings to you so that you can benefit from them, then there you go. Thanks for asking my opinion, genuinely, because people don't often ask me and go straight to your mother."

"Oh, Dad! They're missing out on all of your experience. I'll tell them they should speak to you."

"Oh no, don't do that! I've golf to play!" Frank remarked.

"Haha," she laughed. "I'm sorry I've kept you talking so long. But this has been so helpful. Thanks a million."

"Honestly, you're welcome. So, off to Greece, it is then?"

"Well, there is still much to do, Dad," Rachel replied nervously.

"Yes, but the decision is made," Frank assured matter-of-factly, "The rest is just logistics."

Rachel paused on that comment and thought how wonderfully wise her Dad was. How much she loved him, and how fantastic her family was. How could she have been so blind to the fact that they were all looking out for her? She didn't deserve them. "Thanks so much, Dad. Give my love to Mum."

"Any time, Sweetie. I'm going to have to go. Please drop your mother a message. She'd love to hear from you."

"Bye, Dad. Love you."

Rachel put her phone in the pocket of her jeans and walked along the quayside. Watching the boats, she smiled and thought how amazing it would be to do that forever, with the sun on her back and the Mediterranean Meltemi winds in her sails, having exclusive time with Finn and no boundaries on where they could go. Such freedom, such indulgence!

So, there it was. The decision was made. Why was that so hard? Why did I argue so much to get to this point? But wait! What if Finn doesn't want to do this? Rachel panicked and took her phone out of her pocket. She remembered that he had been out with Sinead last night, so he was probably nursing a hangover but would probably run today. It was

8:17; she might just catch him….It went straight to voicemail.

'Hey honey, just me. Good morning! I hope your head isn't too sore and you had a great evening with Sinead. I'm sorry we've been arguing so much recently. I've just had a great chat with Dad and think I've made up my mind. I should be home in time for lunch, so I would love to talk it over with you. Love you!'

Chapter 13

It's not you, it's me

Sunday, 28th June

Finn sat at the kitchen table, waiting for Rachel to return. Too many drinks last night with Sinead had taken its toll, leaving him with a sore head, a dry mouth and an un-nerving paranoia. They'd spent most of the evening chatting about the "old days" and growing up in Ireland. Reminiscing about how often Sinead skipped school to steal cigarettes and smoke them behind the bike sheds. Finn joked at how she even managed to get a degree after being so absent from school. Sinead reminded him how much time Caitlin spent roller-skating, even to the extent of going to bed whilst wearing her skates. Finn confessed that he used to mess about in church to piss Ryan off. They roared with laughter as they remembered how Fiona would draw faces on biscuits with squirty cream and then shove them in her mouth in one piece. They also spoke a lot about their mother, marrying the laughter with tears. Fuelled by alcohol, it had been a nostalgic and brilliant evening, but he was feeling it now. Rechecking the clock, he was annoyed that he felt too tender to go for a run, as he knew that would make him feel better. There wouldn't have been enough time anyway. She'd said 10, right? He hadn't even managed a shower.

10:09. He was surprised she was late; maybe her train was delayed. Although, things shouldn't be bad on a Sunday morning. Pushing a sweaty hand through his dirty hair, he reached for his glass; it was empty. Why was he so anxious? Last night in the taxi home, he deliberated what Greece represented to Rachel and whether he understood it fully. It was clearly something that she wanted to do, but what about him? Talk of heading off into the sunset muddied the waters of what a simple one-week holiday symbolised. And anyway, he'd decided last night that he wanted to go to Boston. Finn exhaled and stroked his beard growth. Reliving his younger years with Sinead over beer and cocktails had been refreshing and much more fun than arguing about Greece with Rachel. Would they travel to another country and still have these arguments? Probably, based on recent experience. Or was it going to be concentrated time for conflict? God, he hoped not.

How could he talk to Ellie and Gino? From Rachel's description, it was grief-filled and raw, and he wasn't sure that was something he could cope with right now. Feelings about his mother were starting to surface, making him uneasy. Over the last few days, he'd been emailing intermittently with Gino, and he wanted to be there for his friend, so it would be good to catch up in person and talk about the horror he'd been through. But how could he deal with recounting pure grief? How could he honestly support his friend? He didn't feel he had the tools to give any comfort. Last night, Sinead had drunkenly repeated how much she missed the Tuesday morning text from their mother to the point where Finn told her, "I'll fucking send you a text every Tuesday. Now shut up!"

That was his response. That was his empathy. That was him being a complete shit. Why had he been so unkind? Thankfully, Sinead didn't flinch and just punched him in the arm. God, he'd missed her; he knew that Rachel would never let him speak to her like that. He stared out of the window and exhaled. Would Rachel let him say his piece today? Especially since she was doing an excellent job of making all the decisions in their relationship. Where was his voice? Could he tell her that he'd been thinking about whether he should go to Greece at all? He was so hungover and so grumpy and irrationally anxious. If he went to Greece, would that signal to her that he was willing to be there for more than a holiday? What did going mean? They'd only just been planning for Boston. Greece, now? Fuck! What was happening to the Boston scenario? Selfishly, she hadn't given him any time to discuss his prospects. They were obviously not in a good place, and he genuinely couldn't decide what to do. He was starting to see why he was so uneasy; there were far too many unanswered questions. He and Rachel were completely misaligned. Undoubtedly, pointing that out would make her mad; she was so volatile at the moment. He stood up and walked around the kitchen table to the fridge. Refilling his glass with hangover-clearing vitamin-c-packed orange juice, he walked to the sink.

Where was she? This was unlike her. She was never late. Out of the window, he saw a couple joyfully walking hand-in-hand along the pavement. They exuded happiness. Finn sighed. Life was about seeking answers, and Rachel and their bitter squabbling impacted his happiness. They needed to reach a shared, positive and solid ground. Finn sighed again and watched the couple walk out of view. Did he still want Boston? What if he stayed in London and continued doing what he was doing now? What if he went to Greece and sailed off? Why was he so indecisive now? Uneasy, yes. But undecided wasn't like him. He put his hand through his hair again and walked around the kitchen. Perhaps he should go to Greece, talk it through, forget his concerns, and clear the air. Find some direction and clarity and then re-evaluate. Shit! Why couldn't he just fucking make a decision? He was starting to understand Rachel's dilemma, which was more complicated than it looked. There had been so much going on over the last few weeks that he could do with some head space.

He picked up his phone and noticed that he had a voicemail. How had he missed that? He played the two unheard messages. The first was from Rachel. OK, so she wasn't due for a couple more hours. He wished he'd known that earlier. He wouldn't have been so stressed. Why had he not checked his phone earlier? Was he really that hungover? Well, at least it would give him time to clear his head, shower and prepare himself for the inevitable argument, or at least calm himself down and be ready to talk maturely. Maybe he could get a short run after all. The orange juice had undoubtedly made him feel better than when he had first woken.

The following message was from Sinead. 'Bro, I'm banjaxed! What the hell? Fab night! I loved it. But dead, I tells ya. Speak soon.' Finn grinned wryly and remembered how much he loved his sister. It truly had been a great evening. He decided that he would go for a run. He had time now. It would definitely help his thinking and calm his nerves. He went upstairs to get changed.

Rachel sat in an empty carriage, listening to calm jazz music on her AirPods, and stared out of the dirty train window. Hampshire's luscious green trees and fields began filling with unnatural urban construction as she whizzed back toward London. She couldn't wait to speak to Finn and tell him how relieved she was to have finally reached a decision. Talking with her family over the last few days had been so helpful, and her father's gentle encouragement was just what she needed. She was going to take a sabbatical. She smiled. She loved that statement!

"Rachel Logan, you're going to take a sabbatical," she whispered to herself. Her smile widened. *I'll head to Greece, rent a yacht, sail around the islands, soak in the sun, go off-grid and work on my resilience.* She exhaled; that sounded like complete heaven. She stared down at her phone, hoping to see a message from Finn, but the screen was clear. Had he not got her voicemail? Was something wrong? The phone just showed a smiling selfie of the two of them. Greece would be a fabulous opportunity to reconnect with each other since the arguing had been taking its toll on their marriage. On Saturday, they would visit Ellie and Gino to discuss their future plans. Gino could help them source a yacht, and then they would make plans to return as soon as they had sorted their flat and agreed on her time off from her job.

As soon as she got on the train this morning, she'd emailed Bob. Only last week, they'd been talking about the new strategic direction he was taking his team in the next year, and Bob had mentioned that although she'd not taken the interview, he wanted her to join his team in the Spring and be part of his vision. Surprisingly, their relationship had flourished in the light of her decision to decline the interview, and she felt a solid professional connection. Her email accepted his offer. That would give her plenty of time to find herself yet still keep her career prospects. Fantastically, Finn could still do his work in Boston; it was just a slight postponement. She was back on track to deliver what they'd planned for so long. She knew he'd approve. He'd be more than satisfied. Her family would be supportive, too. It kept all her options open and didn't close any doors; it simply took the pressure off her now. This was SO going to work! She stared out the window again, noticing it strangely appeared cleaner. She exhaled. She was so happy.

Finn managed only a 6k run because he felt dreadful. It was markedly slower than usual, leaving him with a headache from extreme dehydration. He wasn't impressed. His phone buzzed as he cooled down on the walk back to his flat. Desperately thirsty, he checked it. He hoped it wasn't Rach; he wasn't ready yet. While running, he mulled over all his options and came up empty. He simply didn't know what to say to her. Thankfully, it was Sinead.

"Hey, you! How are things? Are you as dead as me?" Sinead croaked down the phone.

"I'm not too bad, actually," Finn lied, "Just finished a run."

"Fuck! That's impressive... I feel rubbish. I'll be doing very little today." Finn could hear her light a cigarette. "I had an idea after our chat last night," she continued as she took a drag of her cigarette. "Ryan got back to me, far too early this morning, about the three of us meeting up in London, and he confirmed that he's free next weekend, so perhaps we could get together on Sunday evening for a few days."

Finn was just about to tell Sinead he was heading to

Greece next weekend when he suddenly knew that he undeniably didn't want to go. He stopped walking. There it was, a revelation. He was now convinced that going to Greece was not what he wanted. Knowing it would cause an argument with Rachel if he just said he *"didn't want to go"*, perhaps this was his excuse. Sinead had given him an opportunity. Could he convince Rachel he should stay here? Would that be fair? Would she be annoyed?

"Well, I thought we could go over to him instead. A wee trip home. What do you think? I haven't heard back from Caitlin or Fi yet, but I've asked them too."

Finn exhaled, raised his eyes to the sky and then closed them. After last night, he badly wanted to see his brother and spend more time with his sisters, and this sounded like the perfect excuse. Perhaps it would be better for Rachel to get away on her own and take the time to level her head and come to her senses; after all, this was her dream, not his, and it had all been pretty rushed. Going to Ireland would be the perfect decoy to any argument she could throw at him, which he knew she would. How about thinking about himself for a change?

"Finn? You still there?"

"Sure, sorry, just got distracted."

"So, what do you think? We could fly over on Sunday evening, catch up with Ryan after evening mass, and stay till Wednesday. Caitlin will be nearby that weekend, too, so perhaps we could get her to swing by. I can look into flights. I know it's short notice, but can you get the time off?"

"I actually have that week already booked off." Finn heard Sinead take another drag of her cigarette.

"Oh shit! I forgot you're off to Greece with Rach. Sorry. Oh, don't mind me. Forget about it. The head is mush today."

Finn paused. "No, Ade, I think I'd like to go home. It's been far too long."

"Really? Won't Rach kill you? Or, kill me, at least."

"I need to do this for me. The same way Rach needs to do Greece for her. It's only a week, and I think the space may be good for us."

"Fuck's sake, Bro, I don't want to wreck your marriage! Are you sure?"

"Yea, I'll speak to Rach today. If you could look at flights and let me know, that'd be great."

"Will do. I'll drop you a note later. And I'll see if I can convince Fi to put down the nappies and join us for a drink."

"Thanks. That'd be amazing if we could all get together. I think it'll be a very special time together. The last time was Ma's funeral. Sorry, I've been so remiss, Ade. I do love you."

"Love you too," Sinead whispered back. "Now I need to go and find some more coffee. Bye."

"Bye."

So, there it was. If that wasn't going to be a statement to Rachel, then nothing was. He understood her need to pursue happiness and be able to make decisions for herself, but what about him? He also needed to be more assertive and work out how to make decisions. Hearing Rachel say that she needed to extract herself from her family's influence, he felt it was the opposite for him. He craved family. After spending a small amount of time with Sinead, it showed him that family was everything. How had he been so unkind to his siblings? How had he not been there for them over the last six months? How had he not felt this before? He'd been so busy thinking about Boston and heading off, and Rachel was leading the way. With that now derailed by her, he needed to focus on healing and do that with his brother and sisters.

He missed his mother desperately, and he'd not addressed it. The grief that Rachel saw in Ellie would be complicated for him to experience. He hadn't dealt with his own emotions after losing his mother, hiding them away and focusing his energy elsewhere. He should tell Rachel that. Maybe she would understand, hadn't they both had a similar discovery? How powerful grief is, how difficult it is to overcome, how much soul-searching is needed to cope with it.

Perhaps that is how he should open their discussion today, they've both been exposed to grief, and like her, he needed to learn resilience. And to do that, he needed to go home. Maybe he should consider it an empathetic opportunity rather than a conflict-avoiding excuse. He'd have to work on the explanation better. Spending time with his family would make him happy, and that is what he should say. He walked in the flat's front door and rushed up the stairs. He needed to get ready for when Rachel came in.

Turning on the shower to let it heat up, Finn stared at his face in the bathroom mirror. He didn't recognise the reflection. His mother always used to smile as she reminiscently told him he was the spit of his father, but sadly, he couldn't recall his face. He was glad his mother couldn't see him now. The dark circles under his eyes and a day's beard growth made him look haggard. He stripped off his sweaty running gear and dropped it on the floor. Entering the steamy shower, he put his head under the water so his hair flopped over his forehead. He closed his eyes and exhaled. The water washed away the sweat and alcohol that exuded from his pores. It felt good. He stood with his hands on the shower wall and lowered his head. Suddenly, his breathing started to labour; he tried to cough and clear his throat. Opening his eyes, he moved out of the water flow and raised his head. Finn continued coughing to get some air circulating, but his heart rate increased. Unexpectedly, he collapsed like he'd been punched. Where the hell had that come from?

Panicking, he tried desperately to catch his breath as his heart beat fast and furiously. Attempting to stand up, he grabbed the slippery, wet shower wall but had no strength in his legs. This was an unfamiliar feeling. Perhaps the run had not been a good idea. As an experienced runner, he knew how to calm his heart rate but he couldn't control this irregular breathing. He was consumed with fear and reached to turn off the shower because the hot water was adding extra anxiety to the situation. He needed to get out. He couldn't concentrate enough on finding the taps as a wave of emotion unexpectedly crashed over his whole body, and he began to weep uncontrollably. Slumping into a foetal position, he automatically grabbed his knees as the water continued to fall.

He couldn't think straight. He couldn't focus. He wept. His body had given up on him. Unconsciously, he started rocking as he trembled and tried to get his breathing to a normal level. Gasping between sobs, all he knew was that he felt deeply, deeply sad and physically affected by simply remembering his mother.

Rachel walked in the front door with a joyous bounce in her step. "Hey, Hun, I'm home!" she yelled as she closed the front door.

Automatically, she threw her keys onto the console table in the hallway and skipped into the kitchen. Switching on the kettle, she clattered around in the cupboard, looking for the cafetière. Finn shakily came down the stairs and paused at the entrance to the kitchen. "Do you want a cuppa?" she yelled again, not knowing he was close by.

"I'm good, thanks," he mumbled as he walked in and

headed to the fridge for sparkling water.

"There you are!" Rachel beamed enthusiastically, "I've missed you so much!"

She moved over to Finn and gave him a big hug from behind. He tried to return the sentiment, but he couldn't. He felt numb. They didn't make eye contact. Thankfully, Rachel was oblivious to his melancholy mood.

"How've you been?" she asked as she walked back to the kettle and scooped a heaped teaspoon of ground coffee into the cafetière, "How was your night?"

Rachel lifted the kettle as it completed its boil. Finn was grateful she was looking elsewhere; he didn't want her to see his bloodshot eyes.

"Sorry, did you say you wanted a tea?"

"No, thanks," Finn replied, gingerly sitting at the table with a glass of water. He had just about composed himself after the emotive episode in the shower. Should he tell her about it? Probably not. He wasn't sure he could even explain it to himself. He didn't know where to start with so much on his mind and a pounding head. He sipped his water and decided he wanted the argument to be over.

"Rach, I don't want to go to Greece," he said quietly.

Rachel happily walked over to the cupboard to grab the sugar, not having heard him. "It was so great to see Tom and James. You'd love James's new car. It is so bloody fast. I swear it's going to kill him. God, I got so drunk on Friday night that I felt awful." She pushed the cafetière plunger down, poured a coffee and added sugar to her cup, and then returned the container to the shelf.

"Rach?" Finn emphasised a little louder but still sheepishly.

Rachel studied him. "Blimey, Hun, you look rough. Was it

a big night with Sinead?" she laughed.

"Yeah," Finn replied nervously, "it was." He sipped his water again and waited for the nausea to disappear. "Rach, I don't want to go to Greece," he repeated.

"Huh?" Confused and surprised, as she sat opposite him at the kitchen table. "What do you mean?"

"I think it's all been a bit rushed, and I think it's too early to see Ellie," he continued, trying to find the right words and make his point heard. He hadn't started this right. It wasn't about Ellie; it was about him. Could he start again?

"It's fine," Rachel interrupted as she stirred her coffee, "She said it was fine. And she'd tell me if it wasn't. Gino can't wait to see you. Ellie admitted that he wants to spend time with you so that you can help him get through all the madness that is going on. Why the sudden change of heart?"

"Sorry?" Finn asked, noticing his heart rate rise a little. This was the start of the argument. He could feel it. Why was Rachel being so chatty and nonchalant? At the same time, he knew that he didn't have the energy to quarrel. Tired and hungover and still reeling from the unexpected outpouring of grief earlier, Finn decided to nip it in the bud. What would be the point of being antagonistic? "Look, Rach, I've been doing some thinking over the last few days, and I just don't...."

"So, you want to cancel?" she said in a flat voice.

Finn stood up in a vain attempt to control the situation. He didn't want to raise his voice as he felt exceptionally emotional. He glared directly at Rachel and paused. "Could I finish?"

Rachel's eyes opened wider as she tried not to look indignant. Understanding that Finn was serious, she stayed silent and sipped her coffee.

He walked over to the kitchen window, hoping to eloquently explain all the thoughts he'd worked through over the last few hours. If he didn't look at Rachel's face, he might be able to deliver it in one go. Unrehearsed, there wouldn't be any order, but he wanted to get his point across without contention.

"There's been no change of heart. I didn't decide to go to Greece. You did. Since you delivered the bombshell about not taking the interview for Boston and after your visit to see Ellie, I feel that you've been making decisions without consulting me. The crazy idea of heading to Greece and sailing into the sunset...."

He heard Rachel adjust her position in her seat but was pleased she didn't interrupt him again.

"...without even seeing if I'd like to do that. I know we've talked about it in the past, but it was a pipe dream. It was not something that we were actually going to see through. Constantly arguing with me and complaining that your family hasn't supported you for the last while has been really difficult for me. I know how sad you were about Ellie's news; I was, too. And I understand the need to find resilience, but I think you've been doing it wrong. Fighting with me is wrong. I'm not the problem. And I want you to be happy. Of course, I do. I want to be happy. I want us to be happy. Catching up with Ade last night was so fantastic; reconnecting with her after such a long time honestly made me think. Probably similar thoughts to yours. I need to find some emotional stability. Firstly, I need to address my emotions for Ma...." Finn's voice cracked, and his eyes filled with tears. Another wave consumed him, and he lost his balance a little.

"Finn?" Rachel asked, concerned, and quickly got up to go to him. "Are you OK?"

He blinked and moved towards a kitchen chair. Rachel

pulled it out for him to sit down. The cushion felt good. Finn didn't think he'd drunk that much last night to feel this fragile.

"Just feeling a bit delicate today," he said.

"Are you sure?"

"Yeah, it's been a hell of a day." He knew that he needed to finish his speech while still having the details in his head. "Look, what I'm trying to say is that this has been a fucking terrible few weeks. I honestly hate arguing with you. It makes me feel so crap inside. What should've been a joyous time in finding out about your interview and the prospects of moving to the States has manifested into an acrimonious battle between us. Coupled with the impact of Ellie's news and where my head is, I think going to Greece is not the best thing for me right now."

Across the table, he observed that Rachel's previous bounce and positivity had vanished entirely. He wiped both of his eyes with the palms of his hands and swallowed. Rachel remained silent. Before the argument started, Finn needed to tell her what he wanted to do next. He could see in Rachel's face that something big would soon surface.

"I had no idea just how wretched Sinead felt. I haven't been there for her after Ma died, and I should've been. To be honest, I don't think I've addressed Ma's death at all." The tears came again, and Finn had no idea how. It caught him unaware. Is this what Sinead had described? The churned-up nausea returned to his stomach, and he struggled to breathe again.

"Finn, honestly, are you OK?" she reached across the table and tried to grab his hand, "What's going on?"

"I don't fucking know. Genuinely. I think that maybe I've had a reality check similar to yours. I need to find out how best to move forward with my life because I'm emotionally wrecked right now. And I've only just realised this. After Ma's death, I completely ignored my feelings and separated myself from my sisters and Ryan. I put all my focus on the prospects of going to Boston and spending time with you. When you took that away, it was like having a rug pulled from under me. Coupled with that, I was desperate for a carte blanche and an opportunity to start afresh, but on reflection, that was ignoring the elephant in the room. Sinead told me about her relationship with Ma last night, and it was nothing like mine. I wasn't that close to her, and I wonder why. Ryan is just so amazing and such a rock. God knows what he's had to take care of, and he never asked for my help. Never complained. Why was I not there for him?"

"Do you truthfully feel that way about me?" Rachel asked, visibly hurt.

"Sorry?" Finn responded, still thinking about how he could mend the issues with Ryan.

"That I've taken everything away from you?"

"Well, you sure as hell have been making the decisions for us both recently." he replied, "Until last night, and I know that sounds recent, I didn't know where my head was. I loved the idea of Boston, as you know. I got over the initial worry about how it would work for me, and I was excited about a new adventure for us both. I was following your dream, making myself fit into your life. But I was OK with that. Selfishly, too, I was ignoring the fact that I needed to sort stuff with my family before I even considered heading off to the other side of the Atlantic. And then you unilaterally took it away. Without any consideration for me whatsoever."

"I want to talk to you about that," she interrupted.

"Again, Rach, can I finish?" he asked impatiently. He stood up and went to the fridge to get more water.

"OK, but I do want to talk about Boston."

Finn closed the fridge door and stared at Rachel. It lasted uncomfortably long. He had to say it. He held her gaze, "I'm not coming to Greece next week. I'm going home to Ireland to try and rebuild the relationships with my family. I want to move to the U.S., and I want you to support my options and not make decisions for me."

There it was - out in the open. Boom.

Finn exhaled and studied Rachel to gauge her response. He was desperate to hear her retort, expecting a flourish of shouting. He felt marginally better for saying his piece, although he was not sure he'd explained himself thoroughly. His head was still a mess, and he hoped he'd given her enough reasoning to make her understand. Surely she'd complain that he wasn't supporting her, but he felt strongly that he had shit to sort out.

Rachel sipped her coffee and looked at Finn. "I'm really sorry, Finn. I've been awful to you lately. Not thinking of you at all. You have every right to say these things. I want to go to Boston, too."

Finn stared across the table, stunned. "What?" he frowned, "I don't understand."

"I've decided that I want to go to Boston, too. I emailed Bob and accepted a job offer that will start in the Spring."

Finn stared at Rachel, reeling from the news. He'd spent so long trying to make sure he explained himself that this was not the response he was expecting. He took a sip of his water. "Fuck, Rachel, what are you like?!"

"But I want to go to Greece for more than a holiday. I want us to take some time out and find ourselves on a yacht and…"

"Sail off into the sunset," Finn finished.

"Yes!!" she answered, her face lighting up again.

"You're fucking unbelievable," he vehemently spat out as he walked to put his glass in the sink.

"What do you mean?" she asked, astonished.

"I'm going for a walk," he growled as he headed out of the kitchen. "Cancel my flight to Greece; I'm going home."

He left the kitchen, and Rachel heard the front door slam. What had she done wrong?

Chapter 14

I trace it all back to...

Monday, 29th June

"Why the fuck should I have to compromise?" Rachel blurted out.

Christie stared at Rachel and raised her eyebrows, thankful that no one was too close by to be offended. "No more wine for Mrs Logan, me thinks."

"Oh, give over, Christie. I've only had two glasses."

"Two large ones on an empty stomach," she pointed out.

She gasped across the table to Christie and sighed, "Oh God, and it's a Monday, too. Shit!"

Christie reached over to Rachel and passed her the

previously ignored glass of sparkling water. The ice had melted. Rachel nodded and took a long sip of Perrier.

"I'm sorry, Christie, I'm just so pissed off at the moment. So many things are going on..." she took another sip of water and used her other hand to point her index finger in the vague direction of Christie. "Just when I thought I'd got over the plethora of questions, finally finding my answers and overcoming the hard part of making a decision, all of the tables have turned. Again. And everything is up in the air - again!"

She put her glass down, raised both hands and waved them like a stereotypical Italian gangster. The waiter saw the signal and looked over, but Christie shook her head at him. Nope, it wasn't a request for more drinks.

"I think you should head home and speak to Finn," Christie offered.

"I don't want to speak to him," Rachel confessed drunkenly and childishly.

"You don't mean that, Rach. You've just had too much wine." Christie considered the confused waiter and signalled that she wanted the bill, with the globally understood mock writing on her hand, "I'll call you a taxi."

"Finn isn't at home," Rachel admitted sheepishly, ignoring anything Christie said, "He's staying with Sinead."

"Well, do you want to come back to mine then?" Christie asked.

"Aww, Sweetie, you're so kind," Rachel slurred whilst smiling, "You are the best! But I've got the Bradshaw meeting first thing in the morning, and it's my side of town." She paused and visibly tried to shake herself awake. "Fuck, I'm going to need to sober up for that! Maybe we could get some food?"

"I've got to head, Rach. This was only supposed to be 'one after work', and it's already 8 o'clock."

"Shit! Really? Oh God, I'm so sorry. I totally understand. Let's get the bill, and I'll call a taxi. I'll order food when I get home."

Christie raised her eyes. She'd already ordered two taxis on her app, called the waiter over, and was now paying the bill while Rach rambled. She knew how Rachel got. This wasn't new. "We're good. You owe me £19. Your taxi will be here in 8 minutes."

"Thanks, doll," Rachel was used to Christie bailing her out. It was how their friendship worked. Christie was such an organised person, and they laughed at how much she acted like Rachel's PA, "I'll pay you on the way home." Rachel moved to get up and wobbled a little; this was not how she wanted to feel. Why had she had so much wine? She was furious at Finn, and this was her reaction. Perhaps she needed to think about whether always turning to wine was an issue, but that's definitely for another (sober) day when she wasn't so confused.

After storming out yesterday, he'd texted her to say he'd gone to Sinead's and wouldn't return until Tuesday evening. Why did he react like that? He'd wanted to go to Boston, and she confirmed they would do that. Just a little later than planned. Why was he being so unkind? Rachel stood up and put on her jacket. She stared at the waiter who was looking at her. She grimaced and then mouthed, '*Sorry,*' He nodded and carried on collecting dirty glasses.

"I'm just nipping to the loo," Rachel announced loudly, unsure whether Christie was listening. It was more of an audible thought. Boy, she had had too much wine.

"I'll come with you," said Christie.

Walking to the Ladies', Rachel tried to think about what

she'd done wrong, but her head was too fuzzy. Why had Finn got so upset with her? It was uncharacteristic of him to be that angry.

"Am I being unfair?" Rachel asked Christie as they washed their hands.

Christie considered Rachel's face in the mirror and paused. "No, you're not being unfair," she replied, as Rachel smiled, "But I think you're being selfish."

"What?" Rachel responded as she shook her wet hands.

"Well, you're making massive decisions for you and Finn and doing it single-handedly," Christie calmly answered as she reached into her handbag to find her buzzing phone. "And changing your mind at the same time. No wonder he's confused." She knew how Rachel was, and their relationship was solid enough to be this candid. "Your taxi is outside. We need to go."

Rachel shook her head and tried to regain some concentration. Was her friend right? Shit, so many more questions.

"Yeah, sure," Rachel grabbed her bag and left the toilets.

Christie pointed to the black cab, facing one way, as she got into the other, facing in the opposite direction. "See you tomorrow," she shouted.

Rachel waved, "I'll be in after lunch."

Getting into the cab, Rachel was grateful she had a reticent driver. She had a lot of thinking to do. It was ridiculous to be fighting with Finn and having conflict at a time in her life that should be exciting. Why couldn't she find happiness? Despite Ellie's circumstances, she'd felt so at peace in Greece. Why didn't Finn want to share that experience with her? What was the issue with spending time together and getting off the daily grind? She'd sorted her job prospects to fund the adventure and knew her family supported her; she felt ecstatic. Why didn't Finn feel it? It didn't make sense that he was so mad that she'd returned to the original scenario they'd planned. He'd been happy before all of this shit had happened. She was so confused. Admittedly, she'd gone full circle and caused lots of uncertainty on the way, but they were back to where they wanted to be, so why was he so mad?

She couldn't believe how much her life had changed in under a month. She was heading to Greece on Saturday, alone, and needed to get herself sorted. She needed to sort her head out. Since they'd met in Southampton, Alice had been hinting at Rachel's issues, sending her links to practical books to help her with her relationship with her mother and her dependency on alcohol, pointing out that she'd observed Rachel's tendency to rely on wine, coffee and paracetamol to deal with everything. She responded to Alice's emails with noncommittal statements like *'Shit; I can't do it all at the same time'* and *'Yeah, but surely you know my mother, right?'* Knowing that Alice had her interests at heart and that she was only being kind, Rachel picked up her phone and messaged Alice.

> Hey mate, how's things? Are you free for a chat?
> Could really do with your help. Rx

Her phone buzzed back immediately.

> Sorry currently in an online seminar so can't talk
> But can type
>
> It's nearly 8:30 WTF?
> Some Professor in Chicago is doing a talk on gender roles

> using Piaget's Cognitive Development Theory
>
> Wow! Your world totally rocks
>
> haha - you're just jealous
>
> Yeah right
>
> I've had a fight with Finn and had too much wine
>
> What should I do?
>
> Apologise
>
> And get a chippy

Rachel smiled and looked up from her phone. She could always count on Alice to keep her straight. Even though they had only been together a few weeks ago and had such a fabulous time, perhaps they could get together again and laugh, chat, cry and hug. Maybe Alice could come with her to see Ellie, and they could return to where they were a few weeks ago. They had had such a good time. They could have long beach walks, drink wine, feel sunshine on their backs again, and help Rachel work out what was going on in her head. She was sure Ellie wouldn't mind and was expecting two house guests anyway.

> What are you doing on Saturday?

Alice hadn't replied. The seminar must be riveting. Rachel suddenly felt very dehydrated and hungry. Why had she had so much wine? Contemplatively, she rubbed her lips and scratched her chin. She needed to fix things with Finn. Maybe it wouldn't be a good idea to ask Alice. She sighed and gazed out the taxi window. Her head was so muddled. Thank God she was nearly home. Caught at the traffic lights, her brain started ticking again. Would it be that rude to go to Greece with Alice? Spending time with someone who wouldn't argue with her would be refreshing. It would surely piss Finn off, though, wouldn't it? Rachel sighed. She wanted to get home, eat something, have a glass of water and go to bed. Her head was buzzing with uncertainty, and she could feel a headache coming on.

Finn had explicitly conceded that he wasn't coming to Ellie's, so she did have a spare plane ticket. Although Alice had been pretty brutal when they met in Southampton, her WhatsApp chats and subsequent supportive emails had made Rachel reconsider her actions and helped her make decisions. God, was the Merlot night with Alice only nine days ago? So much had happened! Rachel looked down at her phone, hoping Alice would decide for her because she didn't have the energy. Then again, all those decisions she'd sought out and made had been blown apart, thanks to Finn!

Fuck. Fuck. Fuck. Her phone buzzed.

> I'm going to see Mum, why?
>
> Do you fancy coming with me to see Ellie?
>
> I thought you were going with Finn
>
> Yeah, that's what the fight was about

Before she could continue the interaction, the taxi pulled up outside her flat.

"That's 21 quid, mate," the quiet taxi driver mumbled as he passed her his SumUp device, assuming she was paying by card. Rachel tapped it with her phone, grabbed her handbag, and left the taxi without saying anything.

Feeling marginally more sober than earlier but still tired, she needed something to eat. Knowing that there was no food in the fridge in the flat and that she was ravenous, she walked to the nearby Tesco Extra to grab something.

Deciding, en route, to be good and grab something healthy, she sought out the pre-made salads.

"Good evening, Darling! Is there anything I can help you with?" An overzealous checkout assistant suddenly appeared out of nowhere, startling Rachel. She could only be about four feet tall, with long, frizzy black hair and too much makeup on her face. Rachel tried not to stare, but her slightly inebriated mind meant she looked puzzled at the tiny woman. Surveying the alternating blue and black nail varnish on her talon-like fingernails and loads of gold jewellery on her neck, fingers and earlobes, she was quite a sight! Rachel felt like a giant.

"Just a salad and a sparkling water," she answered, walking towards the fridges.

"We've Häagen Dazs on offer today, Darling. I wonder if I could tempt you with some Phish Food."

"Oh no, thank you! I'm trying to be good," chuckled Rachel, walking away quickly.

She grabbed a few things and went to the self-checkout. It was more items than she'd thought she'd buy. How had she randomly remembered she was out of hand soap? Grabbing a bag-for-life, she started scanning. The tiny woman was loudly helping an elderly couple pay for their shopping with clubcard points, which allowed Rachel to duck out of the shop before needing to have any more conversation. Her phone buzzed.

> Are you sure Ellie is up for seeing you? We were only just there.
>
> Yes. She said so
>
> Was that Ellie saying that or you saying that?

Rachel walked to her flat and ignored Alice's comment. She needed to pee again. Reaching into her handbag, she took her keys out and opened the door. Strangely, no lights were on, no TV or radio to be heard, and no cooking smell. It felt alien. So un-homely. She threw her keys onto the console table and dumped her handbag. Walking into the kitchen, she turned on the lights and placed her shopping on the counter. She went to the fridge and grabbed a cold bottle of sparkling water. Kicking her shoes off, she went to the toilet. Her phone continued to buzz.

"Ach, you shouldn't feel bad. She's being a shite," argued Sinead as she stubbed out a cigarette in the ashtray and took a sip of her gin and tonic.

"You can't say that, Ade," Finn responded, with little conviction, as he took another slug of his beer. Because, sometimes, he felt that way about Rachel.

The last few days had been utter turmoil for him. Walking out on Rachel was necessary because he was so volatile and knew it was best not to be in her company. But he felt awful. He'd never walked out on her before, and the episode in the shower had left him feeling scared. Where had that emotional explosion come from? Had it been lying dormant? Would it surface again? Was it a ticking time bomb? There were so many questions; it was getting ridiculous.

Sinead stood up and left, presumably to get another drink. Finn wondered whether he should text Rachel. Best do it whilst Sinead was not in the room, she was backstabbing Rachel as she felt she needed to protect her brother. He wanted to fix things with his wife and didn't want to get into another fight. Perhaps he should leave it. He'd made his intentions clear that he wasn't going to Greece, and Sinead had already lined up everything for Ireland. A week away from Rachel would benefit them both, wouldn't it? He needed to speak to Ryan; his brother always made things appear better.

He stared around Sinead's little flat and thought how surreal it felt. It was messy, with cushions everywhere, wilting plants in pots with dead leaves on side tables, dirty, empty coffee cups, and a few half-filled ashtrays. Random art adorned the walls, which Sinead had explained had been drawn by Marla's mother and had massive sentimental meaning. He couldn't see it. Sinead agreed she couldn't either but didn't want to upset her prompt rent-paying flatmate. None of the furniture matched; there was a vintage leather sofa, a modern glass coffee table, a tartan wingback chair and a wooden rocking chair. Magazines and books were stacked and strewn across every available surface. An unusual neon light hung on the wall saying 'Hello there' in homage to Cat Woman's apartment from the Batman movie. Every corner of the room had some lamp, all floor-standing in different shapes and colours. This place was nothing like his and Rachel's flat, which was interiorly designed and kept tidy and shipshape. He smiled a little as he felt his love for Rachel wash over him. He couldn't stay mad with her for long. He had a lot of work to do to get on top of his emotions. Ireland was going to be crucial. He needed to find peace.

Rachel returned from the toilet and started delving through her shopping. She ignored the beetroot & halloumi salad with pomegranate and dill and went straight to the Cookies and Cream Häagen Dazs ice cream. Damn that little woman, Rachel thought as she put the peppermint hand soap aside, wishing she hadn't seeded the idea. Grabbing a spoon, the ice cream, her sparking water and her phone, she walked to the sofa in the living room. She sat down and read her messages.

> I really don't think it's a good idea
> I think Ellie needs more time to heal
> Why are you fighting with Finn?
> Does he think it's a good idea to go?
> TT?

OK, so Alice wasn't coming to Greece.

> I'm going on Saturday and Finn isn't coming with me
> Ellie is OK with it
> You OK?
> Not really, But some time away will be good

Suddenly, Rachel's phone rang. It was Alice. So, did she need to talk about it now? She was pretty happy sitting silently, feeling sorry for herself, and conversing digitally. "Hey…" Rachel waited.

"Seminar is over, and I thought I'd call you," Alice said softly. "Are you sure you're alright?"

Rachel sighed, took a large spoonful of ice cream and put it in her mouth. "Bugger! That's cold!"

"What?" asked Alice.

"Sorry, just got brain freeze eating ice cream. Ignore me," Rachel replied.

Alice laughed, "You don't change, TT."

"Yeah, good ole Rach!" Rachel quivered. "Mate, I do need your help. The shit has most definitely hit the fan."

"That's not just the wine talking?"

"No, I don't think so. The last few days have been so rough. Emotional chaos. I fought with Finn; he walked out, Alice. He's never done that before. I must've really pissed him off. Then, too much wine is how I cope with things these days. And then the realisation that I've absolutely no idea what I should do."

"This has changed from when you were down with me. What's happened? Is there anything I can do?"

"Any advice would be gratefully received," Rachel replied resignedly. "Honestly, is there any way I can get my head straight?"

"I can try," Alice offered, "But it might be a bit brutal. And ideally, I'd like to see you in person to ensure I can support you if it becomes difficult."

"Blimey! What are you going to do?" Rachel remarked and laughed nervously.

"Maybe I can help. I know it's pretty late, and it's a Monday, so I'm not sure how much I can help, but I can try to draw some answers from you."

"What do you mean? It sounds like black magic."

"Ha! You've no idea, sister," Alice jested. "We therapists use a method called 'Person-centred therapy', which is based on the view that, given the right conditions, everyone has the capacity and desire for change and personal growth. I can ask you some questions to help you come to terms with any negative feelings you have, and then, over time, I can help you to change and develop in your own way."

"Oh wow..." Rachel put her ice cream and spoon down and quickly checked how much charge she had on her phone.

"So this is far from the right conditions, as we're apart and you've been drinking, but it could work."

"I'm up for it if you are. Anything to help the shit that is going on in my head. Can I grab my AirPods? I think it'll be more comfortable."

"Sure, good idea."

Rachel entered the hall and quickly rummaged in her handbag for her AirPods. Tomorrow meant a client meeting in the morning, but she had time to give them to Alice now. Could this help? Would she get some answers? She hoped so.

Returning to the living room, she opened her sparkling water, took a sip, and put the lid back on the ice cream. Let's try this.

"OK, I'm here, Alice, all plugged in. How do we do this?"

"So we surrender to the truth," Alice said professionally. "And shut up, TT, this is about getting you to focus."

Rachel smirked, amazed at how Alice knew she was making a face and being silently impertinent.

"I'm going to ask you questions and keep pressing you to find the answers; it's an opportunity for discovery. Stay on point, and don't get distracted. Respond directly to my questions. This isn't a conversation; it's about you finding the answers you need."

"What happens if I don't have the answers?"

"Oh, TT," Alice calmly and sweetly assured her, "Of course you do. You don't know it yet."

Finn looked at his phone again, desperate to text Rachel. If he did send a text, he didn't want Sinead to see, as she'd been bad-mouthing Rachel for most of the evening. Sadly, he'd been too distracted to defend her honour, but he knew

Sinead didn't mean it. Both of them got on well, most of the time; this was typical of his sister.

"Ade, please stop slagging Rach off. It's nasty."

"Yeah, sorry. I just get pissed off with her when she calls all the stops. She's lucky to have a husband like you. Not many blokes would stand for it."

He watched her and grinned.

"How do you put up with her? She can be a real prima donna, you know."

"She's had a tough few weeks and some substantial life choices recently, so I'm going to cut her some slack."

"Wow! You've changed your tune!" Sinead laughed, "Didn't you walk out on her yesterday?"

Finn swallowed his beer, put the glass down, looked at his sister, and grimaced.

"OK, TT. Let's see what we can do." Alice paused, rustled down the phone, and then kicked off, "Ready?"

"Sure."

"So, what do you feel is wrong?"

"I'm confused and don't know what to do." She paused. That came out too quickly, surely? It was automatic. Is that how you do this? Encouraged by Alice's silence, she continued, "I'm continually fighting with the most important person in my life, which is killing me, and I hate it. I want to get back to what we were like a few weeks ago. I can't believe how quickly everything has changed. But at the same time, I want him to understand that I'm craving head space and want to take some time away from my current life."

"Why do you want to get away from your current life?"

"Because I don't feel like I own it." She opened her eyes.

Where was this coming from?

"Have you told him this?"

"Yes, and every time I do it, it becomes an argument."

"How do you tell him?"

Rachel wiped her eyes as they'd suddenly filled with tears. She took a sip of her water. Alice remained silent.

"I selfishly tell him what I want." Rachel stopped, sighed and nervously adjusted her AirPods. Bright rotating lights of an emergency service vehicle caught her eye as it whizzed past her window. She looked up, and her voice turned into a whisper, "And the amazing guy that he is, he simply listens and unconditionally supports my choices." She wiped away more tears. She missed Finn. Alice remained quiet.

"After Ellie's news, I became acutely aware of my lack of resilience and general emotional immaturity. It made me think. It made me wonder how I would cope in similar circumstances, and I knew I would fail. I decided I didn't want to do the big corporate thing anymore. I wanted to head off to Greece, sail into the sunset, and find myself. Get away from my current life. Get away from the life I thought I wanted. When I thought about the possibilities, I felt energised. But the timing was so off. Finn was furious that I'd changed my mind."

Rachel knew that Alice had already heard all of these details, but repeating the scenario and investigating the point at which it went wrong felt cathartic. Alice remained quiet.

"My excitement of a trip away to paradise was short-lived as my previous positivity and happiness turned to doubt and worry. Did I genuinely want to jack in the job? Did I want to go into uncharted waters? I reacted, and I argued with Finn. I kept arguing with Finn. He and my family kept challenging me on why I was not chasing my dream career, and I became so confused. Who should I believe? I lost my confidence. I couldn't defend my choices anymore." she gulped, "So I declined the interview and didn't think of the repercussions and who it would impact. I let my husband and parents down."

"How did you let them down?"

"Well, I didn't do what I said I would do."

Rachel stopped and tried to collect her thoughts. Was she making sense? Alice was still silent. Was she getting this right? She decided to continue,

"And when I realised what I'd done, I tried to fix it. Work's been amazing and really supportive of my ever-changing mindset, so I backtracked. I went back to Bob, and I took the job. Well, it was a new job, a different job, but ultimately the same trajectory. It was the answer that Finn and my folks wanted. But that didn't work either."

"Is that why you're confused?"

"Of course! Wouldn't you be?"

Alice stayed silent. Rachel reflected and then remembered Alice's instruction to stay on point. "Sorry, yes that's why I'm confused."

"How are those situations linked?" Alice pressed on.

"What do you mean?" Rachel still felt confused.

Alice appreciated that Rachel was new at this but wanted to ensure she followed the rules. This wasn't a conversation. "How does focusing on your emotional maturity and choosing to turn down a job opportunity equal letting your parents and husband down?"

Rachel took a moment to understand the question. This was a challenging exercise, but she couldn't believe how much she was discovering. She suddenly had a profound respect for Alice.

"For as long as I can remember, I've felt I've had direction and purpose. From a very young age, I wanted to do well and succeed at everything I applied myself to, so I worked super hard. I was proud of what I'd accomplished. I loved being in first place. My family pushed me to achieve as much as possible, and the competition with my peers and brothers was healthy. It even became a little addictive. I recall telling my folks I would never be Prime Minister because I decided not to. I worked hard, and I achieved high. I deserved everything I got."

Rachel stopped. Had she just claimed that she'd always excelled? Did she think this? Well, she'd just said it, right? "Sorry, Alice, I'm not sure I can do this."

"Why?"

"Because I sound like a total dick."

"On whose measure?"

"Wow!' Rachel replied with a slight laugh. The punches kept coming. Having never gone through therapy, this was stripping her beyond her underwear to her lower epidermis.

"Hmm. Surely, it's my conscience?" Rachel asked herself, shaking her head and trying harder, "I should be winning since I've always won in the past."

"What does winning mean to you?"

"Coming first."

"So, when you come first, you feel you've won?"

"Of course."

Alice paused. "Do you ever feel you've won when you haven't come first?"

"Sorry, could you say that again?"

"Do you ever feel you've won when you haven't come first?" Alice repeated.

Searching for an example, a random thought popped into Rachel's consciousness. She felt she was in a mental zone that would allow her to articulate her thoughts comfortably, so she kept talking.

"When I was at primary school, I was in the egg-and-spoon race. My friend Carly was ridiculously nervous about the race. I told her it would be a breeze because I felt it would be a breeze for me. She was in the next lane to me. My Mum, Dad and brothers were there to watch, embarrassingly waving and whooping on the sidelines. I took off first and led the race, knowing I would win. Looking back at Carly, I saw her struggling to hold her egg, so I slowed down to encourage her. She smiled, and we crossed the finish line together. I was so happy that Carly had finished and hadn't dropped her egg. She screamed like she'd won. After the race, my mother told me that I should've pushed on and won and that she was disappointed in me."

The phone line went silent.

"Wow, that's so fucked up," Rachel muttered to herself.

"Does that make sense to you?"

"No, and I can't remember the last time I thought about that day. I've no idea what happened to Carly."

"Did you feel like you'd won in that situation?"

Rachel blinked and took another sip of her water. What on earth was being trawled up here? How in the hell did Carly surface in her mind? Is this what therapy was?

"No, my mother took away any positivity that I felt from helping Carly."

"How did that make you feel?"

"I apologised to my mother and went about proving to her that I was a winner because no one wants to be a disappointment." She suddenly became overcome with emotion and burst into uncontrollable crying. She shuddered and sobbed down the phone line.

"TT, are you OK?" Alice shouted, "TT?"

Rachel pulled out her AirPods, threw them on the floor, and let her phone fall onto her lap. She dropped her face into her hands and helplessly cried. Her palms filled with water as she tried to control her pulsating chest, which was convulsing from the sobbing. Meanwhile, her phone buzzed repeatedly. Alice was trying to call; she must have disconnected the call when she dropped the phone. Where had all these thoughts come from?

She stood up and went to the toilet to wash her face and hands. This had been brutal. She stared at herself in the mirror and examined her puffy eyes. Continuing to stare, she noticed that her face looked weary. Her skin was dehydrated, and she could see a few wrinkles on her forehead. Her makeup had pretty much disappeared from its earlier application. Checking her watch, it was 9:42; she should speak to Alice. That was a bit abrupt to hang up on her; she'd be worried. Walking into the living room, she picked up her phone.

> Please get back on the call
> TT?
> TT?
> Are you there?
> I shouldn't have done it this way
> I'm sorry

Rachel needed to take some time. She took another sip of her water and then called Alice.

"TT? Are you OK?" Alice begged, frantically.

"Yes, mate. I just got a bit sideswiped there. Why didn't you tell me that would happen?"

"Sorry, I did say it would be brutal. It was a terrible idea for me not to do this face-to-face. I'm so sorry. Are you OK?" she asked with genuine concern. "There's no way to know how someone will react to being probed. I didn't mean for you to get so upset."

"I know you didn't, but I'm astounded at what surfaced! I'm so surprised to think about Carly again. Screw my Mum too."

"We're not finished, but I don't want you to get any more upset, and it's getting late."

"So, what constitutes 'finished'?"

Alice went quiet. "Good point."

"Thanks for trying to help, Alice," she said in a tired voice. "I think I'm done."

"Of course, I understand. I just want you to be OK. And I'm so sorry if I've caused you more pain. I so want to give you a big hug right now."

"Me too. I'm so exhausted, I just need to go to bed. Thanks for everything."

"I understand. Get some rest. Please ring me tomorrow so we can talk more."

Rachel's phone buzzed, but she ignored it. "I will. I've just got to go to bed right now. I'm shattered."

"Night, TT."

"Night, Alice."

Rachel walked straight into her bedroom, put her phone on charge, and fell onto the bed. Emotional exhaustion consumed her. She missed the message that had come in.

Rach, I'm so sorry. I had to leave yesterday because otherwise I would've been unkind to you. I would never forgive myself if I were. There's so much we need to discuss, and I'm sorry we can't do that on a yacht in Greece. I need to be in Ireland. I have to deal with stuff and things I need to mend. Let me do that. But, babes, we're good. Honestly, I love you so completely.

Chapter 15
If I hadn't seen such riches

Tuesday, 30th June

Tuesday morning arrived with the regular 06:45 weekday work alarm, surprising Rachel. Grabbing her forehead, she slapped her phone and groaned. Suddenly remembering the previous night's therapy session with Alice, she stared at her ceiling and exhaled. Her head hurt. Evaluating the empty bed beside her, she sighed and came over queasy. Was that the wine from the evening before, Alice's teasing out her troubled inner psyche, the 'feel-sorry-for-myself' ice cream consumption or the sinking feeling that things were messed up with Finn? She was going to struggle to get out of bed today.

Before even considering showering, she decided to make a strong coffee, take paracetamol, and rely on the caffeine and pain relief to get her going. Standing in the kitchen, she noticed how strange the flat felt without Finn. It was too quiet. She had no idea what a noisy person he was. No radio was playing, and even though the coffee machine was bubbling a new pot, the Ninja machine lay silent, void of a high-protein kale-infused smoothie, and the kettle wasn't boiling. It had felt the same last night, and it was genuinely odd.

Waiting for the coffee to brew, she stared out the kitchen window at the passers-by. Even at this early time, people had started their days. Although Rachel felt rough, a certain degree of calm enveloped her. That, too, felt odd. Was it a product of last night's session? Had she performed an emotional detox, and this was the result? Could a revelation bring about a physical reaction? She reached over to turn the radio on and heard *'Sit Down'* by James playing. It made her smile, and she hummed along with the melody. It was a favourite song of hers and Finn's. She'd always loved the line, *"If I hadn't seen such riches, I could live with being poor"*. Was that what Greece was? If she hadn't experienced it with Ellie, she wouldn't have craved the need to escape and then derailed her relationship with Finn. Bloody hell, what had Alice done to her? Feeling nauseous yet calm, numb yet relaxed, she realised she needed to sort herself out. Having managed to articulate many thoughts last night, she recalled the theme of the evening. Confusion. Indecision. Conflict. A heady cocktail of feelings!

As she reached for the largest cup she could find, her phone buzzed. She ignored it and poured the freshly brewed coffee. It smelt divine. She remembered she needed to charge her AirPods, as she'd want to listen to music on the tube later. Were they still on the floor? Walking into the living room, she saw the melted ice cream on the coffee table. Annoyed that it had made a mess, she collected it and grabbed her AirPods from the sofa. As she returned to the kitchen, her phone continued to buzz. She put the ice cream in the bin, sipped her coffee and collected a dishcloth from the sink. Walking back into the living room, she wiped the coffee table, plumped up the cushions on the sofa and made the place look tidy again. She returned to the kitchen, rinsed the dishcloth and took another sip of her coffee. Suddenly thinking to herself, what in the hell am I doing? Feeling dazed and like a zombie who had gone into an automatic clean-up mode, she shook her head and sat at the kitchen table. Stop it, Rachel; you need to focus.

The radio was now playing *'The Sinking Feeling'* by The The. Was this some crazy witchcraft? She'd joked with Alice about black magic, but it seemed that the songs on the radio were spelling out meaning to her. The line, *"You can't destroy your problems by destroying yourself"*, came on, and Rachel laughed out loud. Damn you, Alice.

Resigning herself to address the buzzes, Rachel picked up her phone. She saw Finn's message, read it, and gulped. Placing her hand on her chest bone, she started to cry. This morning had been truly weird. She was definitely going to have to talk to Alice some more. But thank God, at least Finn wasn't mad with her anymore! She swiftly called his number and took another sip of her coffee. Waiting to hear his smooth Irish tones, she was disappointed when it went straight to voicemail. She'd leave a message, but what would she say? Shit! He'd extended her an olive branch, yet despite that, she didn't know what to say to her husband. Panicking, she realised she had more questions. What did he mean by saying he needed to deal with things in Ireland? What was wrong? She reacted by hanging up. Shit! Surely, that wasn't right? She should've tried to say something!

Calm down, woman, you're a mess. Let the caffeine and paracetamol kick in, and call Finn. But be calm!

It was early, and Finn must still be asleep. No doubt he'd had a night with Sinead and alcohol and, like her, had ignored that it was a school night. She redialled his number and said.

'Hi Honey, thanks for your message. We must talk in person. I can't do this into voicemail. I'm sorry for all the shit I've given you lately. I never meant to hurt you. I think you said you might be at a client's today in Fulham. Let me know, and I could meet you at lunchtime. I love you.'

Closing the call, she checked her phone and saw it was 7:12. She still had plenty of time to get ready. The journey to her client meeting in Richmond would only take 45 minutes. Contemplating making breakfast, she remembered there was no food in the house. She certainly wasn't going to eat the salad she bought last night. Still looking at her phone, she saw several messages from Alice.

> Are you OK this morning? I hope you managed to get some rest.
>
> I'm so sorry if I upset you.
>
> That was never my intent.
>
> Do you have time to talk? I want to check you're OK
>
> Please let me know

Rachel thought Alice was probably reeling from last night's session as much as she was. She knew her old friend had a heart of gold and that trying to help her via phone was probably unacceptable; she must feel awful. But Rachel had pushed her, urged her to help. As if it was Alice's responsibility to fix her. Why was she such a bitch to her wonderful friend? Why did she hurt the people that she loved? Rachel's bizarre morning mood morphed, and she became overcome with the sensation of needing to turn the situation around. She felt obliged to give positivity back to her friend and reassure her that she understood her kind intentions. Closing her eyes and breathing deeply, she decided to call. Alice picked up immediately.

"TT, you OK?" she asked nervously.

"Morning, Alice," she replied calmly. "Thanks for yesterday. How are you?"

"I've been worrying all night. I'm so sorry for upsetting you. I shouldn't have done that over the phone."

"Babes, you're the best, it's fine. I pushed you to do it. I wanted you to fix me because you're so good at that stuff. I put the pressure on you, and I'm sorry for putting you in that position. It was my fault. You have nothing to apologise for at all."

"It was so unprofessional," Alice considered sadly. "I should never have done it that way."

"Please don't beat yourself up about it. I was the one that asked. You've been nothing but a supportive friend lately, and I've been a completely selfish cow. All I've done is complain about my life to everyone who loves me and thought nothing about their feelings. How can I be upset with the one person who is looking out for me?"

Rachel couldn't believe where this speech was coming from. Perhaps Alice had unearthed some answers in her head after all. Besides, it felt good to be humble for a change. She took another sip of her coffee, which was turning cold.

"I need to sort my shit out, Alice. You're right. The stuff you've been showing me recently about how I deal with things is so true. Mum, the tablets, and the wine. I've just been ignoring the symptoms and lashing out. I'm so sorry.

You're amazing at what you do. You're professional, kind, understanding and selfless. I can't thank you enough for being there for me."

There was silence on the phone, then,

"Shit, TT, what's happened to you?"

"What do you mean?" she asked, surprised. She thought she'd made her point eloquently and sincerely; the words resonated with her.

"That was a genuine apology," Alice replied. "A fucking first for you."

Rachel laughed nervously. Was she honestly typically that obnoxious? Wanting to dilute her guilt, she dismissed the comment. "You sure dealt the black magic out last night, didn't you."

"Haha," Alice laughed, sounding a little more confident, "We should catch up when you return from Ellie's. I would love to come with you again, but I can't. We still need to talk stuff through. Perhaps I can come up to London. I'm sure you and Ellie will discuss many things when you're together, and if you're off sailing, you'll certainly be contemplating life. So, if you have any new thoughts on what we spoke of last night, write them down, and we can talk when we meet. The headspace will benefit you, so nurture your thinking because the answers will come. But I want to make sure that you feel positive and receptive to the answers you find. Besides, there is so much history you must forgive your Mum."

"Oh, please don't get me started on that! And there was I, thinking I'd made some progress."

"You have, TT, but there is still more to do."

"I'm only jesting, Alice. I know there are shit loads of question-answering still to be done. I need to fix things with Finn urgently; I can't stand where we are right now. You're right, the time with Ellie will give me the headspace to think things through; in fact, I'm depending on it. I'll have to leave the stuff about my Mum until I get back. Oh! And I'll try not to have too much alcohol, paracetamol or caffeine."

"Ha! It's a holiday, so relax and switch off from the troubles that have consumed you lately."

"Aww, Alice, you really are the best."

"FaceTime me when you're with Ellie. It'd be lovely to see her."

"Of course, I will. Gotta go, I need to shower and get ready for a meeting. Take care, and speak soon."

"Laters."

Finn checked the stats from his morning run on his watch as he walked up the stairs to Sinead's flat. It had been a decent 10k, and he was glad he'd been sensible last night, turning to cups of tea even after Sinead's insistent offering of more beer. It was because he didn't like feeling hazy and unsharp in the mornings. Especially since the episode a few days ago was still messing with his head. He was invigorated by the circuit he'd taken; the same paths leading from his flat had become mundane, and taking a different route was a nice change. Reaching into the pocket of his shorts, he took out Sinead's keyring that read, *'I don't do mornings'*. It made him smile. Struggling to get the key in the door lock, he was alarmed when the door suddenly opened. Sinead's flatmate, Marla, appeared in the doorway. Standing six foot tall with long, straight jet-black hair, she wore tartan pyjama bottoms and an ACDC t-shirt.

"You can't wiggle the key in the lock. It won't work," she stated slowly, staring blankly at Finn through her thick, black-rimmed glasses.

"Oh, sorry. I didn't know. Good morning, Marla. I hope you're well."

She turned on her heel and walked off without further dialogue. No wonder Sinead had concerns about this woman. He couldn't live with her idiosyncrasies. Walking into the flat, he could smell burnt toast and hear Sinead cursing at the smoke alarm that was not turning off. It took him right back to a few weeks ago when Rachel was wafting the smoke alarm because she, too, had burnt the toast. Wow! That felt like a lifetime ago.

Last night had been great talking to Sinead about family, and he was looking forward to returning to Ireland, but he realised how much he missed Rachel.

Stepping into the shower, Rachel surveyed herself in the mirror. Her legs and arms were in desperate need of a tan, even after a few days away in Greece earlier in the month. Living in England meant you kept your body covered for most of the year, so she couldn't wait to escape again and get some sun on her skin. She moved under the hot water, letting it run through her hair and down her pale body. It felt amazing and made her come alive. The caffeine and paracetamol had done their job, too, so she felt rejuvenated. As she washed her hair, she recalled her chat with Alice. She was surprised at herself. How could she think that clearly when her head was so scrambled? Where had the clarity come from? She was able to articulate her thoughts and feel genuine empathy. She was not sure she'd liked last night's therapy session; it had knocked her temperamental emotions and affected her thinking, but she felt compelled to have another session with Alice. She felt safe in the company of her good friend. This must be what she was searching for, the emotional intelligence that she saw in droves in Ellie. Alice could be the key. Whilst in Greece, she'd have the time to talk with Ellie and ask how she should progress.

She rinsed her hair and body and reached to turn the shower off. As she did, she heard her phone ringing from the bedroom.

"Shit!" She awkwardly jumped out of the shower and quickly grabbed a towel. It must be Finn. Trying desperately to stop her hair dripping and cover her body as she exited the bathroom, she picked up the phone. It was her mother. Should she accept the call? By the time she'd decided to answer, her mother's smiling face had disappeared from the screen.

"Bugger!"

Dripping everywhere and feeling annoyed, she threw the phone onto the bed. It started to ring again.

"I'm not in the mood, Mum. There is something called voicemail, you know." she snapped in exasperation but decided to check, just in case it was Finn. His face appeared on her phone screen, and her heart jumped.

"Hello, Finn, how are you?" she answered eagerly, desperate to hear his voice.

"Hey, you. I'm good. I miss you," he answered in his soft Irish accent.

Rachel felt immediately relaxed and warm inside; those words were like a physical hug. She walked back into the bathroom to drip there. "So good to hear your voice. I'm so sorry for all the fighting lately. I've been a real shit."

"Me too, Babes. It's been a tough time. I'd love to meet you for lunch today. We can talk it over then. Could you make 12:30 at The Brown Cow?"

"That would be great. But could we do 12? I need to be

back in the office for around 1:30."

"Sure, see you then. I can't wait."

"Thanks."

She hung up and smiled, marvelling at how the morning had changed so much since first waking up.

After hanging up the phone with Rachel, Alice decided to text Ellie. They'd been texting a lot lately, discussing how Ellie and Gino were coping since Alice and Rachel had left. In light of last night's session, she felt she needed to give Ellie an accurate picture of Rachel's mindset. Alice didn't want to say that Finn wouldn't visit, as she thought it was Rachel's business to tell her. Knowing that Rachel was volatile, Alice was concerned that yesterday's session may have taken her over the edge. This had been an emotional rollercoaster for her over the last month, and she wasn't sure whether Rachel would take her angst with her to Greece.

Ignoring the emails offering help from Alice, Rachel had classic denialism. However, Alice had not expected a well-thought-out apology and genuine clarity of thought from Rachel. Was she healing? Was she finding the answers she so desperately needed? Surely not, it was too soon. And Alice wasn't sure that she'd done the session correctly. Yet, she wanted to protect her other best friend, who had been on the biggest emotionally and physically stressful journey of them all. Alice wanted to ensure that Rachel didn't upset Ellie.

Usually, she would call Ellie, but she had to get on the bus and didn't want the morning commuters and schoolchildren to hear her talking, hence the text.

> Hey Ellie, how are you?

Hey you, I'm good.

Just having my morning green tea. You?

                        Just getting on the bus to go to work

I spoke to TT this morning after a pretty dire therapy session with her last night

What? A therapy session? Are you in London?

                        No. I stupidly did it over the phone

After she'd asked for help after a few large glasses of wine

What is she like?

                        I know, but I wanted to help

Did you?

                        Do you know what?

                        I think I did.

Chapter 16

Always friends

Tuesday, 30th June

Finn was sitting at the back of the restaurant, but Rachel saw him the minute she walked into the room as if they were magnetically attracted to each other. The pub was busy, and the smell of garlic and wholesome food made her feel hungry. She strode over to him at pace and grinned.

"Hi, Honey," she cooed, leaning over to kiss him on the cheek but suddenly panicking in case he didn't reciprocate. Finn stood up, hugged her tenderly, and kissed her slowly. It took her breath away. Rachel became immediately aroused and sat down quickly. Checking that no one had seen Finn's public display of affection, she gazed at him with dilated upils and lightly licked her lips.

"Are you blushing, Mrs Logan?" Finn smirked as he sat down.

"Well, that was unexpected," Rachel paused, "...but lovely." She adjusted herself in her seat and grabbed Finn's hand across the table. "I've missed you so much, Finn. It's been hideous without you. I'm so sorry for what a shit I've been. I hadn't meant to be like that. I've been so confused lately."

"Rach, honestly, it's fine," he said squeezing her hand. "You're right, it's been crap, and I'm sorry I stormed out on you. I couldn't control my emotions."

"It was the right thing to do. We would've just started yelling otherwise."

"I thought that too," he replied, looking directly into her eyes. "We good?"

Aware that she was still slightly turned on, she smirked and tucked her hair behind her ear. "Well, with a kiss like that, I can guarantee we're good. What can you follow it up with?"

He lifted his chin and laughed out loud. "Boy, I've missed you."

Alice stepped off the bus and walked to her first meeting of the day with the other partners from her practice. She decided she wouldn't tell them that last night she'd carried out an introductory therapy session over the phone because they'd think that completely unprofessional. She wanted to keep them all on her good side because she had high aspirations for this job and didn't want to mess things up. Still thinking about Rachel's volatility, she was genuinely concerned about whether Rachel was making the right decision. Wanting to help her find answers was exceptionally important to Alice. Apart from being nosy and wanting to help fix her friend, she was invested in the outcome. Ever since they were young, Alice had always seen promise in Rachel, holding her in unattainable high esteem.

Through high school, she noticed that Rachel was developing into an extraordinary woman, and she became her biggest fan. Their relationship started to decline when Ellie went travelling, as they didn't have her to facilitate their bickering when they quarrelled incessantly. Alice's emotions kept getting in the way of being a good friend. Not understanding her feelings and not wanting to wreck their friendship, she decided to go travelling to find answers. Without Rachel, she recognised that her life lacked substance and value, and she tried to fill the void in the bars and clubs of Thailand, Cambodia and Indonesia. After some scary episodes, including being stalked by a scarred Russian man, witnessing a stabbing in a tattoo parlour, taking too many drugs, and being pick-pocketed in Vietnam, Alice found the strength to grow up and move on.

During that time, she decided to get therapy and finally registered that she was utterly in love with Rachel. Having kept in constant contact while travelling, she heard about all of Rachel's antics at university. It made her sad to think that Rachel was making a life for herself without her, but she didn't say a word. She continued getting therapy, funded by several waitressing jobs and concluded that she would never have a physical relationship with Rachel. She questioned whether to divulge her secret. Her mother flew out to visit and gave her a tarot reading that predicted she'd find happiness and that Rachel would remain in her life as a strong presence. Exhilarated by the news, she worked on finding closure. After staying away for another few years and trying a few frivolous relationships in Bangkok, Alice decided she was ready to return home. Only her mother knew about her unrequited love, and she never mentioned it to Rachel or Ellie. Through her Psychology degree, she learned tools that helped her channel her love for Rachel into positive and friendly energy. That was why she was so bothered; she had to be there to help Rachel become the best of herself.

Having swiftly ordered their food, Rachel started talking. On her way to the restaurant, she'd rehearsed telling Finn her thoughts and explaining what she'd been thinking since he left. It felt weird to have to consider how to speak to her husband. Usually, it was automatic and easy, so it would be good to clear the air and embrace the positivity he'd shown her in the kiss he gave earlier. She had a small time window before returning to the office, so she dug in.

"Finn, can we chat over the issues we've been avoiding?"

"We can try."

She couldn't believe how upbeat she felt. He had kissed her with such tenderness, and she wanted to tell him how much she cared for him. They were surely back on track, back to how happy they were a month ago. Feeling that they'd properly reconnected, this outcome was better than she'd expected. "I only have about 45 minutes, so it'll have to be like speed dating."

"I wouldn't say speed dating, but I get what you mean."

Speaking with Alice had been eye-opening for Rachel, and she wanted to express to Finn that she now felt optimistic; her concerns and worries had started to fade.

"I had a therapy session on the phone with Alice last night, and it unearthed things that I hadn't thought about in decades. It was an exceptionally emotional experience."

"Did you find any answers?"

"No, not really, but I do feel calmer. I was surprised by that. I'm shattered but calmer." She sipped her sparkling water, glad she hadn't ordered a glass of red wine. Perhaps Alice's words were sinking in. "I'm sorry. Truly sorry. I've been horrendous. I've had so many things whizzing around my head. But they're my issues; I'm so sorry I've taken them out on you. Alice has been trying to get me to find clarity in the decisions I've been making lately, as well as helping me come to terms with the hostility I feel towards Mum. I've realised that the problem was that there's just been too much going on. I couldn't prioritise the important stuff."

She took another sip of her water and looked at Finn. He remained silent, absorbing her words.

"Between the potential job and transatlantic move and Ellie's news, coupled with fighting with you and wanting to go away and find me, I couldn't see the wood for the trees. It consumed me, and I took it out on you. I'm so, so sorry." She paused and turned her head away. She was proud that she could articulate her thoughts so well without crying. Where was she getting this emotional strength from? Had the session with Alice actually helped? "And then I got scared. I panicked and felt I had to reset. It felt unfamiliar to be lost. It wasn't safe. I desperately wanted to stop arguing with you and take us back to the point where we were happy. So, I took the job and thought that would solve our arguments. And it didn't. In fact, it made it worse. Finn, I am so, so sorry."

She couldn't hold the tears back anymore and started to cry. She tried to blink away the tears as she didn't want to embarrass Finn, and for anyone in the restaurant to see her, so she wiped her eyes with her napkin. Finn picked up the mantle.

"It's been a rollercoaster, Rach, and we've both fuelled the arguments. It hasn't been just you. But I've lashed out with anger and not discussed with you the things that have been going on in my mind. That was unfair of me, and I'm truly sorry about that. You're right; it's been an explosion of questions. I totally get what you're saying. I've had a few episodes myself recently and been in a delicate place, emotionally."

Rachel finished wiping her eyes and looked at him. A boisterous waitress suddenly appeared from nowhere and awkwardly dropped a plate in front of each of them. "Two ham and tomato flatbreads?" she exclaimed far too loudly.

It instantly destroyed their reflective mood, and they looked at each other and laughed. Before they could thank her or ask for anything, she was gone.

"Well, that was nice," Rachel laughed.

"Indeed!" he joked. "Well, Bon Appetite!"

They dug into their sandwiches, staying quiet for a few minutes, digesting the food and the comments they'd both just made. Rachel started.

"So, what's going on in Ireland?" she asked, "Is everything OK?"

Finn exhaled slowly and finished his mouthful. "I'm going over on Sunday with Sinead to catch up with Ryan, Fiona and Caitlin. After Sinead and I went out to dinner last Saturday, I realised that there were too many things I hadn't addressed since Ma died. I had the weirdest thing happen to me just before we last spoke."

"What do you mean?"

"On Sunday, just before you came home, I was in the shower after my run and became completely overcome with emotions. It affected me physically, like being punched. I felt sick, couldn't control my breathing, and started crying. It was fucking awful."

"Oh no! I have to say, you did seem super upset. What happened?"

"I think it was because I'd been talking a lot about Ma to Sinead. She explained to me their relationship. It was frequent, friendly, and unconditional. One that I didn't have. One I wasn't even aware of. Just thinking about her made me feel fragile and powerless. I collapsed in the shower and wept. I've never done that before. Not even after she died."

"You must have felt awful. I'm so sorry, I just put it down to you being hungover. God, I'm such a shit."

"Oh, Babes, you weren't to know. Thankfully, I haven't had another experience like that, and I hope I never do. It was unbelievably scary," He wiped his mouth with his napkin and sipped his water, then paused, looking at her. "We also spoke about what Ryan had been through, and I realised that I needed to do some proper grieving. And I think it best I do it with my siblings. I need to be there for Ryan; he's been such a rock, and I haven't."

"But you've been so strong since you lost your Mum."

"You've always said that Rach, but you're wrong. And that's my fault. I've made out that I was coping, but I think it was just deniability. I haven't dealt with it at all. I still can't even explain to myself what happened in the shower. I don't feel I have any emotional strength at all. I think my reactions to your words and arguments recently came from a place of weakness. I probably had a similar experience to you when you were with Ellie, needing to know how to find inner strength."

"You're not weak, Finn, not at all, quite the opposite. Seeing Ellie overcome such intense grief was inspiring and new for me. I've been trying to explain that to you very badly over the last few weeks. I don't think I can even explain it to myself." She finished her water and refilled their glasses from the Perrier bottle on the table. "I need to speak to Alice more because I'm only addressing the symptoms now. By arguing with you, making reactive job choices, suddenly wanting to escape everything, and showing hostility to my Mum, I'm just ignoring the fact I'm emotionally unstable. If I were stable, I would be able to tolerate these issues and not get so anxious and upset. Through talking about being physically impacted by emotions, when I was on the phone with Alice last night, she helped me remember a day back in primary school, one I had not recounted for decades, and when she pressed me to explain the situation, I was enveloped in emotion. It was like I'd been shocked. It was so brutal."

"Exactly!" Finn exclaimed, "That's how I felt in the shower. I thought I was having a heart attack."

"Blimey! What are we like?" She gazed back at him and remembered why she'd fallen in love with him. She loved that he could show his vulnerability, how much he contemplated his feelings, and how important it was for him to deal with issues. They were best friends, and they'd weather the storm.

"Perhaps I should speak to Alice too? We've both had a hell of a few weeks," he said softly.

"You can say that again. So let's go and find our strength. Let's get back on track. If we need to do it separately, then that's fine. I'll go to Greece and spend some time with my head, and you can go to Ireland and spend some time with your heart."

She looked at Finn and smiled. He paused and then warmly smiled back, "Ooh, I like what you did there."

"Honey, we're going to get through this," she said, reaching over and grabbing his hand. "We're too good together. Let's take some time next week to find answers and collect our thoughts, then we can discuss our next steps together. I promise there'll be no more unilateral decisions from me and more collaboration on our future."

"Yes, I think that's the best way forward. No rash decisions and no more arguments."

"I'll drink to that," she said, raising her water, and they clinked glasses. "Now about that kiss…"

Chapter 17

I'm here!

Saturday, 4th July

Rachel opened her eyes, moved her sunglasses from her nose to the top of her head and sat up slowly. In search of sun cream, she reached across to where she'd left it earlier. She noticed that someone had quietly replaced her condensation-soaked mug with a new Moscow Mule cocktail on the table beside her. Fresh mint, solid ice and an erect paper straw in a new copper mug meant it couldn't have been long ago. She glanced towards the pool and saw a sun-tanned waitress look over and nod, ensuring her guest knew it was her. Rachel thought, it doesn't get better than this.

She had caught one of the first flights out of London, landing early in the day in Kefalonia and wasn't fully awake when the text came in.

> Wait for the surprise, TT.
> And don't say anything until we meet.

The cryptic text had Rachel confused but intrigued, and she didn't know quite what to expect. Walking into the Arrivals lounge, she had been met by an impeccably dressed chauffeur with a sign saying "Lady Logan". She smirked, reached into her handbag, put on her Bulgari sunglasses, and, with a flourish but no words, indicated to the driver that she'd arrived. OK, Ellie, she thought, two can play at this game.

The man didn't say anything either, efficiently taking her suitcase and escorting her outside. An elegant black executive Mercedes-Benz S-Class was waiting, and he opened the door for her. Rachel got into the luxurious car, trying not to break her facade. This was going to be so much fun! Ellie had raised the bar.

Taken directly to an exclusive hideaway unknown by tourists, perched above a secret cove, Rachel stepped out of the pristine vehicle with tentative poise. Where was she? Trying desperately to look composed and blend in, she hastily walked over to Ellie, who was standing at the hotel's entrance. They embraced with genuine friendship as Rachel mouthed, 'What the fuck?' Ellie smiled demurely and said it was a special treat organised by Gino before he'd gone away on business. She gracefully placed her arm through Rachel's arm and headed through the large glass doors. The chauffeur passed Rachel's bags to the bellboy.

Walking through the foyer, Rachel removed her sunglasses and stared at her surroundings, wide-eyed in amazement; she couldn't keep her mouth closed. The place was truly breathtaking. The reception had a vaulted ceiling from which hundreds of small teal, azure, and jade-coloured glass orbs hung. It resembled a crashing wave, and Rachel instantly loved it. It made her think of the artwork in her flat, yet that didn't seem very impressive in comparison. This was something else. It was like the exquisite ceiling installed in The Bellagio in Las Vegas. Highly polished white marble walls were periodically stroked by billowing purple silky fabric cascading from the roof. A gentle sea breeze wafted into the reception and caused this visual event. It was magnificent.

Ellie explained that the hotel was a high-class, elite VIP hangout and that they'd be staying there for two days. She nodded to the reception staff and walked through. Putting her sunglasses back on, Rachel immediately started surveying the area in a vain attempt to see an Instagram celebrity, but only a few people were about. Ellie quietly added that Rachel would need to behave and watch her language.

After a detoxifying breakfast of apricot, pomegranate, watermelon, and chia seeds mixed with Greek yoghurt, Rachel and Ellie enjoyed a hot stone full-body massage, French manicure and pedicure, and exfoliating facial in the hotel's spa. This was followed by a delicious light lunch of mozzarella, tomatoes, fresh basil, and red onions, drizzled in olive oil with koulouri.

They were now sunbathing beside the hotel's pool, overlooking a private beach. Feeling like royalty, Rachel was still stunned by the experience and had to give herself a pinch. Do people actually live like this? Watching a sailing boat in the distance let out its main sail and perform a seamless manoeuvre, she realised she couldn't wait to get out on the water; this place wasn't her, but she enjoyed being indulged. She needed to speak to Gino about getting out onto the water. Whilst staring towards the beautiful Aegean Sea, Rachel abruptly appreciated how lucky she was. She'd patched up things with Finn, left on good terms with her siblings and her mother, Bob had thanked her for taking the job, and the chat with Alice had been constructive. She'd reflected on their chat a lot. Shit, was that only five days ago? She exhaled again and sank into the sumptuous sun lounger cushions. The view was sublime, and life felt good. She could just about hear the fast-click cadence of the cicadas in the nearby mountains over the gentle poolside music, but she focused on the soft, rhythmic lapping of the aquamarine sea against the white coral sand. She couldn't believe she was finally here. The sounds, the smells, and the salty tastes activated her senses, making her feel amazing. The maritime vista filled her vision, and she inhaled the scents of summer. Feeling the heat of the Mediterranean sun on her rarely exposed mid-drift, she reached for her new cocktail and looked across at Ellie.

"Babes, why would you ever want to be anywhere else?" she asked, sipping her new cocktail. "I can see why you're here. Finn is going to be so annoyed he missed this."

Ellie laughed and met her friend's gaze. "You'll have to thank Gino; this isn't my usual daily life, you know! It's a shame Finn isn't here, although Gino is away on business, so maybe it's for the best."

"When did you say he was back?" Rachel asked, putting her sunglasses back on.

"He said Monday evening, but things move around a lot, so that might change."

"But, that's perfect. I have you all to myself for two days! What are we going to do? Can I be Lady Logan for the whole time?"

"I knew you'd like that," Ellie laughed. "It was Alice's idea. She thought you would want to feel like royalty. One step above celebrity, you know."

"Ha, she knows me well. Well, I certainly feel like royalty today. This place is amazing. I could totally get used to this. What about you? Baroness Bianchi?"

"The two of us are going to take the time to chill. We'll talk about all the pain we've been going through over the last few months and try to find some calm."

She clearly hadn't heard Rachel's joke and was just talking. Lying facing up to the sun on the luxurious cream cushions laid out on her teak sun lounger, wearing a floppy, wide-brimmed straw hat and Prada sunglasses, with her left knee bent, she wasn't addressing Rachel, it was more of a statement to the wind, a verbalisation of her thoughts. Her smooth golden skin shimmered and was complemented perfectly by her pale blue bikini. She oozed class. There was no way of telling by her physique what a trauma her body had been through. She was like a celebrity. She fitted in with this place perfectly. Yet she seemed distracted.

"Find acceptance and peace…"

Rachel glanced across and noticed that Ellie appeared slimmer than last month.

"…positively think about the future," Ellie continued to ramble.

"I'm looking after you, is what'll happen."

Ellie stopped as if awoken by Rachel's response. "What? And be Nurse Rachel?" she laughed a little, "No need, TT, Gino has everything sorted. We just have to sit back, relax and work on our tans." She let her left leg straighten and then exhaled. She flagged the attentive waitress and gestured for another round of cocktails.

"So, have you finished all the work on the villa, or is there still stuff to do?"

Ellie sat up and smiled, having temporarily lost her reflective mood. "All the building work is done, but we're still waiting for some furniture to arrive. I've been thinking about what to turn my efforts to now, especially since the baby won't be here." She gulped down the last mouthful of her Bellini and looked to see if the waitress was coming with the next round.

Rachel wasn't quite sure how to address that statement, so she stayed quiet. She desperately wanted to ask her friend how she'd been coping with her emotions since they were last together, but for a split second, she realised that maybe Ellie wasn't. What should she say now? They both remained silent, and this time, the silence was uncomfortable. Rachel panicked and decided to break the quiet.

"Did you know that Alice has become a founding partner at a psychotherapy practice in Southampton?"

"Of course," Ellie responded curtly, "We text each other all the time."

"Oh," Rachel said, surprised and slightly hurt by the response, "OK."

Why was Ellie being this way? She didn't need to be rude; it was just a question. Or was she imagining it? Ellie wasn't usually like this. She was a gentle soul. Maybe Rachel was just tired from the early flight and not thinking straight.

"I think it's great news for Alice," Ellie commented dismissively. "She needed to find something positive for her. She'll be brilliant."

The sun-tanned waitress walked over with two fresh cocktails, two glasses of water and placed them on the teak table between their sun loungers. Rachel realised that this would be her third cocktail of the day, and she could hear Alice's voice in her head, so she thought that perhaps she should slow it down, especially with the sunshine bearing down on her.

Ellie picked up her glass and raised it, "To friends and cocktails!"

Rachel picked up her half-finished second cocktail and clinked glasses but didn't take a sip. How had the mood changed so quickly? She watched as Ellie elegantly sipped her Bellini.

"I think I'm going to go for a swim to cool down. It's pretty hot."

Rachel stood up, took her sunglasses off and threw them onto the sun lounger. Ellie nodded slightly and continued to sunbathe. Walking to the pool's edge, Rachel saw a ridiculously good-looking couple walk into the pool area. They must be famous, she thought; real people don't look like that. Slightly intimidated, Rachel sucked in her stomach, dropped her shoulders, stretched her legs and adjusted her posture as she walked into the pool. She dived under the surface and let the cool water encapsulate her body. It was so refreshing. Instantly forgetting everything, and with her eyes closed, she swam strongly below the surface, letting the temperature slow her heart rate. It had an immediate effect on her mind. Through the mixture of the topical temperature change to her skin, the oxytocin release from her earlier massage, and the vodka from her second cocktail, Rachel felt herself grow calm. She slowly glided up to the surface and turned to float on her back. She opened her eyes and stared at the perfectly clear aquamarine sky as the water fell from her face. Not a cloud in her whole view. The airy vastness of the sky had a different ambience to the soothing translucence of the moving water she'd surveyed earlier, yet they had a similar hue.

God, she loved the Med. It was just so beautiful. Floating carelessly, she felt the sun start to warm her skin and had a pleasurable serotonin rush. The pool water bubbled in her immersed ears, and she remembered when she used to joke with Tom about wanting to be a fish. Keen sailors, they both had a strong affinity to water. It was their happy place, and Rachel was happy right now. She turned over and dived under the water again, feeling its cool tranquillity. It naturally soothed and relaxed her. She couldn't wait to get into the sea and float aimlessly in the salty water.

She was finally here! It wasn't a dream anymore. She was in Greece and had a week to enjoy her surroundings and unwind. Would she find her answers? Her direction? Rachel sculled around for a few more minutes, wanting to maintain the feeling of serenity, yet something wasn't right. Had she pissed Ellie off? Where did her sudden change in tone come from? Maybe it was too soon to have come to visit. Perhaps Alice was right. Rachel's sense of calm slipped away. She had to speak to Ellie. Standing up in the pool and going over to the steps, she was greeted by a smiling woman holding a white fluffy towel. Rachel thought, Blimey, that's service for you! Taking the towel and returning the smile, Rachel dabbed her face and arms and wrapped the towel around her body. Looking over to the sun loungers, she saw that Ellie had not moved.

"That was so refreshing!" she said as she walked over to her.

Ellie looked over but kept her sunglasses on. "It does look good. I might go in soon."

Sensing that the mood was still slightly off, Rachel

decided not to point out Ellie's antagonism. Instead, she meticulously laid the towel on her sun lounger in preparation to assume her frontal sunbathing position. She was about to lie down when Ellie turned towards her and grabbed her arm.

"I'm sorry, TT."

Rachel turned and sat down. "Are you OK?"

Ellie took off her sunglasses, and Rachel could see she'd been crying. Ellie kept her sun hat on, as she wanted to keep some degree of dignity, and thankfully, there were not many people around to see. "No, not really."

"What happened? We were talking, and then it just went to shit. Was it something I said?"

"No, it wasn't you. And I'm sorry I snapped like that."

"It's alright, honestly. Look, maybe it's too soon for me to be out here. Maybe I shouldn't have come. I've been thinking about that…" she suddenly became over-anxious. "Alice said it was too soon for me to be out here. God, I'm such a cow. I've been so wrapped up in my world and trying to deal with my shit that I ignored whether you would be OK with this."

"No, it's fine. Really… it's fine. I'm glad you're here. Gino needed to go away on business and didn't want me to be alone. Honestly, TT, it's fine."

Rachel reached across, lifted her third cocktail, and focused on Ellie. Something was going on, and she needed to sort it out, as much for herself as for Ellie. "I'm going to have to do an Alice on you."

Ellie's eyes widened, and a small smile slowly surfaced. She gently wiped her eyes with both hands, so she didn't smudge her mascara and adjusted herself on the lounger. Rachel sat down on her towel and sipped her cocktail, ignoring Alice's voice in her head.

"OK, so I don't have Alice's amazing skills, her training, her experience, her patience, or the qualifications, but I get what she tries to achieve."

"What do you mean?"

"So, you know the therapy session she gave me on the phone? It was so bizarre. In a very short time, she reached inside my head and helped me find what had been bothering me. There is still much to do, and I will need to catch up with her when I get home, but it was enlightening."

"Oh, so should we be speaking to Alice?"

"Probably, and I know she did want us to FaceTime her, but we can try it. I hate to see you so blue. Can I try?"

Ellie looked at Rachel softly. She could see the genuine care she was trying to demonstrate. What could go wrong?

"I'm going to talk to you, and then you have to do all the talking," said Rachel. "You have to answer the questions I ask you. But I can't answer you, as it's not a conversation." She saw Ellie appear confused. "I think Alice explained it a lot better than that."

"You think?" Ellie laughed.

"Look, Bianchi, you said I could come here. You gave me permission. I will try to fix you, and you'll feel better. We're going to find answers, and we're going to do it together."

Ellie stared at Rachel in disbelief. Rachel was surprised at herself. How had she managed to turn an anxious situation into a positive one? It must have been because it was Ellie, and Ellie was so important to her. She would do anything for her friend. And then Alice; what had Alice done to her?

"OK, that was a little harsh, rude, and unkind. But I've been up since four thirty this morning, am on my third cocktail and had more sunshine on my body than I've had in months. So, you're going to have to cut me some slack."

Ellie laughed out loud and reached for her cocktail. "You always find a way to make it about you, don't you, TT?"

Chapter 18

Timeless treasures of the heart

Sunday, 5th July

"You're such a shit driver, Bro!" Sinead exclaimed. "How the hell did you pass your test?"

"I'm not, Ade. You can't navigate for shit."

Finn had hired a ridiculously small - five-seater, my arse - manual Daewoo Matiz at the City of Derry airport and was driving his two sisters to Ryan's house in Donegal. Since living in London, he didn't drive very often, and the last thing he needed was to be told what to do by his younger sister.

"I told you exactly where to go, and you took the wrong turn."

"Aye, you did, Finn," Caitlin added from the back seat. "And you should know where you're going, anyways."

"Enough, both of you!" Finn spat as he stopped the car, reversed it into someone's driveway, thrust the gearstick into first gear, and took off, at speed, in the direction he'd just come.

"Ooooohhhh!" joked Sinead. "What's up with you, ya bollixya?"

"You. Arse."

"Flip's sake, you two, do you ever stop arguing?" Caitlin asked. "I would've got a taxi if I'd known you'd be like this."

Sinead turned around in the front passenger seat and smiled at Caitlin. "What? And miss all this class banter!" She turned and lightly punched Finn in the arm as he changed gear.

"Fuck's sake, Ade, what did you do that for?"

"Turn right!" Sinead shouted.

Finn turned the car sharply and headed up a narrow street, where he saw a wooden sign indicating The Church of the Sacred Heart to his left. The familiar sight was comforting. There were several cars slowly coming out of the car park; evening mass must have just finished. Finn thought all the inhabitants of the cars looked sufficiently absolved of their sins to return to their lives. He hoped that Ryan could do the same for him. He needed to calm down, at least. How had he taken a wrong turn? He'd been here so many times before.

"See, I can navigate perfectly!" Sinead piped up.

"Thank God we're here. I couldn't take much more of you two," Caitlin added.

Pulling into the church car park, past the graveyard, and avoiding the leaving parishioners, Finn drove around to the back of the church. There was a small, grey-rendered house on the church grounds, given to the serving priest of the parish. Ryan had been there for twelve years. Surrounded by a well-tended garden, it was a lovely little home that Ryan took care of with pride, as if it was his own. As Finn parked, Ryan came out of the front door, wearing a smile and his pristine white vestments, which floated ethereally around him. He walked towards them at pace. Sinead and Caitlin got out of the car, heading towards Ryan.

"Bro!" Sinead shouted as she ran around the car to embrace him.

They hugged hard, and he reached out to include Caitlin in a three-way hug. Finn turned off the ignition, picked up his wallet, and unplugged his charging phone. He got out of the car and slowly walked over to his brother.

"Hey, Ry, thank fuck we're here. I swear I was going to kill Ade."

Sinead and Caitlin pulled away, laughing. Finn walked up to Ryan and gave him a solid hug. It felt wholesome.

"So good to have you here, Finn. Thanks for coming."

"Thanks for having us to stay," Finn replied. He wasn't that angry with Sinead. In fact, he enjoyed the banter. She was always good for that. No offence was taken.

"Come in, guys. Dinner should be ready in about an hour. You can dump all your bags in the hall. Later, we'll sort out where you're all staying."

Collecting all their bags from the car and walking into the house, Finn felt an emotional pang of nostalgia. Before she was sick, his mother often stayed with Ryan and made jam from the blackberries she'd forage on her daily walks. She baked fresh scones with lashings of butter, cream, and her jam and then served them after mass. They were a firm favourite. Finn thought that the parishioners probably missed her, too.

"Ooh, something smells good," Caitlin said as they walked into the kitchen. "What's cooking?"

"Oh, don't give me any credit for the food. It's a stew made by Mrs O'Sullivan. I just put it in the oven. Did you bring the potatoes I asked for?"

"Yup," said Caitlin as she lifted them from a bag, "I'll wash them and put them in a pot."

"Thanks, Sis."

"I can't believe you still call her Mrs O'Sullivan!" Sinead retorted. "Her name's Niamh."

"I know," Ryan laughed, "It's mad, isn't it? I can't help it. I've just always called her that."

"When is Fi getting here?" Finn asked.

"She said around eight, so I thought we'd wait to eat with her. Is that OK?"

Caitlin, Finn and Sinead nodded and started unpacking the other groceries they'd brought for their stay. Smoked salmon, hummus, peanuts, crackers, stilton, brie, goat's cheese, crisps, strawberries, grapes and copious amounts of Malbec and Chardonnay were unloaded quickly and efficiently.

"Look, guys, I need to get out of my vestments. I'll be about five minutes. Put the kettle on and make yourselves at home."

"Do you have anything stronger than tea, Ryan?" Sinead asked cheekily.

"Remember, I got whiskey in duty-free," said Finn.

"Check out the drinks cabinet. I got you in some gin!" Ryan laughed as he left the room.

"Superstar!" Sinead shouted back.

"Do you think we've enough booze?" Caitlin asked.

"Enough to sink the Titanic!" Sinead laughed.

Looking around Ryan's tidy kitchen, watching his sisters busy themselves, Finn decided to text Rachel to let her know he'd arrived.

> Safely at Ry's and about to open up the Logan Reminisce Shop.
>
> I hope I survive!

Finn watched Sinead and smiled. He could see his sister was happy. What a perfect idea to all come away. He was genuinely looking forward to this time together. His phone buzzed back.

> Thanks for letting me know. Spend time mending your heart with your lovely family. All good here. I love you and miss you. R xx
>
> Right back atcha babes. xx

Finn put his phone on the table as Sinead handed him a gin and tonic.

Ryan removed his vestments, folded them neatly, and put them in a cupboard. He then put away the purified chalices and blew out the votive candles. As he walked to lock the church door, the phone in his trouser pocket buzzed.

> Hi Ryan, please take care of Finn. You're probably the only person who can help heal his wounds right now. Please don't tell him I sent this. I don't want him to think I'm interfering. And you don't need to respond. I'm sure you're all celebrating

> by now. Speak soon. Love Rach x

He put the phone back in his pocket. He paused and pondered Rachel's message as he approached the light switch. Was Finn that fragile? What had his brother not told him? What was happening in his life? They were too far from each other to have regular conversations, and Finn and he obviously needed to talk. Of course, he would offer unconditional support, love, and understanding. But why did Rachel not want Finn to know she was concerned? That was a natural thing for someone to say about someone they cared deeply about. Ryan turned off the lights, locked the front door and returned to his house. He didn't have to serve Mass until Tuesday so he could have a wonderful evening together with the most important people in his life. His phone buzzed again. He lifted it out and saw a message from his sister, Fi.

> Making great progress, should be at yours for 7:30.
> Cannae wait to see yous. Fxxxxx

Ryan smiled; that was excellent news. It was going to be wonderful to have all his family around him. It had been too long since they'd all been together. It was Ma's funeral, and that was too sad to be enjoyable. He was so grateful to Sinead for organising it.

"Yes! But that was MY relationship with Mum, Finn, not yours. They're not comparable," Sinead said a little too loudly, reaching to top up her wine.

"Well, perhaps that's what the issue is, Ade. I didn't have that relationship. And, right now, I'm feeling fucking guilty about it," Finn replied.

"You shouldn't," Fiona added.

"Why?"

"Because I didn't have it either, and I don't feel guilty."

"Yes, but that's you, Fi. You've got this incredible gift to move on once something is concluded."

"Whoa! That's a bit harsh, Finn," said Caitlin, filling her glass with more Chardonnay.

It was nearly midnight, and the Logans had been talking and drinking since Fiona had arrived at seven-thirty. They'd got up to speed with the pleasantries of jobs, Fiona's children, annoying work colleagues, Ryan's parishioners, Donegal neighbourhood gossip, Marla and her appalling mother's art, Rachel's career crisis, and life in general whilst consuming Mrs O'Sullivan's mince stew. They'd moved beyond warmed rice pudding with cold tinned fruit onto cheese and biscuits. As the drink flowed, they were now getting into the emotional part of the evening.

"I don't mean it like that, Fi. I LOVE the fact you can close stuff down. That's how you've dealt with so much. It wasn't meant to sound cold. I wish I could be like that."

"Why do you feel guilty, Finn?" Ryan asked.

"Because I wasn't there for Ma. And after her death, I didn't reach out to any of you. You especially, Ry, when you had to fucking deal with everything, I was such a shite brother. I'm so sorry," Finn said as he grabbed his chin to try and stop himself from crying.

"It was hard for all of us," said Fiona.

"I know, Fi, but what did I do after Ma died? I did fuck all, is what I did. I didn't come over here to see if you were all coping. I kept away. I wasn't even there for Ade in London. And it wasn't as if I was dealing with it whilst I wasn't here; I ploughed my energy into my work and supported Rachel with her decisions. I appeared strong. I wasn't dealing with it at all. Nothing…I just put my emotions on pause."

"Why do you think I drink and smoke so much?" Sinead dropped into the conversation.

All five of them fell silent, a hard stop.

"I need to go pee," said Fiona suddenly, "My bladder has been shite since I had kids."

They all burst into laughter, and the tension vanished.

"I need a smoke, anyways," Sinead added.

"Ooh, can I nick one?" Caitlin asked slyly. "You know what I'm like when I drink."

"Sure," Sinead said, "You're so naughty!"

The two of them laughed as they left from the back door. Ryan stood up and moved to sit next to Finn. They looked at each other kindly and sat silently for a moment.

"Don't say it," Finn said.

"What do you mean?" Ryan asked. "Where is all this anger coming from?"

"I don't want you to tell me it's OK, Ryan. You're so good at being this benevolent, calm and understanding person who is eternally optimistic and able to deal with layers of shit."

"It's my job, Finn."

"Yeah, I know that, but this was Ma, Ryan. That's got to be different, right? It can't be as measured and automatic as how you deal with death amongst your congregation. I've only recently realised how fucking rubbish I'm at this stuff. All the crap going on with Rachel has made me, well, both of us, question our emotional stability. I've struggled to get Rachel out of her psychological rut because I don't think I've anything in the tank to offer her. I'm broken."

As she returned to the kitchen, Fiona said, "You're not broken. You're grieving."

She sat beside Ryan, not looking at Finn, and reached for her wine glass. Slowly, she filled it with the remainder of the open bottle of Malbec. It was a spectacular display of composure. Finn and Ryan just watched her as they considered her statement.

"Finn, you're not emotionally unstable, you're not depressed, you're grieving," she said, putting the empty bottle back on the table as Sinead and Caitlin returned to the kitchen, and she didn't lose the rhythm of her message. "You're empty, you're numb, you're lost, and it's hard. Really fucking hard. And no one can help you. No one can take it away. Death, even though it's something that every living being has to deal with, is such a difficult thing to experience. You have to endure it because it's so personal. It's your cross to bear; only time will heal you."

"Is that how you've dealt with it?" Finn asked Fiona gently.

She nodded as the words she'd said resonated in her mind. She wiped her eyes and took another sip of her wine.

"I think it would've been better if we'd shared our feelings, though," said Caitlin. "If we'd had the opportunity to talk it over this candidly and honestly with each other, without feeling shite. I can only speak to you guys this way, my friends are always so fucking tetchy."

"Oh, tell me about it!" Sinead interjected, "No one speaks to me like you all do."

"So this isn't just my story, then?" Finn asked, looking around the table at each of his siblings. They all returned his gaze and nodded. "Thank fuck, 'cos I was getting a little uncomfortable about it being the 'Finn show'. You're telling me it wasn't just me, that we've all struggled with how we should've been after Ma's death?"

"Yup!" Sinead said drunkenly, raising her glass.

"Aye, I've been shite," Caitlin added, clinking glasses with Sinead.

"Of course, we've struggled," Ryan replied.

"I had to go away, or should I say, stay away," Fiona added contemplatively. "It was how I coped. And, yes, it was probably shite, but I had to be selfish. I put all my energy into my kids, using them as an excuse not to return home. Sorry if that's horrible to hear, Ry, but it's what I needed to do."

Caitlin stood up and went to hug Fiona. Sinead joined her, and they embraced in a messy, sisterly fashion. Ryan and Finn looked at each other and softly smiled.

"You took the lion's share, didn't you, Ry?" said Finn. "How are you doing?"

Although momentarily distracted, the women sat back down and focused on their eldest brother.

"Blimey! It's all about me now?" Ryan laughed as he nervously took a sip of wine. Everyone remained quiet and stared at him. "Come on," he said, looking at each of his siblings, "I was always going to look after her, wasn't I? That was the deal, right? She lived near me, and none of you did." He paused and looked around the table again. "Fi, you have your kids, Caitlin and Sinead, your high-powered jobs, and Finn, you have Rachel. I simply had more time to give her. Ma was never going to leave Donegal, and neither was I."

"How did you deal with her illness?" Sinead asked quietly.

"My faith gave me strength, and I let the doctors do their job for her. That's all I could do. I devoted as much time to her as was possible with my work. You don't get compassionate leave as a priest! It was important for me to make sure she went to hospital appointments on time and was eating well. Mrs O'Sullivan was a trooper, ensuring we had hearty meals every day. I will never forget how generous she was. I don't know what I would've done without her."

Ryan swallowed hard, and Finn could see he was starting to falter.

"I was also able to give her the peace she craved in her final weeks, and I was grateful that I was there when she died. It was brutal to see such a fiercely strong woman fade into a shadow of herself."

Ryan rubbed his eyes as they started to fill up with tears. Watching his brother show emotion this way was unfamiliar to Finn. It made him sad. It must've been a devastating period for Ryan. Why had he given him a hard time? There was nothing automatic about dealing with dying. He shouldn't have said those things. Ryan's tears started to flow fully now. Perhaps he realised he was allowed to relax, as he was amongst family; this was a side of Ryan he hadn't seen before. He was usually always such a tower of composure and fortitude. Perhaps Ryan needed emotional decompression as much as he did. They all needed to let it go. Wash out the grief from their veins. Sinead stood up, walked over to her brothers, and hugged them. Caitlin and Fiona stood up and joined her. They stayed in the awkward 'I'm-sitting-you're-standing' embrace for at least a few minutes until Sinead broke the mood.

"I need a smoke."

They pulled away and adjusted themselves, all individually wiping their eyes. Finn couldn't believe how much weight had been lifted from his shoulders. That simple contact with his siblings had taken away months of pain. These few days together would be a fantastic opportunity to pull apart all of the guilt and sorrow and discuss how they could all come to terms with the loss of their amazing mother. Finn loved the way his siblings were able to swing from deep emotion to humour in a heartbeat. There was so much unsaid history that they didn't need to explain; it was unique, and he missed it. Although perhaps the alcohol helped.

"Anyone for an Irish coffee?" Finn said, standing up and moving towards the kettle.

"Yes, please!" shouted Sinead as she walked out the back door with Caitlin.

"Ach, why not?" said Fiona. "I'm going to have the hangover from hell tomorrow, anyways. Why stop now?"

"That's the spirit, Sis!" laughed Finn.

"Not for me, thanks," Ryan replied, "This is the most I've drunk in years."

Finn started making the Irish coffees and suddenly saw an old photo of his mother on the windowsill. "When was that photo taken?"

Ryan looked up and smiled. He stood, walked to the window, and lifted the wooden frame. "That was when Ma came back from Lourdes." He started to laugh, "It was shortly after my ordination, and she brought me back some holy water in a Ballygowan plastic bottle. She said that it would give me an advantage. I have no idea what she meant by that."

Finn laughed.

"She brought me a bottle back, too," Fiona laughed, "I accidentally drank it one hungover morning! Who in the hell puts it in a water bottle! I expected it in a plastic Our Lady."

"What?!" Finn laughed even harder. "Ma had such a wicked sense of humour."

"Do you remember when she made raspberry jam and decided to smear it over her arm, lie in that armchair and pretend she was dead until Mrs O'Sullivan came in?" Ryan laughed wholeheartedly.

"What did we miss?" asked Sinead as she and Caitlin walked in smiling.

"Ryan was telling us about the time Ma pretended to be dead," answered Fiona.

"Wow!" said Sinead, "That's inappropriate, Ry, after what you just talked about."

"Oh shit," Ryan gasped, grabbing his face, "Wrong context Ade. That wasn't meant to sound like that."

"I'm joking, Bro," Sinead quipped, and they all laughed.

"I'll make you a cup of tea," Finn declared. "You probably need to stop drinking now."

Caitlin and Fiona had decided to call it a night at two a.m. Sinead, Ryan, and Finn had moved into the living room and were still talking at three a.m. The banter was greatly influenced by an evening of cocktails, wine, and Irish coffee.

"But do you feel fragile?" Ryan asked, having moved onto the whiskey after one cup of tea.

"Well, let's refer back to Fi's comments, which, let's be honest, were stellar, telling me that I'm not broken," Finn was quite animated as he spoke. He was loving the time with his brother and sister. Despite the alcohol, he felt he was finding clarity in his thinking; this was the best he'd felt in a long time, "So then I mustn't be fragile."

"You can be fragile and not broken. Think of a vase," said Sinead. The men looked at her and burst into laughter.

"Ssshhh!" Ryan insisted, raising his finger to his lips, "We mustn't wake the others."

"There's no fucking way they'll wake tonight, Bro," Sinead replied.

"OK, maybe I should reword it. Do you feel vulnerable?"

Finn looked across to his brother and dropped his head. "Do you know what, Ryan? This is the strongest I've felt in ages, having the time to talk to you all, taking the piss out of each other, talking about Ma, and understanding that it's not only me that misses her and that it's OK not to be OK, gives me huge strength. We're all vulnerable, right? So, no, I don't feel fragile. Well, not anymore. I feel like I'm not alone in this."

Finn gulped and recognised that spending time with his family was essential. In one evening, he'd recharged his batteries and reset the negativity. Fiona had said that time was the healer, but Finn realised that love was a pretty close second. It felt so good to be home.

"I love you guys so much. This has been just what I needed. Thank you. I somehow feel whole again." Finn raised his glass to Ryan and Sinead and smiled.

Chapter 19

I see you

Sunday, 5th July

Rachel and Ellie had just finished a late breakfast of fresh fruit, Greek yoghurt, brioche and strong black coffee, and were walking over to the pool for some morning sunbathing when Ellie's phone buzzed. It was already scorching, and Rachel was looking longingly at the pool. She was going to need a swim very soon.

"Gino has organised a three-night charter on a Sun Odyssey 33 for you. You can collect it from Georgios early Tuesday morning."

"Oh my God!" Rachel yelped, "Really? He's so amazing!" She reached into her bag and took out her phone.

> Grazie mille, Gino. You're the best! I can't thank you enough! Thank you, thank you, thank you xxx

As Rachel texted, Ellie pointed to two sun loungers, and two very tanned, young pool assistants started putting up the umbrella and laying fresh towels out for them. Rachel got a response.

> You're welcome, Rachel. It's a thank you for taking care of my girl x

"Two Mimosas, please," she instructed as she laid her bag on the teak side table and sat on the lounger. The pool assistants nodded and left quietly. This celebrity life was unreal!

"I can't believe you've only been here a day. Thank you so much for coming," Ellie gushed as she stretched out on the sun lounger, feeling positive and calm. "Even if you did nearly push me over the edge yesterday."

"Yeah, sorry about that! Still, Alice saved the day," Rachel laughed, "But seriously, are you kidding? I wouldn't have missed this for the world. It was just what we both needed. And I'm going sailing in less than two days! I can't believe it." She placed her bag next to Ellie's and took her sunglasses off. "I know this is a horrible thing to say, but I think it's good that Finn isn't here. It means I can have special time with you. You've treated me like royalty and made me think about what I could do with my life. I should be thanking you!"

"Don't worry, I'll send you my bill," Ellie replied, pulling her sunglasses down her nose and looking at Rachel over the top of them.

Rachel laughed as she walked away to take a swim.

The previous day, Rachel thought about how to start the therapy session with Ellie. How did Alice start? She adjusted herself on the sun lounger because her bikini was still wet from her swim and was sticking to her bum. Water was slowly dripping down her back from her hair and bikini top. Thankfully, the towel absorbed it, and the sun started drying it out. She crossed her legs into the Sukhasana pose so she could face Ellie.

"Listen, Ellie, I won't make this about me. Well, maybe a *little* bit about me. This is all about you. Because I've so much to learn from YOU. You're the reason I've been having my crisis of conscience. You're my inspiration to find emotional stability and resilience. You rock at being strong. You're the epitome of courage. It pains me to see you sad, and I want to help you find, what did you call it? Acceptance and peace, and to positively think about your future."

"Wow! That's quite a speech, TT."

"Did I rush it?" Rachel smirked, "I didn't actually get time to practise."

They both reached for their cocktails and smiled. Only true friendship allowed them to switch quickly between laughter and tears, sadness and happiness.

"Well?" Ellie said, sitting up and looking at Rachel, "What do I do?"

"Let me remember what Alice said." Rachel paused, trying to remember the instructions Alice had given her. "So, I can't talk to you, I can only ask you questions. You must find the answers through your words and thoughts. I'm not allowed to respond to your questions. We should talk later about the thoughts Alice unearthed in my psyche. It's unbelievable what came up."

"What came up?"

"She made me remember - and trust me, I have no idea how - Carly Phillips. Do you remember her?"

"Didn't she have mad curly hair and always wore super shiny patent shoes? I think we called her Curly Phillips."

"That's her! Somehow, Alice made me remember helping her win the egg and spoon race in primary school!"

"Wow! How long were you under?"

"It wasn't hypnosis, you muppet, it was just a you-talk-and-I-don't-talk kind of thing. But she did warn that it can be a bit brutal as you can remember stuff that'll upset you. I certainly had a strange turn when I started talking about my mother."

"Goodness," Ellie raised her eyebrows, "That sounds a bit ominous."

"That's exactly what I said! But we'll be fine. We can always ring Alice." Rachel took another quick sip of her cocktail, her first-day tiredness forgotten, "You ready?"

"No, but go ahead. I've had enough tears in the last few months, I don't think anything can derail me today. Shoot."

"OK," Rachel started, "What do you feel is wrong?"

That was how Alice had begun her therapy session; that would be the best place to start.

"I've lost my baby." Ellie looked expectantly at Rachel.

Remembering that she wasn't supposed to respond, Rachel searched for the next question.

"How does that make you feel?"

"It makes me feel unbearably sad, TT. What do you think?"

Rachel nervously picked up her cocktail and took a large gulp, realising how skilled Alice was, how much she'd underestimated her expertise, and that this was probably not a good idea. OK, she thought, stop thinking about what Alice asked you and ask Ellie the questions you want answered.

"Do you have the strength to overcome this sadness?" That was surely a good question. It would allow Ellie to articulate how she'd find acceptance and peace because Ellie was strong and always overcame things. That's what she did.

"No," Ellie answered.

Shit. Rachel realised that she shouldn't ask closed questions. This exercise was meant to help Ellie, not just answer Rachel's questions.

"How have you overcome sadness in the past?" Rachel continued.

Ellie exhaled and looked away from Rachel. It was apparent she was considering her response. This question was better.

"By asking myself whether I should."

Rachel remained quiet, frowning slightly; that was an interesting response.

"If I hadn't chosen to overcome the death of my parents and get on with life, what would I have done? What was the alternative? To give up? Shut off my emotions and move on. I'd never have met Gino. I'd never have been open to happiness and love. If I'd immersed myself in the massive void that losing my first baby left in my life, I would never have left my bed, and my marriage with Gino would've suffered. Possibly even ended. And right now, it's still too raw to think how I will address the emotional lake of feelings I have for losing this baby."

Rachel couldn't believe how much Ellie was divulging. And so quickly. This approach genuinely had a way of getting someone in the thick of it. Thankfully, everything looked OK. Should Rachel carry on? Because she had no idea what she was doing! Ellie kept talking,

"But losing a baby again is making it harder and harder to overcome the sadness. It's like sadness is a person in my life, I've met it so often. Why do I always have to be strong? Why do I always have to prevail? I'm struggling to find the resolve to get up and try again. I've been getting up too often. Being brave is exhausting."

Ellie lifted her sunglasses and wiped the tears from her eyes. She didn't seem to care about her mascara anymore. Rachel was desperate to intervene and hug her, but she remembered what Alice had said, this wasn't meant to be a conversation, it was for Ellie to find answers.

"I've had to be courageous. How else would I deal with my life?" She replaced her sunglasses and looked around. Rachel couldn't believe how much she was talking. This process was so damn cathartic.

"But courage comes from fear, yeah? I was so scared after I lost Mum and Dad. Seriously, who can deal with losing their parents at the age of seven? I had to deal with being alone for the whole of my childhood, having to be brought up by a sterile great-aunt who couldn't care less about me. I had to start fending for myself, and I grew up really quickly. Thank God I had you and Alice; you've no idea how much strength you both gave me. Watching you both helped me see how to behave, how to endure, how to achieve, how to fight and how to win."

Rachel listened intently. Was Ellie saying that SHE gave her strength? How was that the case? Rachel always thought Ellie was invincible; did she say she looked to her for inspiration?

"As you know, I became a rebel at boarding school, but problems came with being a maverick. I started to have a serious issue with authority. Actually, when I hit puberty, it was your Mum who put me straight."

Rachel looked at Ellie indignantly. "What?" It was an automatic reaction to a statement like that, even though she knew she should remain quiet.

"Yep, your Mum told me that I shouldn't think short term and that messing with the people that would ultimately help me prepare for adulthood was a bad idea. She told me to become strong, cheeky, bold, and mouthy so that people wouldn't bully me but also so I could stand on my own two feet. She impressed on me that I needed to understand my strengths, forgive my weaknesses, and know I could overcome anything. Yep, Rach, your Mum, and Alice's too, kept me straight."

Rachel looked away from Ellie as her eyes filled up with tears. Why had her Mum never been like that to her? Hold it together, Rach, this isn't about you. Let Ellie speak.

"Sorry, I didn't mean to interrupt."

"Do I keep talking?" Ellie asked.

Rachel nodded. It was bizarre where this was going.

"What your Mum told me to do was a great approach to dealing with losing my parents. At the earliest opportunity, I left my great-aunt and went to Europe to get into fashion and start my adult life. I often rang your Mum for advice; I still keep in touch with her now. When I lost my first baby, I thought that my despair would consume me. It would end me if I didn't choose to cope with the heartache. I had to go back to how I dealt with losing my parents; I had to remember what your mother told me. And Alice's Mum, too, was a total brick. Actually, she came out to see me a few months ago and gave me a tarot reading." Suddenly, she burst into tears. It was like she'd been slapped.

"Ellie!" Rachel scrambled off her sun lounger and moved to sit next to Ellie, "What's wrong?"

"Oh my God! Why didn't I make the connection?"

"What do you mean?"

"When Isla did my reading, the Death card came up. She reassured me that it didn't mean death in the true sense of the word but signified major changes in my life. I assumed that it meant the death of my infertility and the big change to becoming a mother. I was so wrapped up." Ellie continued to cry.

"I'm calling Alice," Rachel interrupted.

Ellie stood up and walked away from her. Rachel lifted her phone and called Alice. What had she done? This had been a terrible idea.

"Hey you," Alice answered on the third ring.

"Alice, can you talk? I've done something awful."

"What's happened?"

"I tried to do that thing with Ellie that you did to me where I don't ask questions, and Ellie finds all the answers, and I think I've upset her."

"What the fuck, TT? You're not qualified!" Alice shouted down the phone. "Is she OK?"

"I think I prompted her to remember your Mum's tarot reading and the Death card, and it's all gone wrong. Shit, Alice, what do I do?"

"Hug her and tell her it's going to be OK. I'll set up my laptop, and we can do a FaceTime. I'll get my Mum on it too. Fuck, TT, what were you thinking? I'll text you when I'm online."

"I know. I just wanted to help," whispered Rachel.

Alice hung up abruptly, and Rachel started to cry. What WAS she thinking? Why was she such an arse? Selfishly looking for answers and not thinking about how it might affect Ellie. Rachel was so confused. What was going on? Tired, slightly pissed and overwhelmed, she stood up and looked around to see where Ellie was. She saw her in the middle of the swimming pool, lying on her back, staring up at the sky and slowly sculling. Rachel threw her phone on the lounger, rushed into the water and swam over to her.

"Are you OK?" Rachel approached slowly.

Ellie turned over, ignored Rachel and walked over to the pool's edge. Rachel didn't want to make a scene. What should she say? Thankfully, the pool only had one other couple on sun loungers, and they were on the other side, sleeping in the sunshine.

"I'm so sorry that I upset you," said Rachel, walking behind her, "I shouldn't have done that. I'm such an arse. I've spoken to Alice and…"

"The water helps take away the pain," Ellie interrupted pensively, "it has a great way of calming my soul." She held onto the pool's edge and slowly moved her legs under the water's surface. "I imagine it feels like being in the womb. Besides, being in the water doesn't show I've been crying."

"Alice wants to do a FaceTime with us now and help get you back. I should never have tried to sort anything. I'm not qualified. I'm selfish. I wanted to fix you. I wanted to take the pain away."

Ellie slowly looked over to Rachel and smiled.

"Do you know what? I think you did."

"What?!"

Ellie stayed quiet. Rachel was confused by her poise.

"You asked me the questions I didn't want to ask myself, questions that no one but you would ask. You made me face the fear of my baby's loss. You made me realise that I needed to pick myself up and overcome this sadness because no one else will do it for me."

Rachel stared at Ellie, blinking away tears. So that was the definition of resilience. That was the panacea. That was how you dealt with what life threw at you. You picked yourself up, wiped yourself down and got on with it. Then you question yourself, falter, and pick yourself up again. That's why Ellie was so strong. She kept getting up.

"I'd forgotten that. I've done it my whole life, but I'd forgotten. You're such a good friend, TT, the best. You've always been there for me, and I treasure your friendship. I love you, and I always will. You helped me to remember that I can overcome. I'll get through this; it's what I do."

Rachel burst into tears and reached towards Ellie in search of a comforting hug. They embraced, cried, and accepted each other's need to break down completely. Rachel was glad they were in the pool, as she wasn't sure she would've been able to remain stable if she was standing up. They held the embrace, and after a few moments, both slowly dropped below the surface and let the water consume them. It was symbolic as if they were trying to absolve themselves. Coming up to the surface, they looked at each other.

"It wasn't me, though; those questions you asked yourself were all on you. I wanted to fix you, but that was wrong. I love you, Ellie. You're truly amazing. I don't care what you say. You're my hero."

"I love you too, Sweetie. Thanks for being here for me."

Wiping the water out of their eyes and squeezing the water out of their hair, they looked at each other and laughed.

"You've got mascara all down your face!" Rachel quipped.

"You don't look that good yourself!" Ellie responded, wiping her face and smiling.

They both spotted the helpful poolside assistant hovering near the steps with two fresh towels for them. She was clearly unsure if she was intruding, so they walked over.

"Shit, we need to go and talk to Alice before she has a meltdown!" Rachel exclaimed. "She's going to kill me."

Chapter 20

Gone sailing...

Tuesday, 30th June

Desperate to start her adventure, Rachel left Ellie's early. Feeling like a child on Christmas Eve, she hadn't slept at all the night before. Tip-toeing around the villa, she snuck out before Ellie and Gino even stirred and went to collect her charter. The night before, she'd instructed the taxi to collect her from down the street. Armed with a small bag of clothes, her passport and paperwork, her credit card and mobile phone, she ran to meet it and jumped in enthusiastically. She sat in the back seat with the broadest beam across her face. The waiting was over.

What would today bring? Back at home, on cloudy or

rainy days, something was uplifting about going sailing. The thrill came from preparing a boat, checking the tides, reading the charts, leaving the harbour and wishing for the weather to improve. On windy days, with all the checks in place, and regardless of the weather, it was utterly exhilarating. But what would the Ionian Sea show her this day? The anticipation consumed her. She couldn't sit still in the seat of the taxi.

Before leaving London, she'd looked on Google Earth at the surrounding area but had not planned a route and had no idea where she would go today, yet she felt no anxiety. She just wanted to stretch her sea legs and be on the water; this was what she'd dreamt of. Thankfully, the petite taxi driver, who couldn't speak English, knew exactly where to go. She pulled into the marina and showed Rachel the fare by pointing at the meter, smiling and then nodding. Paying with her phone, Rachel grinned and jumped out quickly.

As the taxi pulled away, Rachel dropped her bags on the ground. Purposefully breathing in the fresh morning air, which was a lovely smell of salt, warmth, seaweed and a hint of eucalyptus and olives from the nearby trees, she exhaled it slowly. It was distinct from the dewy fragrance of an early morning in Hamble Marina but held the same promise. Surveying the magnificent yachts all tied up and bobbing in the water, she tried to guess which one would be hers. Which one would be her companion for the adventure ahead? What relationship would she start today? The endearing and familiar sound of main halyards hitting against aluminium masts caught her attention; the ting-ting-ting was like a call to arms. Rachel, this is it, babes! You're here, and you're going to be sailing in a few hours. You'll be on open water soon with everything ahead of you. The possibilities are endless. A tear welled up in her eye, and she suddenly thought of her father, remembering his kind encouragement.

Perhaps she would let him know how she felt. Walking over to the breakwater, she sat down and watched the boats sway in the gentle morning swell. Their movement was smooth and continuous, rhythmic and mesmerising. It made her feel incredible. Brimming at the seams with positive energy, she became overwhelmed with pride. She was going to do this! Reaching for her phone, she texted her Dad.

> I'm here, Dad…and it's amazing. You were right.
> Love you so much. Rach xxx

Looking out to the horizon, she breathed in the air again. This time, she could taste the sea. It was exquisite and overwhelmed her senses. All the past worry, confusion, and arguments with Finn and her family drained away like she'd pulled a plug; this was the feeling she'd been searching for, the serenity mixed with excitement. Being here early, before a sail, was undoubtedly the best part of the day. There was such potential to watch how the day would unfold. The wind hadn't awoken, and the sky rapidly changed colour as the sun rose. It was Rachel's ultimate happy place.

Finn had texted yesterday to tell her he was having a fantastic time with his siblings. Knowing Sinead, there was a possibility they may still be awake even now, chewing the fat and having special family time over whiskey. She decided to text him.

> OMG I'm at the marina and about to find my boat. It's SO EXCITING!
> The weather's fantastic, you would LOVE this.
> Should be on the water at around 10. Will try to text you later.
> I love you. Miss you, Rach xxxxx

Perhaps Finn would text back. Either way, it didn't matter; she'd wanted to let him know because he'd love this, and it was a shame he wasn't there. The Mediterranean sky was perfectly cloudless, turning from the dark red Rachel had seen when she started her taxi ride to orange to pink to purple; the blue colour was waiting in the wings to appear. Today would be awesome.

Adjusting her position on the breakwater because the hard rocks were beginning to dig into her bum, she looked higher up into the sky and asked herself, *'what will the weather throw my way?'* It was teasing her right now, not showing its cards. She exhaled again and had to pinch herself; she still couldn't believe she was there. The sea had a calmness that Rachel had not seen before. Perhaps it was because she was so calm? It would be like her previous visit, but she would now have a chance to indulge herself. When she came here with Ellie and Alice, she hadn't had the opportunity to take it all in fully. The mercury-looking water rippled and pulsed slowly, reflecting the sky beautifully. She felt spellbound, the sea was captivating her. Remembering the countless times she'd left Hamble Marina and headed into The Solent, the thought of leaving Agia Evfimia Marina and heading into the Ionian Sea was thrilling. She'd left there before, but this was going to be different. She knew the wind would blow when the Greek sun rose and the temperature increased. It was a unique phenomenon in Greece and could mean strong winds without visual indication that anything was happening. Rachel wasn't expecting to have that today as the forecast was for light winds and unbroken sunshine, but she liked to be prepared.

With plenty of time before she could pick up her yacht, but eager to find out which one would be hers, and in desperate need of a coffee, she decided to explore. She jumped off the breakwater and headed towards the main part of the marina. When she'd come previously with Ellie and Alice, all the details had been dealt with, and she hadn't clocked the available facilities. Marvelling at how bustling it was, even at this early hour, she watched people busily preparing boats for departure. It was obviously a handover day, and it would get pretty crowded soon. Crew members were rinsing salt from teak decks, wiping guardrails, adjusting fenders and returning ropes to their organised state. Charter staff were filling the boats with supplies for the exploits ahead, and Rachel struggled to contain her excitement. It would be her soon!!

"Can I help you?" a well-dressed, sun-tanned, and very smiley Greek man asked, having suddenly appeared.

"Sorry?" Rachel replied, a little surprised.

"Are you looking for anything in particular?" His English was extremely impressive, and Rachel immediately felt inadequate, as she knew no Greek.

"I'm picking up a charter today, but I'm a little early. I was looking for somewhere to get a coffee."

He continued to smile and became overly animated as he said, "One cannot start their day without a decent coffee. Please, follow me."

Rachel raised her eyebrows. Surely this guy was having a laugh? He flamboyantly turned on his heel and walked away from her. She couldn't help but notice that he had the shiniest of shoes. It made her think of Carly again. Strange for a sailor. Watching him walk off at pace, she decided to follow him. She did indeed need that coffee. Walking through glass double doors into a plush room filled with sumptuous seating, laid out with crisp white tablecloths, fresh flowers and bone china cups and saucers, Rachel looked over to the spirited man for direction; this didn't look at all like the marina coffee shop.

"Lady Logan, please take a seat," he said, pointing towards a dark green, comfortable-looking armchair, "We will bring over some coffee and pastries shortly. It is black with one sugar, yes?"

She stood aghast. How did this strange man know who she was? What had Ellie done now? He paused, staring at her, and then laughed.

"I'm so sorry, I just had to hold that look," he smiled. "My name is Ioannis, and I'll be helping you today. Gino and Ellie have instructed me to assist you with whatever you need to get sorted."

"Really?" she laughed, relieved and overwhelmed that Ellie had organised this for her, too. She'd been so generous with the stay in the exclusive hotel, and now this. What could this woman not do?

"Would you like some fresh fruit and orange juice too?" Ioannis asked.

"That would be lovely, thank you," she replied, smiling.

Ioannis walked away. She sat in a luxurious armchair and looked around the room. Several photos hung on the walls showing stunning images of sailing yachts gliding through the water with athletic individuals at the helm. They seemed so exhilarating. The next few days were going to be the best fun ever. The butterflies started to rise in Rachel's stomach as she turned away from the room to look at the view through the windows; her excitement returned. Shaking her head, she still couldn't believe that she was there. The first pier was less than five metres from where she sat, and she could see every detail of the beautiful boats: the exquisite lines, the smooth teak decks, the craftsmanship, the glistening glass, the polished GRP. It all shone in the emerging sunshine. Thinking back to just over two weeks ago, when she was sitting in Ocean Village with Alice, her head was in a different place back then. How was this so unlike all those times she had set off from Hamble Marina? Why was the excitement too difficult to contain? It just was. She beamed until her face hurt. She had to thank Ellie.

> Ellie, you're the greatest; you really are.
> I can't thank you enough for all your generosity, this was so unexpected. Thank you!
> I can't believe I'm here. I'm in heaven. x

"Your breakfast, Lady Logan," Ioannis said as he walked over with a large tray. He placed down a white china cup and a silver cafetière, then added a silver sugar pot with a small plate of pastries. He expertly filled the small table with a plate of finely sliced apricots, peaches, watermelon, cherries and figs and a tall glass of freshly squeezed orange juice.

"Wow, thank you so much," Rachel said as she sat up in her seat, aware that she was dressed more for a boat than a posh restaurant. She placed a linen napkin on her lap. It was the least she could do! She heard her phone buzz from where she'd put it on the small table.

"Is there anything else you would like?" Ioannis smiled, "Perhaps some yoghurt or some nuts?"

"No, thank you," Rachel said, thinking she couldn't pronounce his name correctly, so it was probably better not to attempt it. "This is more than enough."

He walked away, and Rachel looked at her feast. Waiting for her coffee to brew, she picked up her phone to take a few pictures of the bounty and saw the text,

> You're getting used to being called Lady Logan, aren't you?

After finishing her enormous breakfast, she sat back in the armchair and looked out at the boats again. Checking her phone, she saw she still had plenty of time before she was due to pick up her yacht and felt relaxed that Georgios would help her. Surprised by how hungry she'd been, she wiped her lips with her napkin and laid it on her empty plates. Opening the WhatsApp group "Bitches behave", she posted pictures of her breakfast with the comment that she was getting used to this lavish lifestyle of being waited on. She smiled when her phone buzzed back straightaway.

> I trust Lady Logan is pleased with the hospitality.
>
>   I am, thanks, Baroness Bianchi. It's amazing.
>
> Whoa! What's this? Lady Logan and Baroness Bianchi - what am I?
>
>   Countess Carmichael!
>
> Really?
>
>   What's wrong with that?
>
> It's lame and makes me feel like the Sesame Street character
>
>   Ah-Ah-Ah
>
> I'd say it's more like someone who runs a brothel...
>
> Fuck off, Ellie

Rachel couldn't believe how much these women made her smile. Looking out again, she saw that the sky was now a beautiful clear azure. It reflected on the water, and the previous mercury glint had changed to a sparkling blue mirror. It reminded her of the beautiful glass orbs that hung from the hotel ceiling; they completely captured the essence of the sea perfectly. No wonder she'd loved the installation. More people were walking around the marina, about to start their daily chores. Being around boats was second nature to Rachel; she'd been immersed in a marine environment since she was young, but why did this feel so dissimilar? How did her excitement as a sailor in Southampton differ from the exhilaration she felt right now? What was this unfamiliar thrill?

> How you holding up, missus?

A text from Alice; it was like she knew how Rachel thought, that she could tell Rachel would be asking herself questions.

> I'm great, thanks. Just taking it all in. It's so beautiful.
> How's things with you? x
>
> That's awesome, I'm so happy for you.
> Just about to head to a pilates class. Have a quiet day today of paperwork. Jealous of you.
>
> I'll send you a pic when I'm out on the open water.
>
> Stay safe. Ax

Rachel smiled and put her phone on her lap. *Why was this so different, Rachel? How does this environment make you feel, Rachel? Why are you even comparing, Rachel?* She paused and reached for her coffee cup. She finished the dregs of the strong, sweet coffee and suddenly recalled drinking the coffee Christie had given her in the office last month. How much her head and heart had changed since that time; it felt like a lifetime ago. She'd been on an emotional rollercoaster, navigating between anger, confusion, expectation and duty. Yet, today, she felt calm, hope, excitement, and peace. She wasn't anxious at all. She was serene.

What had she asked herself a few weeks ago? The

question that made James laugh so much. *'What is the cost of inertia? What am I not learning to do while spending so much time doing the stuff I've always done?'* Recalling it made her laugh, too. It was so different now. What she'd been searching for wasn't a destination at all, it was the journey. She'd found what she was looking for by simply looking for it. *It's different because I'm different. Whoa!*

Ioannis appeared and started clearing her table. Since everything had been eaten, he didn't ask whether she had finished, but it broke Rachel's concentration.

"Thank you, that was delicious," she said, feeling a little embarrassed that she'd been so greedy and didn't know how to pronounce his name.

Georgios suddenly appeared. "Rachel, how are you?"

"Georgios! How lovely to see you!"

Rachel stood up, dropping her napkin onto the floor. She hugged him and kissed him on both cheeks, European-style.

"Are you ready to start your day, Lady Logan?" Georgios asked, winking at Rachel, knowing that Ioannis was listening. "I'll take you over to reception in about twenty minutes to go over the particulars of your charter."

"That would be great, Georgios, thank you."

"Would you like anything else?" Ioannis asked.

"Just a glass of water would be good, thanks."

Rachel's emotional state swung between exhilarating excitement, trepidatious anticipation, upbeat optimism, and comforting nostalgia. It was a giddy concoction that made her feel dizzy. Reaching into her handbag for paracetamol, she remembered Alice. She took her empty hand out of the bag and smiled; she didn't need that, but she did need the toilet.

Returning from the Ladies', she recalled talking to Tom

about how the mood of a sailor was intrinsically linked to the weather. The clouds, the moisture percentage, and the sea swell were all indicators of how a sail would play out. Would it be invigorating? Would it be frustrating? Would it be challenging? Would it be ecstatic? Rachel smiled as she remembered her sailing days in Southampton. Surely Greece was the ultimate upgrade because her current mood was euphoric! It didn't get better than this. Grabbing her things, she searched for Georgios.

Stocked up with fresh water, food, fuel, and all the instruments and charts checked, Rachel was finally out on the open water. Her charter was named 'Signora del Mare', a fitting translation of 'Lady of the Sea', which Georgios said Ellie and Gino had explicitly requested. It was a beautiful yacht and she fell in love with it the minute she stepped onboard. Knowing they'd be acquaintances for the next few days, she settled into her routine.

The yacht was smaller than the one she'd sailed last month with Ellie and Alice, but it was utterly perfect for just her; she didn't need it to be that grand. It had a smaller galley and only two cabins. It had a single wheel at the helm making it more manageable for a solo adventure. The weather was tantalisingly good, so she decided to see what the Lady could do. After leaving the marina under the motor, she removed all the fenders from the guardrails and placed them in the boat locker. Even though the winds were light, she put the engine into neutral, pointed the boat into wind and pulled the mainsheet. She raised the sail fully before turning to port. She trimmed the mainsheet on the winch, and the white sail billowed against the clear sky. The warm breeze stroked her face, swishing her hair around. Gaining a little speed, she turned the engine off, and the sound was terrific. It was a smooth swooshing sound as the bow of the Lady glided cleanly through the water. The fabric of the mainsail luffed a little, so she extended the mainsheet to get an optimal sail shape. And she did this all automatically.

Through all the arguments and indecisions of late, she'd forgotten that this was what truly made her happy. Why hadn't she known that? It was so familiar and rewarding. It was much more than an adventure sport, it was something spiritual, something in her DNA. She felt at home on the water, making informed decisions about wind direction and sail placement. It was so natural for her to be out here. Looking out to the water, she smiled with great pride. Grabbing her phone, she took a selfie.

Chapter 21

It's the price of love

Tuesday, 7th July

Unable to run on Monday as he'd been way too hungover, Finn was desperate to get outside and stretch his legs. Feeling markedly better than yesterday, he'd been up since six o'clock and had read and addressed his work emails, even though he was meant to be on holiday. It had been raining solidly for the last two days; nevertheless, he was determined to do some exercise and intended to brave the elements. Leaving Ryan's house at seven, he'd got caught in the rain. It was a weird type of rain, more of a haze of dampness that you didn't think would get you wet. You could even miss seeing it if you had slightly poor eyesight.

So you'd venture out without an umbrella and then arrive at your destination absolutely soaked.

Walking back into Ryan's house after completing his run, he stripped down to his pants and dumped his sodden running gear near the entrance before deciding to head for a shower.

"Whoa! Don't you be leaving your stinking gutties there!" Mrs O'Sullivan barked. "You know yerself you gotta leave them outside."

"But they'll get wet out there," Finn objected with a smirk.

Mrs O'Sullivan stared over her reading glasses at him in silence. "C'mere till I tell ye," she said, putting down the sewing she was doing for Ryan. "I'm up to me oxters in sewing your brother's vestments, and I don't have time to rewash the floor today."

"Don't you worry, Niamh, I'll do it," Sinead said as she walked into the kitchen. "Have to say, it makes me laugh that you haven't mentioned the fact me brother is standing there in his knickers."

Finn grabbed a tea towel from the Aga and wiped his face, hair and arms. He was drenched.

"Ha!" Mrs O'Sullivan laughed heartily, "Mother of sweet incarnations, I didn't even notice!"

"I'm going for a shower," Finn laughed, "Could you put the kettle on, Sis?"

He headed out of the kitchen, desperately trying to cover himself with the tiny tea towel.

"Sure, Bro, and don't mind me," Sinead joked. "I suppose you want a bacon sandwich too?"

"If you're making!" he shouted back.

"Wee critter," Sinead laughed.

"Ach, he's a jammy git, is what he is," Mrs O'Sullivan said as she put her reading glasses back on and returned to her sewing.

Freshened up and in clean clothes, Finn walked down the stairs. He could smell the bacon and coffee that Sinead was preparing, and he was ravenous. Checking his face in the hallway mirror, he could see that the lines reflected in his bathroom mirror ten days ago had faded, and these last few days had been an absolute tonic. Catching up with his siblings, revisiting his childhood town and seeing old friends had given him such an emotional boost. He'd already vowed to come and visit his brother more often. Talking with Fiona about how he needed to learn how to grieve, understanding from Caitlin that it would be best to share it with those who loved his Ma too, and Sinead's upbeat humour had all helped him shake off his melancholy mood of late. Also, he was comforted by Ryan, saying they would help each other get through it.

Being away from Rachel had helped, too, not in a nasty way, but just the break felt healthy. It let him focus on himself and his feelings without needing to accommodate hers. Smiling at his reflection, he brushed his wet hair back with his hands and smoothed his eyebrows. Turning towards the closed kitchen door, he could hear the strong accent of Mrs O'Sullivan, his brother's deep tones, and his sister's laughs. The familiar sounds hit him. It was like his mother was there, the other side of this door. Just like the old days.

He stumbled slightly and sat down on the penultimate stair to collect himself. There it was again, the unexpected jolt of emotional pain. Fuck! He looked up and exhaled. It was going to take him time to deal with this grief. He had so much to learn. Even though Fiona and Caitlin had headed back to their homes yesterday, he felt he had the best people in his life to help him heal. They'd agreed to meet in London in a couple of months and spend more time together; the family felt strong again. He stood up and headed for the kitchen.

"Top o the mornin' to ya!" Sinead joked as she turned from the stove towards him, reverting to the stereotypical greetings she always gave her brother. "Here's your breakfast."

Faced with a plate of bacon, sausages, scrambled eggs, grilled tomatoes, fried potato bread and baked beans with a massive cup of coffee on the table, Finn's hungry stomach won out on his sensitive head, and he sat at the kitchen table.

"Ya legend," he said hungrily, picking up his cutlery and digging in. "Not as healthy as I'd have liked, but spot on."

Ryan was seated at the kitchen table, drinking his third cup of tea.

"This is delicious, Sis, thanks," said Finn.

"Now we're suckin' diesel," Sinead joked as she sat beside Ryan and devoured her bacon sandwich. They watched Mrs O'Sullivan expertly tidying up the kitchen, having finished her sewing.

"I was thinking we could go for a walk, Finn, after you've eaten," Ryan said.

"But it's raining, Ry," he replied with a mouthful of food.

"Don't ye be speaking with your mouth full, Finn, you wee toe-rag. Your Ma didn't raise you that way," Mrs O'Sullivan snapped as she zestfully wiped the kitchen table again and repeatedly rearranged the condiments.

"Sorry, Mrs O'Sullivan," Finn said timidly, looking at his brother and sister.

Ryan and Sinead tried their best to stifle their laughs. Mrs O'Sullivan was oblivious to his insolence and continued to tidy up efficiently.

"It's always raining, Finn," Ryan added, "If we didn't go out because it was raining, we'd never leave the house!"

Finn looked at him, nodded, and continued to stuff his face.

"Do you never stop, Niamh?" Sinead asked, wiping her greasy hands on a napkin.

Mrs O'Sullivan stopped in her tracks. "What d'ya mean, my dear?"

Sinead laughed. "Apart from doing Ryan's sewing, I haven't seen you sit down since you arrived this morning."

"Well, there's always so much to do," Mrs O'Sullivan explained.

"I don't make that much mess," Ryan shrugged at his sister.

"Your Ma and me came from a time when we'd have to sort everything. No washing machine, no dishwasher, no microwave; we'd have to do it all ourselves. I suppose I just never adjusted. However, the one thing that hasn't changed is that things still get manky, especially when I need to pick up after you rapscallions."

"We haven't made that much mess," repeated Ryan.

Mrs O'Sullivan had walked over to the windowsill and was wiping the side with a cloth when she reminiscently looked at the photo of Finn's mother and smiled. "I must say, it's been bleedin' deadly having yous all here. Mary would've loved this."

"Are you feeling any better?" Ryan asked as they slowly

walked around Saint Peter's Lough, both carrying umbrellas and staring out at the rippling water. The raindrops dimpled the Lough, making it look like a bubbling cauldron. Although damp and bleak, the view was calming and beautiful.

"Thank you so much, Ry, it's been a real tonic," Finn replied. "And just what I needed."

"Thank Sinead, not me. She organised it all."

They stopped walking and looked out across the Lough.

"Ma always loved it here," Ryan whispered, "Even when it was raining."

"Which is all the time!" Finn laughed.

"Yes," Ryan laughed, "But you do get used to it. You've just forgotten."

"I feel her presence here," Finn whispered back absently. They stood in silence and let Finn's words sink in. "I just can't believe how much I miss her, Ry. Why didn't I spend more time with her? Why did I shut away all my feelings when she died? And why didn't I come to see you and her when she was sick?"

Ryan didn't respond straight away, taking time to collect his thoughts. He felt those sentiments, too. What should he say?

"Sorry, that's for me to answer," Finn interrupted the rhetoric, "I shouldn't lay this on you."

"These are questions you'll need to work through slowly over the coming months and years. As Caitlin said, we'll all be here for you. But you must forgive yourself."

Finn wiped his eyes and continued staring at the water; he couldn't look at Ryan. The rain was becoming stronger now, yet the noise on their umbrellas was strangely muffled. The sound had an irregular rhythm that broke Finn's concentration.

"Can you forgive me, Ry? Because I'm so far off finding forgiveness for myself. All I've managed to do is acknowledge that I've been a shit brother to you."

"You haven't, Finn, that's a lie."

"Where was I for you through all that happened? Why did you have to deal with it all on your own?"

Ryan exhaled; his emotions were starting to fray. As a priest, he controlled his feelings and stayed calm. Now, he needed to be there for his younger brother and show him the support he promised Rachel, yet he just wanted to yell at him and say that it was the most impossible thing he'd ever experienced. Watching his Ma leave this world, cradled in his arms, was the hardest thing he'd ever had to endure. It still haunted him, and he clearly remembered how her last breath sounded as it left her frail, bony, tiny body.

"I wasn't on my own. I had my faith, which is so important to me. Fiona and Caitlin were amazing. Mrs O'Sullivan was incredible, too. As I've said before, I don't know what I would've done without her."

"But I wasn't there for you, and I'm so, so sorry." Finn turned to Ryan and awkwardly tried to hug him while holding his umbrella. "You were such a rock for Ma. I can't imagine how you must be feeling. My pain is nothing in comparison to yours."

Ryan closed his eyes and started to cry. He tightened Finn's embrace and began to shake faintly. Then, his body collapsed as his emotions completely unravelled. He'd tried to keep it all together for so long it was good to break down. Finn didn't know how to react. Suddenly, the rain stopped, and the noise on their umbrellas ceased. They hugged harder and dropped their open umbrellas to the ground.

"I miss Ma so fucking much," Ryan whispered through his tears. He pulled away and reached into his coat pocket for a tissue. Opening the packet, he handed a tissue to Finn, who took it and noisily blew his nose. "Jeez," Ryan guffawed at Finn.

They laughed timidly, wiped their faces, and blew their noses in unison. Catching each other's eyes, they smiled.

"What are we like?" Finn chuckled.

"We're real, is what we are," Ryan said as he leaned over to pick up his wet umbrella and collapse it. Finn did the same but first gave his umbrella a vigorous shake. "Grief never ends, but it does fade, and it'll become manageable," Ryan reflected as he wound the tie wrap around his closed umbrella, "You'll get over the initial pain, but it's more of a journey of acceptance than a calm end. That's where you'll find your peace."

"I'm not your congregation, Ry. Stop with the preaching."

Ryan raised his eyebrows. "That's what I do. Don't question my job," he replied indignantly.

"Wow! And there it is."

Ryan stared at his brother. His emotions were still tender from earlier. Should he go there? "I'm a priest, Finn. Don't have an issue with how I deal with things. Don't question me on how I can help you or ask what help I can give. And definitely don't have a go at how I deal with things."

"I'm not arguing with you. I'm turning it on you." Finn had changed his tack, "You're a dependable pillar of strength in the community, and you offer incredible help to everyone around you. But what about you? What fallback do you have? Who do you have?" Now, Finn chose to hold Ryan's gaze. It felt necessary now. Much more than earlier. They'd made a connection with their earlier hug.

"What are you saying?"

"Is that where you're at?" Finn asked.

"Sorry?" Ryan answered abruptly, slightly distressed.

"Have you accepted Ma's death? Has your faith let you let her go? Are you good?"

The men stared at each other for an awkwardly long amount of time. "No," Ryan said quietly, caving in under the safe presence of his brother.

Finn's eyes immediately swelled with tears, and he wept; it was genuine and raw. Both men held each other's gaze as they cried away their sadness. It was a significant shared experience, and they didn't want to break it.

Suddenly, Ryan's phone rang. He lifted it out of his pocket and answered.

"Are you guys wanting lunch?" Sinead asked happily. "I can make something. I don't want Niamh to do any more work. She is tiring me out, and I'm just fecking watching her."

"Hey, Sinead, that'd be great. We'd love that, thanks," Ryan replied politely, disguising his emotions. "We'll be about half an hour."

"It won't be anything better than a few toasties and perhaps some soup," Sinead laughed.

"That sounds perfect, Sis. Thank you, you're the best." He hung up his phone and looked at Finn; they stared silently at each other. It lasted a few moments more than it should have.

"How can you be so unbelievably magnanimous and supportive of my selfish needs whilst being in pain yourself?" Finn asked, "And please don't say, 'It's my job'."

"When did this become about me?"

"When didn't it?"

"Sorry?" Ryan asked, confused.

"This past weekend, you've all been nothing but supportive of me. You have excused the utter rudeness that I showed when Ma died and given me the comfort and love that I've craved. But I'm only just seeing now that it isn't just my loss. It's all of ours."

"That's transference, Finn."

"What?" Finn asked, derailing himself from his line of conversation.

"You're trying to make this about me when you need it to be about you."

"No, I'm not Ryan. I know this is about me. All of you have been unbelievably generous with your love and support and told me you'll all be there for me. I've spent so much of these last few days making this selfishly about me that I didn't ask you about you. As I said earlier, this has been an absolute tonic; it has given me hope and consolation, but now I see it's much more than me. I need to be there for you. It's not bullshit."

They hadn't noticed that it had started raining again; their umbrellas were tied up and in their hands. The damp haze had already soaked them.

"We'll always be there for each other; we're family, and we love each other completely," Ryan said. "And before you have a go at me, this isn't a sermon for my congregation, this is a Logan statement. Ma wouldn't want us to be like this; she'd want us to prevail, the way she did when she had the four of us as babies when Da died. She overcame."

Finn wiped the raindrops from his face and pushed his hand through his dripping hair. Ryan continued,

"She had the most incredible fortitude, the most amazing drive and tenacity. We must remember that strength comes from overcoming adversity; Ma showed us that. She was the epitome of resilience. We'll get over the sadness. After all, we feel it because we loved her so much. We'll get over the pain. And we'll do it together, and we'll be OK."

Finn looked at Ryan and smiled. He noticed his brother's furrow was deeper than when he'd last looked. He needed to fix that. This conversation was timely and important. Although he'd come to Ireland under the premise of finding answers for himself, he'd learnt that he was not alone with his issues. He'd replenished his emotional stores and spent some precious time with his siblings, but if he was ever going to get Ryan to forgive him, he needed to reciprocate the love he'd been shown. He needed to demonstrate courage.

"I love you, Ryan, and I'm going to try to be a better brother,"

Ryan looked at him and smiled. "I love you too, Finn. Spending time with you and having conversations like this has been just what we needed."

"Yes, it has," Finn replied, hugging Ryan. "We must help each other be brave."

Pulling away again, they looked at each other. Finn laughed out loud as he shook the water from his hair. "I really had forgotten how fucking wet you get here!"

Chapter 22

I'm onboard with that

Wednesday, 8th July

Even though Rachel's first coffee of the day was made from instant granules in a plastic mug, it was the best coffee she'd ever tasted. Blowing steam off the surface, she sipped the hot liquid and watched the horizon. She'd had thousands of coffees in the past, and the taste of this one wasn't anything special, but what it evoked in her was a positive sense of belonging, a familiarity; the way the smell of apple pie cooking in an oven always made her think of home. The comfort it elicited in her made her feel like she had a genuine connection with her environment. Standing in the cockpit of the Lady, she slowly inhaled the salty air and closed her eyes, realising that this was her Eden. Interrupted by a splash in the water, she opened her eyes, regained her concentration and took another sip.

The previous night, Rachel had moored on an anchorage just outside a tiny fishing village on the east side of Ithaca, an island off Kefalonia. After leaving Georgios and having a wonderfully long and relaxed sail, she'd arrived late in the evening and decided to stay off-land and spend the night on the yacht. She was stocked with plenty of supplies onboard and didn't want to spend any time away from the water. She'd gone for a long midnight swim in the bay and enjoyed repeatedly kicking her feet to create a light show in the bioluminescence of the sea. Mixed with the exquisite clear night sky, filled with millions of pinpoint lights, her vision was overloaded with stars in every direction. It had been sublime.

Dried off, wrapped in a soft blanket, and lying on the boat's deck, she stared into space and opened Spotify on her phone. She chose to listen to "Dancing in the Moonlight" and smiled. She picked up her phone and texted Finn. It was 2 a.m. with her, and she knew Finn was travelling early, so he'd be asleep now. She was desperate to speak to him but knew the timing was off.

> Hey, babes, I miss you, and although we only spoke a few hours ago, I wanted to let you know again how much I love you and miss you.
>
> This experience has been incredible, and I wish I could've spent it with you.
>
> Please promise me you'll come with me to try it out.
>
> Maybe not for the long time I've spoken of before, but at least for some time.

She looked up at the sky. The difference between the artificial bright light of her phone screen and the beautiful, delicate dark abyss was extreme, and it took her a second to regain her focus. Suddenly, the constellations of the heavens came into view, and she was blown away. Was this real? *That's the fucking Milky Way!!!* All she could think of were the songs that could hold her in this mood and allow her to wallow in the moment. She picked up her phone and added Simply Red's *'Stars'*, Coldplay's *'A Sky Full of Stars'*, Rihanna's *'Diamonds'*, and David Bowie's *'Starman'* to her playlist. She placed her phone down, wrapped the blanket around her, looked up to the sky as the Lady gently rocked her like a baby, and lay back to enjoy the soundtrack.

Wednesday morning, Rachel picked up her anchor, cast off her bowline and left her anchorage at dawn. Despite having gone to bed late, she couldn't stay asleep. She was up and ready to roll. Today was a new day, and it held masses of potential. There was no other soul around, and she was phenomenally happy. Having put Eva Cassidy on the sound system when she got underway, the beautiful music encapsulated her mood. Her VHF radio was buzzing a little with static noise, but it didn't interrupt the caramel tones of the fantastic singer, and her heart soared as she heard Eva hit that top note in *'Somewhere Over the Rainbow'*, bringing a tear to her eye. Although the Lady was pretty close to land, Rachel felt free. Views from the boat's deck were like nothing else, the immense sense of space was breathtaking, an uninterrupted panorama that blended the sky into the sea like a Renaissance painting. She wished Finn could see this. Taking a picture wouldn't do it justice.

The sun rose rapidly in the sky, and the water was like a millpond. She had to have the motor running as there was not enough wind to be under sail yet, but she kept the revs low so the noise wouldn't disturb her thoughts. Drinking her coffee, she felt calm and at peace. She gently caressed the wheel as the yacht headed north. Wearing cut-off denim shorts and a bikini top, she noticed that even after a few days, she'd got a tan on her body. It made her feel good.

"Life is so fucking great," she muttered to herself, smiling. "This one's for you, Honey," Rachel said as she cheered her blue plastic mug above her head and finished her coffee.

She reached for her phone and texted Finn. Even though it was early, she wanted to share the moment with him.

> Babes, it's just glorious here. I left at dawn and aim to go around the north of Ithaca and head back to Kefalonia tomorrow.
>
> Perhaps we can chat when you wake up? You would love this.
>
> Let's plan to do this properly. Rach x

Rachel put the Lady on autopilot and checked the charts, navigation and weather on the onboard computer. The forecast was for wind within the next two hours, giving her an excellent ride for most of the day. It wasn't due to be too strong, but it was a weather system that could bring strong gusts and some challenging times. She was elated; this was what she'd been craving.

She'd planned her route around Ithaca, giving herself time to hit any weather, anchor overnight in the north of Kefalonia, and return to Agia Effimia Marina by dusk tomorrow. It wasn't enough time to stretch her sea legs but enough to enjoy the experience. She'd thought about going further afield than Ithaca and perhaps having a night sail, but she wanted to leave that for when she was with Finn. Missing him so desperately, this was totally his type of thing: fresh sea air in the face, freedom to go wherever they wished, and no one else around. Rachel knew her husband; that would be his kind of heaven!

Suddenly, her phone rang, and Finn's smiley face appeared on her screen. She picked it up excitedly.

"Hey, you!" she answered cheerily.

"Well, hello back! How's it going?"

"Oh, Babes, it's amazing. This is just so much fun. I've no wind now, but it's due to blow in a few hours. I've planned a good route and should be at my mooring just after sunset. How are things with you? You're up early."

"Sinead and I are heading to the airport in an hour, as our flight leaves at eight o'clock, and I still need to return the hire car."

"Have you had fun?"

"I really have. It's been a blast. It's so great to have spent time with Ryan. Sinead and I have promised to do this again very soon."

"I'm so happy to hear that, Hun. Just what you needed. It seems we've both had a good time. I'm glad we decided to do it this way."

"Me too. Although I miss you terribly."

"I miss you too. But this has been such a great time to clear all the shit away from the last few weeks. Besides, I'm back tomorrow night."

"I can't wait to see you."

"I can't wait either."

"Please take care and drop me a text when you can."

"Of course I will."

"Stay safe. I love you."

"I love you too, Babes."

Reaching for the winch handle, Rachel placed it in the winch and tightened up the mainsheet, which brought down the boom and trimmed the mainsail. The tell-tails fluttered perfectly as Rachel executed the textbook manoeuvre. The wind had picked up quickly, and the Lady was now making seven knots. The sun was beating down on Rachel's back, and she was sweating. The physicality was exhilarating! Heading away from the land and off her desired course, Rachel decided to make a tack. She moved the bow of the boat towards the wind and waited until the mainsail luffed. Bringing in the mainsheet to stabilise the transition and bending down slightly to avoid the moving boom, she continued to turn the wheel to port. The mainsail started to luff, and Rachel could feel Lady's power easing.

Wanting to maintain her speed, she completed the turn to port, and the boom moved over. A gust of wind filled the mainsail. Her speed returned, and she let out the mainsheet to allow the boom to move and use all the available wind. Releasing it further, she watched as her speedometer told her she had hit 7.2 knots. Tightening the kicker to increase the tension on the mainsail, Lady soared up to 7.5 knots. Rachel was ecstatic!

Back on course, she exhaled. It didn't get any better than this. She'd had the most incredible morning. The conditions were perfect; probably a Force 5, gusting to Force 6 with little spray coming from the water. Wiping the sweat from her brow, she checked her phone to see the time. It was 11:34 a.m.. She noticed that the battery had sunk to 15%. That was a pain; she must've turned off the Wi-Fi, so it would've been trying to find a signal repeatedly while sailing. She quickly took a selfie and sent it to Finn. Looking at the picture, she decided to send it to her brothers, too, to make them jealous.

> Living the dream, guys! Tom, you would LOVE this. Rxx

Deciding to put her on phone charge, Rachel scanned her surroundings for any obstacles or other boats, checked her course, turned on the autopilot and went below deck. She suddenly realised she hadn't eaten yet; she'd been up for hours and only had a coffee. All of the exertion had made her ravenous. She put on the kettle for another coffee and reached into the fridge for some fruit. Yesterday, Georgios had given her a little picnic in a white cardboard box, and she didn't know its contents. When she opened it, she saw an array of sweet pastries, bread rings, walnuts and almonds, and a little tub of Greek yoghurt.

"You dancer!" Rachel exclaimed as she grabbed her blue plastic mug and spooned some instant coffee granules. Grabbing all the items of her hearty meal, she returned to the deck and sat in the cockpit. The Lady was cruising perfectly, and Rachel wouldn't need to do another tack yet. After dipping a pastry in her coffee, she bit into it and licked her lips; it was delicious. It was unbelievable how hungry she was. She'd forgotten how famished you got when sailing. Tom and she always joked that they'd eat ANYTHING when they were on a boat. It was often a cup of hearty soup and a Spam sandwich when they were doing night manoeuvres on a wet and cold winter evening in Southampton, nothing like this environment or Georgios' treats.

She looked out at the glistening water as the Lady glided through it at an impressive speed. The instruments confirmed what she was expecting; it perfectly demonstrated her sailing expertise. Nibbling on an almond, she finished her coffee. Deciding to get back on course and test the Lady's agility, she turned the yacht into the wind to perform another tack. Following the same process, she got back on course with little change to her speed.

"I'm good!" Rachel humorously exclaimed, putting both thumbs up, extending both elbows outwards, and dropping her shoulders.

She reached into the cardboard box and grabbed another pastry. Everything about the moment was perfect; the conditions were optimal, the sun shone, and the Lady ran smoothly, yet she felt a little sad. Perhaps the caffeine and sugar injection had been too stimulating. Everything was perfect...apart from the fact she had no one to share this glorious moment with.

"Pan-pan, pan-pan, pan-pan. This is vessel Serendipity, Serendipity, Serendipity. Pan-pan Serendipity. Call sign Charlie-niner-seven-two-Foxtrot-Papa."

Rachel heard this call for help coming from channel 16. She jumped below deck, switched off her music, and turned up the volume on her VHF radio.

"Our position is three-eight-degrees, two-niner-minutes, three-two-seconds-north and two-zero-degrees, four-zero-minutes, five-zero-seconds-east. We have a damaged mainsail and blocked fuel lines and cannot use our motor. We need assistance to get us to an anchorage. We're on a southerly course at a speed of one knot. We're heading for the Melissa Cape. There are four adults onboard. No one is injured. Over."

Rachel quickly checked her maps and realised that she was close by. She grabbed a pencil and wrote in her notebook what she remembered. She picked up the radio handset and pressed the button.

"Roger that, vessel Serendipity. This is vessel Signora del Mare. Can you repeat your coordinates, please? Over."

Her fingers trembled as she wrote down the location of the troubled vessel. She rechecked her maps and saw that if she maintained her speed of 7 knots, she could be with Serendipity in about half an hour. She checked the weather for the next hour and saw that the wind would be constant.

"Vessel Serendipity, this is vessel Signora del Mare. I'm four miles south of you and should be able to be at your location in approximately three zero minutes. My call sign is Mike-eight-four-four-Lima-Bravo. Over."

Rachel's mind raced into overdrive. She needed to get to them as soon as possible. This is what sailors do; safety is paramount. Thankfully, the conditions were perfect, so it shouldn't be a problem. She had no idea what to do when she got there, but she'd work that out on the way. A static noise came on the radio.

"Vessel Signora del Mare, this is the Frikes Coastguard. Can you confirm that you can reach the vessel Serendipity in the next hour? That will be before 1900 hours. Over."

Rachel's breathing increased, and her palms became sweaty. Although she knew this was common practice when a vessel made a distress call, it became more official now. In all of her training, she'd never had a situation like this before.

"Frikes Coastguard, I will change my course to reach the vessel Serendipity in the next hour. Aiming to rendezvous before 1900 hours. Over."

"Can you move to channel 13 so that we can monitor your progress, vessel Signora del Mare? Over."

"Roger, Frikes Coastguard. Moving to channel 13. Over."

"Frikes Coastguard, this is vessel Serendipity. We will move to channel 13 too. Over."

There was a buzz of static noise again, and Rachel turned the dial of her VHF radio from 16 to 13.

"Frikes Coastguard and vessel Serendipity, this is vessel Signora del Mare. I'm altering my course and heading to three-eight-degrees, two-niner-minutes, three-two-seconds-north and two-zero-degrees, four-zero-minutes, five-zero-seconds-east. I will keep you updated on my progress. Over."

"Thank you, vessel Signora del Mare. We will await your arrival. Vessel Serendipity, out."

Rachel sat at the chart table and exhaled. This day was definitely going differently than when she first awoke. She picked up the mobile radio and went up on deck.

"Oh my God, are you serious?" Finn exclaimed, wiping his hand across his forehead in disbelief, "Is he OK?" Holding his mobile phone in his left hand as he paced the living room.

"I don't know yet," Tom replied anxiously. "I've just had a call from Mum, who said that the ambulance has attended the crash, and they're taking him by helicopter to A&E at the Royal Free Hospital."

"Shit," Finn mumbled, "Is there anything I can do?"

"Have you spoken to Rachel today?"

"I spoke to her this morning from Ireland, but not since I returned to London. She did send me a few photos, but I haven't replied. Do you want me to tell her?"

"No, not yet," Tom said quickly. "I don't want her to worry until we know exactly the situation. She also sent me a picture; she looked so happy."

"I can go to the hospital to be with Lynn if you want."

"Would you?" Tom asked, relieved. "That'd be awesome. She's in a real state, as you can imagine. Lucy and I won't be able to get there until later. Lucy is dropping Beth and Joseph off at a friend's and as soon as she's back, we'll get in the car and drive up. But we might not get in until midnight."

"No problem, Tom. I'll get myself sorted and leave in the next fifteen minutes."

"Thanks, Finn, I really appreciate it."

"Do you want me to call her and tell her I'm coming?"

"I'm going to call her now to let her know what we're doing so I can tell her," Tom replied.

Finn could hear the fear and pain in his voice. "It's going to be OK, Tom."

"I'm not so sure."

Rachel had not seen many boats nearby, just a few off to the northeast. The sea felt like it belonged to her, and she was making excellent time. She'd let out her jib sail and managed to speed up to an exhilarating eight knots and was flying through the water now. She felt so alive! The wind direction had changed slightly, and because of the course change, she didn't need to tack much; she was at an optimum beam reach. The Lady's sails were shaped superbly and using all the available wind. Earlier, she'd flown past a ferry slowly moving between the islands. It made her feel like a superhero; her pace had a purpose.

Whilst gliding along, she'd thought about what she would do when she rendezvoused with Serendipity, and she had a plan. Firstly, she would throw a line aboard, which was probably the most challenging task. As long as she maintained her course and the wind didn't throw her balance, she would succeed. Once she had Serendipity tied to the Lady, she would have to motor to a nearby anchorage.

Having looked around the surrounding area, she found something suitable, but the tow would be slow. The next stage was to anchor in a safe bay for the night and then leave early in the morning to head to the Port of Frikes and hand over Serendipity to the Coastguard and Port authorities. That messed with her original plans to go around the north of Ithaca and have enough time to sail back to Kefalonia and drop off the Lady tomorrow, so she needed to speak to Georgios about either extending her charter or asking them to organise a pick-up from Frikes.

"Vessel Signora del Mare, this is vessel Serendipity. We've observed you off our starboard bow. Over."

Rachel smiled. She saw a tiny shape in the distance just off her port-side bow and assumed it was Serendipity. Picking up her binoculars, she looked in their direction. She saw a yacht with no visible mainsail and four men waving enthusiastically from the deck. She was getting close.

"Vessel Serendipity, this is vessel Signora del Mare. I can see you and am on my way. Have any circumstances changed since we last spoke? Over."

"We have the engine ticking over, but it's pretty useless as there's little power. We can manage about 1,000 revs, so it will only be good for maintaining our position with a little steerage. Our mainsail is no longer helpful, so we've stored it safely in the sail bag. We're all well and cannot wait to see you. Over."

"That's great, I'll be there shortly. I aim to throw you a line from my stern to your bow, so can someone be ready when I arrive? It would be good for you to have a line ready on your bow just in case the line I throw doesn't make it. Over."

"Of course. We'll have that ready. See you soon. Out."

Rachel opened the locker and found the longest line; it was shorter than she'd have liked, so she hoped her throwing arm would be precise. She tied it off on the back cleat and prepared it to be thrown. Not wanting a gust of wind to take her off course once she approached Serendipity, she brought in her jib sail. Perhaps she would lose some speed now, but she needed stability once she got close. With the jib sail safely secured and lines stowed, she looked out to her port side. Serendipity was clearly in view. She turned on the engine in neutral and gave it a little rev. It was ready.

"Vessel Serendipity, this is vessel Signora del Mare. I'm ready to come alongside shortly, so I will bring down my mainsail now. I'll come along your starboard side and turn on your stern. Once I'm on your port side, I'll throw my line to your bow. Please be ready to catch it. I'll have momentum, so please tie it off immediately. Over."

"Roger that, vessel Signora del Mare. Out."

Rachel turned into the wind, released her mainsheet, winched in the main halyard, and let her mainsail drop. Her speed plummeted. She was sweating from the activity and the adrenalin. She brought in the mainsail with efficiency and haste.

"Ahoy Signora del Mare!" one of the occupants yelled at Rachel.

Rachel waved as she concluded the manoeuvre to bring in the mainsail. She quickly cleared the cockpit of loose lines. That was what she'd been taught all those years ago, never leave a trip hazard, keep it tidy. She grabbed two fenders from the locker and attached them to her starboard side in preparation for coming alongside. Suddenly, she was very thirsty; all this exertion was taking its toll on her. But she had no time to go below for a drink. She was parallel to Serendipity now and could see it bobbing up and down in the water. She sharply steered the Lady around the stern of the boat and saw two men on Serendipity standing at the bow, ready. She turned on the autopilot, on a course that would take her away from Serendipity, to avoid collision. The wind was still gusting; this throw would need a bloody miracle.

Coming up on their port side, she reached for the line tied to her boat's stern. She was so close she could see the anxious expressions of the two men on the bow. One held a spare rope to throw, and the other stood ready to receive her line. This was it.

Rachel took a big breath and stood on the transom, holding her line, "Ready?!"

As the Lady cruised past Serendipity, Rachel used all of her strength to throw the line as accurately as she could to the man on the bow. It made the distance! And the man managed to catch it. They were elated.

"Get it under the guard rail and cleat it off!" Rachel yelled. There was no way she would ever manage to do that again.

The man panicked as he realised only he was holding the line as the Lady continued past Serendipity. He hastily got the line under the guard rail and tied it off on the port side cleat. Rachel put the Lady in reverse and gave her a little blast of power. She didn't want to snap the line. There was a noticeable lurch as the line took the tension between the two boats, but the line held.

"Throw me the other line!" Rachel yelled.

The man on the starboard side threw the line from their boat but had forgotten to cleat it off, and the line came over in its entirety. Rachel caught it before it fell into the water and played havoc with her propeller.

"Sorry!"

"Fuck's sake," Rachel muttered.

She cleated it off and decided to try another throw. The Lady was moving away from Serendipity, and she only had one chance.

"Catch this!" Rachel yelled again.

She threw the line with all her might. It was a longer throw than before, but thankfully, it was a longer line. The man who successfully caught the previous line caught this one, too.

"Yeah!" yelled the incompetent other man, somewhat relieved.

The man tied this second line to the starboard cleat, and the two boats were successfully connected. Rachel's radio crackled.

"Vessel Signora del Mare, that's some impressive throwing. Over."

Rachel laughed and wiped her sweaty brow. She was thoroughly exhausted.

"Vessel Serendipity, welcome aboard. I've plotted a course of 212 degrees. We're heading for a bay called Marmagkas. At this speed, it should take about an hour. We should be able to anchor there overnight safely. Over."

"Vessel Signora del Mare. Thank you so so much. We'll have a cold beer ready for you when we stop. Over."

"We'll need to keep an eye on how close we get. The wind is due to drop around 2000 hours, making the journey more comfortable. Over."

"We'll try our best to keep our distance. Out."

Rachel turned to the agreed course, switched on the autopilot, scanned the horizon and went below deck in search of a glass of water. What an experience! How had she managed to do all that? She heard the radio crackle again.

"Frikes Coastguard, this is vessel Serendipity. Vessel Signora del Mare has successfully rendezvoused with us, and we are now under tow. We will stay under anchor at Marmagkas Bay tonight and come to Frikes in the morning. We'll report our timings in the morning. Over."

Rachel smiled as she finished her glass of water. She did that. She fucking did that! She reached for her phone, desperate to speak to Finn, but she saw it had no charge. She'd plugged it in earlier but had not switched it on.

"Shit!"

Turning on the plug, she grabbed her water and returned to the deck. She'd phone Finn and Ellie later tonight once she was under anchor. For now, she needed to bring both boats to safety. She would sleep like a baby tonight.

Chapter 23

I wasn't expecting that

Thursday, 9th July

Rachel arrived in Marmagkas Bay at 2130 hours, as the sun was setting, to the grateful applause of the Serendipity crew. Throughout the hour-long voyage, she'd spoken on the radio with four enthusiastically happy, middle-aged men from Maryland who had never sailed in the Mediterranean before. While standing in the cockpit and navigating the Lady, Rachel learned that the men were corporate insurance brokers. They described themselves as "wannabe sailors" who weren't very good at sailing but wanted to try island-hopping in Greece. More interested in expressive theatre than sports, they acknowledged that their decision to experiment with sailing was somewhat misguided. Discussing with Rachel how stressful the whole experience had been, they asked if they could relinquish all responsibility to her, as they'd probably made a massive mistake in renting a yacht. Not sure whether to be boosted by the vote of confidence or annoyed at their lack of ownership, Rachel told them she'd need a little help to secure them in the bay but would deliver them safely to Frikes in the morning.

Piloting the two boats into a safe position out of the prevailing wind, Rachel looked for a suitable place to anchor for the night. Her phone was on charge and repeatedly buzzed from the chart table, breaking her concentration. Assuming the phone was trying to find a signal in this remote location, she went below and turned the ringer off.

The bay was beyond beautiful, with a tiny islet just off to the east that housed an ancient church. Olive and eucalyptus trees bordered the beach, and the hills in the background rose to touch the shimmering sky. As the boats settled, the translucent sea caressed the shoreline, gently lapping over the marble-coloured pebbles. The beauty was breathtaking, but she hadn't had time to appreciate it yet.

She instructed the Serendipity to drop their anchor and waited for them to get a hold. Once held, she removed the two tow ropes. She then moved away and dropped the Lady's anchor, wanting distance between the two boats in case of movement during the night that might cause damage. Not concerned that the boats were now separate, she surveyed the area, seeing that the bay was well-protected and shallow enough to reconnect in the morning. She told the crew to put out their fenders and did the same. She was being overcautious.

By now, she was tired and sweaty. Knowing she needed to ensure that Serendipity was extra safe for the night, she dived into the water and swam over to the yacht. The water was magnificently refreshing as it enveloped her fatigued body. She considered taking a more leisurely swim and letting the water wash away her mad, insane day, but she knew she needed to conclude everything and secure the yachts for the night. She swam to Serendipity's transom, where the crew met her with grateful smiles and enthusiastic exuberance. She boarded their boat and mentioned she wanted to put out an extra anchor as a precaution so they wouldn't swing due to their limited power. She didn't want anything to happen that might require them to move quickly, as they wouldn't be able to do so.

The crew asked why she was so cautious when the water was like a millpond, and they were safely under anchor. Rachel explained that the weather could change in the blink of an eye, and it was best to be prepared. They gestured for her to go ahead, their lack of knowledge and relief was visible on their faces. Reaching into the locker, she grabbed the spare anchor and tossed it over the stern. Winching in the line to ensure it was settled, she was happy that the boat was secure. While she was busying herself with checks, the crew set about entertaining. They brought out several cold beers and a small feast of cheeses, hummus, meats, salad, and bread. They handed her a towel to dry herself off, gave her an overzealous hug, and remarked on what an amazing young woman she was.

When Rachel was happy that everything was safe, she sat on the deck of Serendipity and sipped a well-deserved beer. Nibbling on some goat's cheese and staring up at the stars, it hit Rachel how mad the day had been. How *really* mad the day had been. Seriously, nothing could've prepared her for this situation or what she'd overcome. She couldn't quite digest what the day had brought. *Well done me*, she whispered to herself proudly. Remembering why she'd chosen to do this trip, that she wanted to find herself, test her resolve and have an experience. Well, that was three big fat ticks in the box today, eh? She couldn't wait to tell Finn.

Beaming as the adrenalin coursed through her veins, she realised that she had done good, and perhaps she was a bit fantastic. She leaned back into the cockpit and reviewed her surroundings. It was utterly breathtaking. High up in the heavens, the starry sky twinkled like millions of diamonds glistening in harmony. She would never have seen this place if not for this detour. How serendipitous!

For the next hour, they talked about Rachel's sailing prowess; they joked about how useless Thomas was, the one who threw the untied rope; they praised Richard's skills on a VHF radio from his Scouting days and how lucky they were to have someone so competent, and supremely kind, to rescue them. Rachel tried her best to smile and listen to their chatter, but she was beyond exhaustion now. At midnight, she stood up because she couldn't last any longer. Instructing the men to be up at dawn so they could leave at first light, she made her excuses and said she had to go and get some sleep. Diving into the water again, she swam over to the Lady, leaving a celestial trail of bioluminescence behind her.

"You're our guardian angel!" the crew shouted behind her.

Rachel boarded the Lady, waved back to the Serendipity, crawled below deck, stripped off her wet clothes and collapsed into bed.

"Vessel Signora del Mare, this is vessel Serendipity. Good morning, Rachel. Over."

Rachel stirred in her sleep. What was that noise?

"Vessel Signora del Mare, this is vessel Serendipity. Rise and shine! Over."

She sat up abruptly. "Fuck!" She yelled as she grabbed the sheet that lay over her naked body. Rushing into the main cabin, she picked up the radio handset.

"Morning, Richard. Sorry, I forgot to set my alarm. Over."

She picked up her phone to check the time - it was 6:14. She saw 17 missed calls and nine messages.

"No problem, Rachel. Get yourself a coff...."

"Richard, I'll get back to you. Out."

She released the microphone, dropped the radio handset absentmindedly, and turned to her phone. What the hell was going on? She opened her phone to see who'd called. Ten missed calls were from Finn, two from Tom, one from Alice, and four from Ellie. What the fuck?

Wrapped in the sheet she'd slept in, she quickly went above deck to check her position; all good. The boats hadn't moved. Looking at her phone again, she called Finn before checking the messages. He picked up immediately.

"Finn, what's up?" she asked nervously.

"Rachel, are you OK?" he asked quietly, "I've tried to call you but didn't get an answer."

"What's up? What the hell is going on? Is it Dad? Mum?" she asked frantically, crying, "Tell me, tell me now."

"It's OK, Rachel," Finn tried to reassure her. "Are you sitting down? Is anyone with you?"

The crew of the Serendipity waved at her from their cockpit, which was an annoying distraction. She went below deck again.

"Just tell me, Finn. What's going on?" Rachel sat at the chart table, apprehensively tightening the sheet around her.

"It's James…" Finn paused, trying to sound strong. "He's been in an accident."

Rachel gulped as her eyes immediately filled with tears. "And?" She closed her eyes, fearing the worst.

Finn paused again. He knew Rachel would want to know all the details, even if they were devastating to hear.

"He's in intensive care and unconscious. They had to perform emergency surgery last night to repair a punctured lung. He has broken four ribs and a broken right ankle, and his left wrist and hand are pretty messed up. He has multiple deep lacerations to his face, legs and torso."

"Oh my God…" Rachel could barely speak. She covered her mouth with her left hand in disbelief. "Is he going to make it?" She couldn't even believe she was asking that question; the words automatically came out of her mouth.

"The doctors told us that the surgery went as well as could be expected at this stage. But the next twenty-four hours are the most critical. But Rach, we need to stay positive," Finn added quickly, feeling Rachel's devastation.

She remained silent, trying to process the information.

"He's in intensive care so that they can monitor his blood oxygen levels and check for infection. It was pretty extensive surgery; he was in there for six hours. Once he's breathing without the chest tube that they put in last night, they'll have a better idea. He's a tough cookie, though, right?"

"Mum and Dad? How are they?"

"Destroyed, as you can imagine. I've never known your Mum to be so quiet. Frank keeps going away and bringing everyone coffee. We're all here. Tom and Lucy have come up too."

"How did it happen?" Rachel moved from her fearful state to anger, "Was it that fucking car?"

"He was involved in a five-car pileup on the M1, coming into Brent Cross."

"Shit! Was he speeding?" she asked numbly.

"We don't believe so. The police said there had been a previous incident at the M1 junction joining the A406 and that the accident James was involved in was probably caused by poor observation and rubberneckers. If James was speeding, then that might be why it happened. We won't know until we speak to him."

"Fuck," she yelled as she stood up and paced the cabin, nearly tripping on the sheet draped around her. "I need to get to him. I need to come home. You say the next twenty-four hours are important…I need to see him."

The VHF radio buzzed; she turned the volume down so she couldn't hear it. She didn't need that right now.

"Where are you?" Finn asked. "We all tried to call you yesterday. I even rang Ellie to see if you'd been in touch. Last I knew, you were heading north from Ithaca."

"Still on Ithaca, but I'm in the middle of fucking nowhere after rescuing a damaged boat and bringing a crew of inept Americans to safety."

"What? A rescue? What happened?"

"I'm on the east side in a picturesque bay with no one else around except a bunch of blundering insurance brokers. It's just beautiful hills, an aquamarine sea, and white sandy beaches; it's heavenly, and of course it is! But it also means I'm far away from you."

"And the inept Americans?"

"Don't ask. It's not important," she'd already transitioned into solution mode. "I need to work out how I get back to London."

"I think Ellie may have a solution," Finn offered. He could

tell that Rachel was already getting organised.

Rachel was pacing the cabin. "I do have some missed calls from her. Let me give her a ring." She was alert and hadn't realised that she'd dropped the sheet that was covering her body and was walking around naked.

"Thanks for being there, Hun, I know they'll love you for that." She exhaled, numb from the disbelief of the news.

"Of course," he said gently. "Rach?"

"Yes?"

"Are you going to be OK?"

"I just need to get sorted."

"Rach?"

"Yes!" Rachel answered impatiently.

"Are you OK, Babes?"

She closed her eyes, wiped her left palm across her forehead, and exhaled. "Sorry, that was really rude of me. I'll be fine. I need to work out how to get home and see James. This is just a bit too much to take in. Sorry. Please tell everyone I send my love, and I'll get there as soon as I can. Love you, Babes. I'll keep you posted."

"Love you, too. Be safe."

After hanging up from Finn, she continued to pace the cabin naked, working out her options. She called Ellie.

"Rach, how's things?" Ellie asked with concern.

"I can't believe what's happened."

"Finn rang me yesterday; I'm so sorry to hear the news. I tried to call you, but it just went to voicemail," Ellie said kindly. "We've been thinking how we can help."

"I need to get home, Ellie," Rachel whispered.

According to her calculations, it would take about two

hours and fifteen minutes to get to Frikes if she travelled at the sedate speed of one knot whilst towing Serendipity. The weather forecast said there would be no wind until late afternoon, so if she ditched the Serendipity, she could manage nearly six knots under power, which would take about half an hour to get to Frikes. Which option should she choose?

"I need to see when the next flight home is."

"We've looked, and the next one to London from Kefalonia isn't until half past one. Gino has managed to organise a helicopter to pick you up from wherever you are and take you to the airport. Do you want me to book the flight for you?"

"So it's quarter to seven now…" Rachel paused as she considered, "I could be at Frikes for ten at the latest if I take Serendipity."

"Serendipity?"

"Yes, yesterday I rescued a damaged boat being sailed by some truly incompetent guys. We're currently in a stunning bay on the east side of Ithaca. I've promised them safe passage to the port of Frikes. If the flight doesn't leave until then, I can still see that promise through. How long would it take to get from Frikes to the airport? I'd hate to abandon them here, even though they're inept and should never have set foot in a boat."

"That's unbelievable!" Ellie said. "You'll have to tell me the details."

"One for wine and another time when all of this is over," Rachel said restlessly. "Could you check if I can get to the airport in time if I get into Frikes at ten? Would you mind booking the flight then? I'll ring you once I'm on my way. What do I do with the Lady?"

"Of course," Ellie replied, "Whatever you need. I'll book

the flight and tell Gino to get the helicopter to Frikes. I'll check with Georgios about picking up the charter. I'll be in touch."

"Fuck, I've never been in a chopper before!" Rachel laughed nervously.

"You'll love it, you adrenalin junkie. Speak later."

"Love you so much. Thank you, thank you, thank you."

Rachel had a pee and a speedy shower and got swiftly dressed. Whilst brushing her teeth, she checked the weather and charts. Picking up the radio, she buzzed Serendipity.

"Vessel Serendipity, this is vessel Signora del Mare. Good morning, Richard. Over."

"Good morning, Rachel," Richard responded immediately. "Everything OK? Over."

"We need to get underway in fifteen minutes. Can I ask you to bring in the stern anchor and store it in the locker, put your fenders away and be ready to bring in your bow anchor when I move around? I will throw the two tow lines again. Please be ready to receive them. Over."

"Roger that, Rachel. We'll be ready. Over."

"We'll be sailing at 1.2 knots, so you must watch for the distance between the two boats. Please look out. Over."

"Of course. Michael and Thomas will stay at the bow for the whole journey. Over."

"That's good," Rachel said efficiently. "Oh, sorry for waking up late. Out."

At 07:06 a.m., the two boats left Marmagkas Bay in tow with a course set for Frikes. Rachel pushed the Lady to 1.2 knots and told the Serendipity to stay alert. By then, they'd realised she didn't want to talk, so the radio remained quiet.

> Flight booked
>
> I have your paperwork
>
> Helicopter will take 15 minutes from Frikes to the airport so you have time
>
> Georgios will take care of getting your charter back, so you don't need to worry.
>
> Sail safe and speak soon. Ex

Rachel smiled at her phone; she had the best friends. She would have to do something extra special to thank Ellie and Gino for their unbelievable generosity and hospitality. She went below deck and made herself a coffee. Grabbing Georgios' cardboard box, she finished the remaining stale pastries. The coffee tasted shit today, plasticky and bitter and nothing like yesterday's. Not believing that experience was only yesterday, Rachel realised that today would be a painfully slow journey. Fidgeting, she couldn't stand still as she watched the autopilot steer the Lady. The speed was frustrating, but she knew this was how it needed to be. She was desperate to get home, see James, and hug Finn. Wanting to know the time, she picked up her phone— 07:59 a.m.

"Shit!" she exclaimed, still fidgeting, "Why is time taking so long?"

This was not what she thought today was going to be like. Of course not. How could she have expected this? Fuck, James, why did you have to buy that car? She sighed and resigned herself to her thoughts. What if James didn't make it out of intensive care? What if he never woke up? What if he died? She gulped and burst into tears.

What if her flight got delayed and she couldn't see him in time? What if she hadn't come on this trip? She would've been able to be at the hospital right now. Why did she have to make it all about her?

Such deep thoughts rocked her to her inner core. She felt so sad, the exact opposite of the chilled thoughts she'd had whilst happily sailing yesterday before she picked up the doomed Serendipity. Again, was that only yesterday? It made her think of the song *What a difference a day makes* by Dinah Washington. She missed Finn; she wanted to feel his positive vibes and hug him so hard. He was a star, always looking out for her and thinking about her well-being. She would have to thank him sincerely for not biting her head off when she was rude. Thank God he was with her family right now; he would help her parents stay calm, and she knew he'd keep her well informed.

Overcome by desperation to get home, her thoughts diverged in many directions, from calm to panic, organised to chaotic. Why was this boat going so fucking slowly! She stomped around the cockpit and continued to fidget. She missed her family, too. She reminisced about their fun times growing up, the love and support they showed each other, and their closeness. Thinking this, Rachel became sad again and felt sick at the thought of not seeing James again. Her family were exceptional individuals, and she needed to tell them that more regularly. She needed to get home and tell James and Tom how much she loved them. How important they were to her. How much she needed them. Like Finn, she needed to spend more time with her siblings and be more forgiving and accommodating to her mother. Alice was right; she really needed to cut her some slack. And just like that, Rachel's phone started to buzz, it was Alice.

"Hey TT, how are you doing? I heard the terrible news."

"Yup, it's shit," Rachel answered resignedly, "I'm in the most beautiful place in the world, having had the most exhilarating and challenging day of my life yesterday, and now today is this."

"So, coping well?" Alice tried to lift the moment, "And there was me thinking you'd make it about you."

Rachel laughed, letting the pressure release, wiping a tear from her left eye. Alice was so good at this stuff, cutting through the crap. She knew how to handle her.

"I've never had such an intensely emotional 24 hours in my whole life!"

"Well, you did want to go there and test your resolve. That was the goal, wasn't it? Be careful what you wish for, TT."

"Yes, but I wasn't expecting this!"

"You weren't expecting Serendipity?" Alice asked. Rachel paused. "Don't panic, Ellie told me," she added with a small laugh. "I'm not a clairvoyant, so don't worry. But isn't that a sign, right there?"

"Ha, but what she didn't tell you was that I had to rescue these four maladroits who don't know their arses from their elbows and that I single-handedly brought their boat and mine to safety!"

"Even without knowing the details, that sounds impressive. How do you feel now?"

"Exhausted, elated, proud, yet exhausted. But this thing with James has floored me."

"Those are all good things, TT. This is what you went to Greece to overcome. You should be very proud of yourself. The experience will make you stronger."

"Yes, and thank you, but now I'm travelling at a snail's pace in the middle of nowhere, towing a dead boat, trying to get back home to see my sick brother."

"Which you had no control over. You'll be able to handle this horrific situation; trust yourself."

"But I'm not there. I'm here, and I need to be there." Rachel stared out at the horizon and blinked back her tears. "How will I ever forgive myself if something happens to him and I'm not there?"

"You can't think that, TT. That's the ultimate 'What If?' scenario and you cannot hold that guilt. What is going to happen is going to happen. You're doing your best to get to him, and that is all you can do."

"I know, but it's painful to endure. I just want to be with him."

"Seems like Ellie has come up trumps on the travel arrangements," Alice joked, "Gino has organised a helicopter; for fuck's sake. How the hell does he do stuff like that? That guy is like an Italian 007."

"I know!" Rachel replied, happy for the lighter mood. "Coupled with the exclusive hotel we stayed in, I have to ask what Gino actually does for a living."

"You and me both, sister," Alice laughed.

"Thanks for calling, Alice. This is just what I needed. You're the best."

"Not at all. I'm glad you've found some answers in Greece. And remember, you couldn't have planned for James's unfortunate accident," Alice said calmly.

"When will I next see you? Please come to London soon. I need to give you a massive hug for all the support you've given me."

"Of course, call me when you're home and keep me updated on James. Give your family my love."

"Love you," Rachel replied.

"You too, Babes."

Just as Rachel hung up the phone, it buzzed.

> Hello sweetie, I understand you are on your way home. Please stay safe. The doctor has just updated us, and they say James is comfortable. What a lovely doctor - I think his name is Mr. Savage. I don't know what comfortable means, but I think it is good. It has been such a terrible shock for us all. It is wonderful that Finn is with us. We do love him. Dad has been keeping us filled with coffee and tea. Get to us as soon as you can. Love Mum xx

Rachel reread the message; she could only imagine what her mother must be going through. She understood that her mother had moved to stating facts as a coping method. She must be hurting.

> Mum, I'm getting to you as soon as I can
> It's going to be alright
> Please give everyone my love. I love you. Rach xx

Rachel rechecked her phone to see the time; it was only 08:13 a.m. This was worse than watching paint dry. How could time go so slowly? Her phone buzzed again.

> James has been moved to Ward 7 in the ICU. He is still unconscious but stable. We are all here. Keep me posted on your progress. Travel safe, and I CANNOT wait to see you.
> Love Finn xx

Rachel smiled and placed her phone on the cockpit table. She stared out at the beautiful view as she slowly headed south. This had been the strangest few days!

"I'm not sure what a difference a day makes, Dinah; I'm certainly coming back from here a different person."

She picked up the phone and replied to Finn,

> Thanks for letting me know, sweetie. I'll text when I'm at the airport. I've missed you so much. Give my love to everyone.
> Love you. Rach xx

The Lady would be arriving in Frikes in fifteen minutes. The voyage had been uneventful, and Rachel was happy it was over. Her head was not in the right space to enjoy it, as she'd spent the whole journey worrying. She'd only spoken to the crew on Serendipity occasionally, but it was more out of instruction than for banter. During the sail, Rachel had gone into über-efficient mode. She'd packed up all her things and got her paperwork ready for the port authorities so she could disembark as soon as they were safely moored. Ellie had texted to say that the helicopter couldn't land nearby because of the masts of the yachts, but that a taxi would be waiting for her at the port to take her to the land site. Rachel had spoken to Georgios and confirmed how the Lady would return to Kefalonia; he told her to leave the keys on the boat and that he would organise everything. The crew of the Serendipity would have to deal with the coastguard themselves.

She'd sorted out all that she needed to; she was homeward-bound.

Chapter 24

All hands on deck

Friday, 10th July

"I've packed everything that was in your room, including the stuff in your bathroom," said Ellie. "If I've forgotten anything, I'll post it over."

"Thank you so much, Ellie," Rachel gushed. "What would I do without you?"

She hugged her friend as they stood at the security entrance at Kefalonia airport. Gino was there, too. He stepped towards Rachel and offered a hug.

"Mio caro amico, thank you for coming to see us," he said softly, "Give my love to your family at this difficult time."

"Thank you, Gino," Rachel returned his hug. "I cannot thank you enough for your kindness, love, and generosity. I owe you both so much. I'm so sorry it has ended like this."

"Not at all; you couldn't have thought this would happen, no?"

"Don't think that, TT," said Ellie, "It'll be OK."

Rachel stepped away from Gino as Ellie handed her the boarding pass. She rifled through her handbag, checking for her passport, purse and AirPods. Looking up at Gino, she smirked a little.

"I don't know how you managed to get that helicopter, Gino; really, I don't. And, honestly, we'll have to talk more about that exclusive hotel when all this is over."

"Of course," Gino laughed gently. "Come over again soon, and next time, bring Finn."

"I will...we will," Rachel smiled, "Thank you again." She leaned over to Ellie and gave her another hug. "I love you so much. Thank you for everything."

"You've got this," Ellie whispered. "Ring me when you've seen James."

Rachel pulled away, grabbed her suitcase and nodded, trying not to cry.

"And give our love to your family," Ellie added as Rachel walked away, heading towards security, waving without turning around.

On the flight from Kefalonia, she stared out of the window, sipping red wine. It was cold and tasteless. She'd ordered it as soon as the hostess passed as she needed to calm her nerves, but she wasn't enjoying it. Observing the coastline and sea disappear into the haze, she could just about see the tiny yachts below heading off on their adventures. The tiny rice-shaped outlines were scattered across the blue like confetti. This time, it didn't fill her with excitement and yearning. Instead, it reminded her how far away from home she was.

How was she going to deal with seeing her brother? What state was he in? Would he be able to talk to her? Was he still unconscious? How was she going to speak to her mother? Even after the olive branch texts, Rachel wasn't sure if she could be civil to her. Why was there so much animosity between them? Why could she not just not get on with her mother? They'd kind of sorted their differences before she headed off to Greece, and now she would need to talk to her in what was going to be an emotionally charged environment.

She adjusted herself in her seat and finished her wine. She realised she had to think that nothing would happen between now and her getting to the hospital. That was the only way she could cope with this. She'd made significant progress since hearing the terrifying news this morning. This morning? What was going on with time?? So much had happened. She put her plastic cup on the tiny flip-down table and eased her fingers through her hair. She looked up and exhaled. She stared at the sterile plastic vents serving the plane with dry, germ-riddled air. It made her feel slightly claustrophobic, so different from the limitless horizon and fresh sea air she'd experienced yesterday.

Yesterday? Fuck, what a whirlwind! In the last 48 hours, she'd endured every emotion and experience she could ever have wished for. Without time to digest it fully, she needed to hold it together; she was already an hour into a three-and-a-half-hour flight and then just a 40-minute taxi ride from Heathrow. She was on the home straight. Thanks to Ellie, who had organised everything, she'd even known to book a flight that landed close to the hospital. Honestly, that woman was amazing. What a superstar!

Looking at herself, Rachel saw that she was still in her denim shorts and yellow bikini top. She'd thought to quickly put on a black tank top when she left the Lady, but she wasn't dressed for a hospital or meeting her mother. She could see that her skin had turned a little 'crispy'; that would have been the salt left on her skin from her yachting exploits; she would need to wipe that off. She opened the overhead locker and rummaged through her suitcase for something less revealing. Looking around, she saw that she had attracted attention; reaching up to an overhead locker whilst wearing a bikini top was not a good idea. She grabbed her toiletries to freshen up and went to the toilet to change.

Rachel rushed through the doors of A&E at the Royal Free Hospital, frantically looking for Ward 7. Wheeling her suitcase and carrying her handbag awkwardly, she scanned the walls for directions. All she saw was an abundance of coloured signs showing her how to get to the Radiology Department, Rheumatology, Haematology, Trauma and Orthopaedics, Oncology, or Department of Infectious Diseases, but not any wards. She panicked and hurried up to the busy reception.

"Excuse me, I'm looking for..." Rachel gasped.

"Please wait," the translucent receptionist replied, raising her right palm derogatorily without making eye contact.

"Sorry?" Rachel gulped, staring at the older woman with the thin skin. Rachel thought she didn't look well. Several staff members in blue uniforms worked around her, equally nonchalant, checking paperwork and writing notes on clipboards. Five or so members of the public were wandering around in varying states of distress, trying to get answers, too. The receptionist tapped away on the keys of her shiny keyboard; it looked like it had been wiped, sanitised and polished every minute for the last year.

"I'm looking for the Intensive Care Unit," Rachel asked more pressingly, "Ward 7,"

"I'll only be a moment," replied the receptionist impatiently. She looked in Rachel's direction as she grabbed paperwork from the nearby printer and attached labels to random parts of the page. Rachel could see that she was very stressed and looked deeply unhappy.

"It's my brother; he's been in an accident," Rachel tried to hold it together.

"Right, Dear. Now, what's his name?" The receptionist softened a little but remained notably belittling. Rachel could see she was tired. It must be hell to work in an environment like this.

"James Templeton, he came in yesterday," Rachel's voice quivered.

"Rach!" Finn came briskly down the corridor.

She turned, dropped her bags and plunged into his arms. "Oh, Finn! Thank God you're here."

They embraced strongly, and Finn buried his head in Rachel's hair. She reached for his face and kissed him gently. The receptionist went back to her keyboard, printer and label-covered paperwork.

"How is he?" Rachel asked, picking up her handbag.

"He's still unconscious, but the doctor says his vitals look good."

"Oh, thank God."

"Come this way. It's not far. It's on the fourth floor."

Finn grabbed the handle of Rachel's suitcase. They walked

towards the lift. Rachel grabbed Finn's hand nervously and squeezed it hard.

When they entered Ward 7, she saw her Dad walking towards her. He was holding two paper cups, one in each hand, and he looked tired.

"Rachel!" he smiled and put the cups on the side of the nurses' station. "I'm so glad you're here."

They gently embraced, and Rachel could smell her father's familiar aftershave, Old Spice. It was comforting and nostalgic.

"Dad, how are you?"

Frank looked at Rachel silently and then blinked like he was thinking of a decent response. "The doctor said that James' surgery went well, but I'm not sure he is out of the worst," Frank said flatly. "You must come and see your mother. I've got you a coffee."

He retrieved the paper cups and walked towards the bed in the far corner. Rachel looked at Finn, raised her eyebrows, and opened her mouth slightly in disbelief. Frank was a shadow of himself. Finn stared back at her, signalling, 'See what I mean?' Frank tried to find the break in the curtain but struggled with a cup in each hand.

"Let me get that, Frank," said Finn, opening the curtain.

"Thank you, Finn."

They walked in, and nothing had prepared Rachel for what she saw.

A sterile metal contraption in the middle of the space caged a fragile-looking body. Rachel silently covered her mouth with her right hand in disbelief. Was that James? Fuck. He was bare-chested with a thin blue blanket covering him up to his waist. His chest was stained with iodine from the surgery, and several wires stuck to sensors were attached to his skin, which was alabaster-coloured and unnaturally shiny so that it resembled marble. There were bandages and gauze wrapped around his torso and jagged cuts all over his shoulders and upper arms. Rachel couldn't see his face clearly because it was covered by two large plastic tubes; another plastic tube was plugged into his throat and connected to the same apparatus. They were helping him breathe, but it made him look like a futuristic scuba diver. All of these tubes were hooked up to a ventilator to the right of his bed. A monitor to the left of his head showed his vitals and beeped with a reassuring, constant rhythm. He had an IV inserted into the back of his right hand that was taking fluid from a bag that hung up above his head. His left hand was in a plaster cast, as was his right ankle, which peeked out from the blanket. He looked so vulnerable, and if she didn't know otherwise, she would have thought he was a corpse.

Rachel took in all these details in three seconds and wanted to collapse. She steadied herself and looked around a little more. Lynn was sitting in an armchair beside the bed, reading a newspaper with her glasses on. Tom was sitting beside her, looking at his laptop computer with AirPods in his ears. Rachel watched as her father walked over to Tom without a word and placed one of the paper cups next to his laptop. A nurse entered the space to check the instruments and see how James was doing. There needed to be more space for everyone to be there, but she assumed no one wanted to leave. Lucy was not around.

"We need to have the curtain open so we can observe him," said the nurse as she opened the curtain to the wider ward.

"James?" Rachel whispered, trying not to cry, hoping he would stir.

Lynn looked up and took her glasses off. "Rachel, you're here!" she smiled, stood up, and put her newspaper on the chair.

"Hello, Mum," Rachel said softly.

"How was your trip?"

"Could we chat later?" she replied dismissively.

Tom had seen Rachel enter the room. He removed his AirPods, closed his laptop, and approached her. "Sis, so good you're here," he said, embracing her firmly.

"Hey Tom," she returned his hug but immediately turned her attention back to James, "Has he shown any life at all?"

Tom looked in her direction, but she didn't register his gaze and kept staring at James.

"No, we haven't had anything since we've been here. But the doctor seems happy with his condition."

Lynn walked forward, hoping for some physical contact from Rachel, too. "Yes, Sweetie, Mr. Savage said the surgery went well, and they just need to watch for infection."

"Are you OK?" Rachel asked, giving her a gentle hug.

"Well, you know," Lynn replied, "I've had better days."

"Mum, could I have a moment alone with James?" Rachel asked, turning towards Tom and Finn, who were standing behind her. She raised her eyebrows and looked at them, hoping they would understand the meaning behind her silent glare.

"Oh," Lynn replied, slightly put out.

"Could I have some time with him?"

"Mum, why don't we go for a walk and find out where Lucy has gone?" said Tom. "She said she'd only be a short while, and I'm worried she's bought all of the chocolate in the cafe." He gently held Lynn's arm and turned her away from the bed.

Finn turned towards Frank. "Why don't we get some fresh

air, too, Frank? All that coffee you've been bringing me has given me a headache. Why don't we take a walk around the car park and leave Rachel for a little while?"

"That would be nice, Finn," replied Frank blankly, looking like a deer caught in the headlights. "I do actually need the toilet."

Within ten seconds, the space was empty, apart from Rachel and James, the beep, beep, beep, beep of the heart monitor, and the rhythmic whoosh, whoosh, whoosh of the ventilator. The nurse returned to check something on the machines and wrote some comments on James's notes. Rachel said nothing to her, and the nurse seemed to know not to interrupt her thoughts.

Rachel turned the chair her mother had been sitting on so it faced the bed, sat down, and put her head on her arms. She grabbed James's right hand, being careful not to disturb the needle administering his IV fluid.

"What the fuck were you thinking?" she asked quietly, looking down at his hand and gently stroking it. They were the most beautiful hands; she'd always thought his fingers were so elegant and had asked why he didn't play the piano like Tom. She started to cry as she stroked his hand, contemplating the moment. Her emotions were flying around, whizzing between relief that she was here and nothing had happened to him before she arrived, to the realisation that his condition was extremely serious; then, from pure agony that her little brother was so badly messed up to the love that she felt for him in this very second. She continued to hold his hand and suddenly remembered when he was six years old, and she used to paint his fingernails, using the excuse that she needed to practice.

"Why did you never tell me to get lost?" she asked, "You never minded that I painted your nails. Why would you let me do that? Why were you always so fucking accommodating and never complained?"

She rested her head on his hand and cried uncontrollably. It had gotten too much. The thoughts that had raced around her mind whilst she slowly sailed to Frikes were hazily surfacing as the tears fell. She was here, but look at him! He looked powerless, the antithesis of the last time she saw him. Where was that cheerful, happy, funny man? How was he going to get better? How could she help him? He had to get better; this wasn't right! She wanted her baby brother back.

"Just be OK, James. Get better," she pleaded. "Please! You can't end like this; it isn't your time. We've got so much to do together. I need to see you make Partner at work and get you a nice girlfriend, and you need to see me be a Mummy at some point. We have so much more to experience together."

She continued to stroke his fingers in rhythm with the beep, beep, beep, beep of the heart monitor and the whoosh, whoosh, whoosh, whoosh of the ventilator.

"Who's going to take the piss out of me if you're not here? Who's going to embarrass me when we go out to dinner? Who will come up with the ridiculous one-liners that always make me laugh?" she gulped, "Can you remember that time you introduced yourself to one of my female work colleagues and said, 'Hi, I'm Michael - More Buble than Jackson?' Honestly, James, there's no one like you, you can't leave me."

She continued to cry and didn't notice Finn walk in. "Rach," he whispered as he walked over to her. She looked up and wiped the tears from her eyes. He handed her a coffee and smiled gently. "Sorry to interrupt you, Honey. I thought you might need this. Did you want anything to eat? I was going to go and get some sandwiches or something.

Are you hungry?"

"No, thanks, I'm not hungry at all. Where are the others?"

"Lucy is talking to your Mum. We've all been outside to get some fresh air, so I reckon they'll be back up in about fifteen minutes."

She nodded as she adjusted her hair.

"How are you doing?" Finn gently asked, laying his hand on her shoulder and squeezing it affectionately. "I can get them to stay away a little longer if you wish."

"No, it's alright, Babes, but thanks. I'll freshen up and come to the canteen in a bit."

"OK, see you then." Finn walked out of the room.

Rachel listened again to the heart monitor and ventilator and stared at her brother. He looked dreadful. So different to the vital, handsome young man she'd seen two weeks ago. The accident had quite literally pulled the life out of him. The last time they'd spoken, she'd spent the whole time talking selfishly about what she wanted to do with her life, and now, as she sat next to James, Rachel realised that she was a self-absorbed, selfish sod. She'd spent so much time thinking about herself that she didn't think about anyone else. She needed to turn things around. Look how sweet Finn had just been, how kind and selfless. She went to Greece to find emotional resolve and work out how to cope with this exact situation, how to deal with something terrible happening to someone she loved. And here she was. She was living that fear. And she had to do better. She had to be better.

James didn't move; the machines ticked along, keeping him alive. She was going to do whatever she could to help him get better. She wanted to spend time with him, to be part of his life. She reached into her pocket for her phone and opened the WhatsApp group "Bitches behave".

> James is so ill and looks absolutely awful. Unconscious and covered in cuts and bruises. He's on a heart monitor and ventilator. Mum and Dad are devastated, dealing with it in their own way. I haven't spoken to the doctor yet, but I will talk to Tom shortly to get more details.
>
> I feel so sick.

Standing up, Rachel walked toward the small sink on the wall and washed her hands and face. As she dried her hands, she heard her phone buzz.

> Sending huge hugs, babes. You'll get through this. At least you're with him. Ax
>
> Hold his hand and let him know you're there. He'll sense your presence. So glad you made good time. Ellie xxx

Rachel looked at herself in the mirror and exhaled. She needed a shower, a change of clothes, and to speak to her mother properly. But not today.

A nurse came across and rechecked the instruments; they were taking excellent care of him. Rachel hoped that they weren't worried about his condition. Turning away from the mirror, she looked at James. No movement. Nothing had changed.

"I'll see you soon, little brother," she said, "We're going to get you through this."

She walked away.

Chapter 25

You can always come home

Saturday, 1st August

"But, Mum, it isn't about that."

"Well then, Rachel, what is it about?" Lynn answered calmly.

Rachel gulped, not making eye contact with her mother. They were having lunch in The Roebuck, a country-style pub across the road from the hospital. James's condition had not improved, and they'd all taken turns to be with him. The mood in the hospital had been getting quite fraught, so Rachel had asked for some time with her mother. Lynn was slightly taken aback, but Finn and Frank encouraged them to leave the hospital and have a change of scenery. Since returning from Greece and being prompted by Alice, Rachel realised she needed to mend her relationship with her mother, but she wasn't very patient. She hoped a lunch date would allow them to talk.

"You've always pushed me to work hard, supported my career, and encouraged me to achieve high, and yet when I want to make a decision that doesn't match your plans, you undermine my confidence and make me feel terrible."

"So, you're mad at me for being supportive? Is that why you're being so cold with me?"

"No, that's not what I meant." Rachel had been preparing this speech for the last few days, trying to stay calm and rational, but it wasn't going as planned. "I'm annoyed that you're so disappointed in me when I don't do what you want."

"That's very harsh, Rachel," Lynn said, moving the cutlery on the plate of her finished starter. "I'm not disappointed in you. I never have been and never will be. I don't know why you would think that. And you're being a bit immature in getting annoyed with something you haven't confirmed to be true."

"But you keep telling me how much work I need to do, how I need to keep striving for more, hurtfully saying that I should be a Mum by now, too. I can't do everything! Because every time I achieve something, you raise the bar. Am I ever going to be good enough for you?"

"Oh my goodness, Rachel," Lynn answered with a nervous laugh, "You've no idea." She looked away and out of the pub's window. At that moment, the waitress came over and removed the dirty plates from their first course. "Excuse me, could I get two large glasses of your Malbec, please?"

"Of course," the waitress answered.

"Mum?" Rachel asked with surprise.

"I think it's time to have a proper chat about our expectations, don't you think?"

Rachel was stunned; what did this mean? "Well, yes, perhaps we should," she said, sitting back in her chair. She felt very uncomfortable.

Lynn straightened the cuffs of her blouse and adjusted her wedding ring. Rachel could see she was nervous; perhaps her mother had been practising a speech, too.

Lynn took a breath and looked at Rachel. "Growing up for me was hard, with your grandfather travelling around the world with the Army. I hated having to keep moving from one boarding school to another. I never had any true friends, and your grandmother was always so hard on me, saying I needed to work extra hard to fit in. She'd come from an Army family, too, and that was what her mother told her. She never understood how lonely I got or how all I wanted were consistent relationships in my life. Well, we never talked about it anyway. Support and love were all I craved during my childhood."

Rachel stared at her mother in disbelief. She hadn't known her to be this candid. That short speech contained so much information that she'd never heard before. She knew her mother had a delicate relationship with her mother, but they'd never really talked about it. James's accident must've been a terrible shock for her; it was unearthing some fundamental truths here.

"I lost a brother when I was young. Your grandmother had a terrible time with post-natal depression after his birth, they didn't know what it was back then, and he died of cot death at eight months old. Your grandmother never fully recovered. I was seven." Lynn adjusted herself, losing eye contact with Rachel. "I used to get into trouble at school, and my mother would tell me off for not conforming. I hated it. I had no stability; what was I supposed to do?"

Was her mother a troublemaker? Really?

"Is that what you used to tell Ellie?"

"Yes! I saw so much of the sadness in her, the same as I'd experienced. I desperately tried to gain my mother's love, but it never came. I wasn't as strong as Ellie. My strength came later in my life. I didn't have you and Alice."

The waitress came over with two glasses of wine and put them on the table.

"Thank you, Dear." Lynn reached for her glass and took a sip. Rachel did the same. She stared at her mother, suddenly seeing her in a different light. Her mother had had to deal with conflict and pain, too. She suddenly felt genuinely awful for being so mean to her.

"The sisterhood you three had when you were growing up, and thankfully still do, is so unique and special. I tried explaining to Ellie that having a strong emotional foundation was important. To be the best person she could be by overcoming adversity and forgiving her weaknesses."

"Why did you never speak like that to me?" Rachel asked sadly. Forgiving her mother was one thing, but she needed to know why Lynn had treated her the way she did.

Lynn sighed and looked away. "Because you're my daughter, and it was my responsibility to prepare you for the future. To bring you up the best way I could. I love Ellie, I always have, but you're my little girl, Rachel. I had to get it right. I didn't want to be like my mother was to me. I needed to succeed, to be a better mother than she was. I needed to guide you away from the pitfalls, teach you how to be resilient, push you to achieve, encourage you to learn how to lead and to know when, or when not, to back down. To do everything for yourself and not change to make anyone else happy. And most of all, persuade you to chase your dreams.

My mother never did that for me, and I didn't want to disappoint you."

Lynn reached for her wine glass and took another sip. "I was so overwhelmed when you spoke about not having resilience and how you wanted to head off somewhere to seek it out. I felt that I had failed you; that is probably why I reacted the way I did. I'm sorry if I did it wrong."

Rachel's eyes filled with tears as she stared at her mother. Who was this woman who sat opposite her? She'd gone from being a nippy, accusatory and annoying mother to a strong, eloquent role model in one speech.

"Oh, Mum," Rachel couldn't say anything else. She'd got it all wrong. So completely wrong. Her mother was amazing, but she had been dreadful to her. How could she have been so selfish?

"I've only ever wanted the best for you, Rachel. And you've exceeded any expectations I've ever had for you. I must've done something right because, honestly, Sweetie, you're amazing. I'm so sorry if I haven't celebrated that more with you along the way."

Rachel grabbed her napkin and wiped her eyes, numb from this revelation. How did she not know this woman? This formidable being. How had she fought with her and not been interested in finding her back story? Always turning to her father for comfort, she should've spoken to her mother more.

"When you described your valiant rescue of Serendipity, I was so proud of you. Who else would do that? You do this stuff. You're bold, courageous, fearless, and coupled with that, you're kind, thoughtful, and loyal. I have no idea how you think you're not resilient. I'm not disappointed in you; I'm curious that you don't know yourself."

"Mum…" Rachel whispered, still wiping her eyes. Did her

mother mean this? She'd never heard these compliments before.

"I'm sorry if I've been hard on you. I should've realised that you're hard enough on yourself that I no longer need to do that. You've grown into an amazing woman, and I love you very much. And I don't tell you enough. Thanks to you, you have an incredible husband, a successful career and a steadfast friendship group." Lynn took another sip of her wine. It became apparent to Rachel that Lynn needed to say this as much as Rachel needed to hear it. "You're all I ever wanted to be." She looked at Rachel with a gentle smile.

"What?" Rachel automatically responded.

Since coming back from Ireland, Finn had felt like a caged animal. Sitting in a hospital bay with Rachel and her family for hours on end was incarcerating. He was desperate to run and be out in the fresh air, away from the beeping machines and bitter smell of antiseptic. It was such a waiting game, yet he felt that if he left and anything happened to James, he'd never forgive himself. After a few days of pacing around, the whole family realised that being in the ward simultaneously was not a good idea; they were starting to get short-tempered with each other. Perhaps it wasn't just Finn who was feeling trapped. Finn could see that Rachel was losing her patience with her mother, and Tom was trying to be magnanimous about the whole situation, but it was starting to take its toll on his calm demeanour. They needed a change. The doctors told them that James was stable, his vitals were good, and he was void of infection, but until he awoke, there wouldn't be much they could do except keep him comfortable.

Rachel suggested that the Templeton family moved on from the idea of all keeping a bedside vigil onto a more proactive rota of people by James's side; she drew up a schedule, which they were all happy with. Lucy returned to Southampton to deal with Beth and Joseph, and Tom booked a nearby hotel so he could continue to work. Frank was less vacant, and his persistent nervous coffee-buying had stopped. Lynn took the opportunity to go for walks with Frank and seemed much calmer.

Finn decided to run before his 'shift' with James and brought his running gear in so he could leave the hospital and run around Hampstead Heath. It was a glorious day, and he looked forward to a new route and being out and about. The family's stress levels had dropped since they'd given each other some space, and he was happy that Rachel would get some time with her mother. They needed to clear the air between them, and he hoped it went well.

Rachel wiped her eyes and watched her mother straighten the cuffs on her blouse.

"You're my hero, Rachel," Lynn said quietly.

"Oh, Mum," Rachel stood up, moved around the table and hugged her mother. "I've been such a pig. I love you, Mum, and I'm so, so sorry for fighting with you."

Lynn patted Rachel's hands, which were wrapped around her shoulders. "Aww, Dear, I know you do," she said sweetly. "I should've said this stuff to you years ago. I should've explained why I was so hard on you. I didn't want to fight with you either. Your father, the sweet thing, had been telling me how confused and worried you were. I even spoke to James abou…" This was Lynn's turn to cry.

"Mum?" Rachel asked, concerned, sitting back in her seat and grabbing her mother's hand.

"I'm sorry, Rachel, I just had a little wobble there, I'll be fine." She adjusted herself in her seat and wiped her eyes, trying to be discreet. At that moment, the waitress returned to the table with the main course of fish and chips, which she placed on the table.

"Could we have two more glasses of wine, please?" Rachel asked.

"Sure," the waitress replied.

Lynn wiped her eyes, and Rachel looked at her.

"I can't believe I'm crying in public," she said. "This is so embarrassing."

"It's fine. We're in the corner, and no one is looking. And besides, we're just across from the hospital, I'm sure there are a lot of tears shed in here. He's going to be OK, Mum. You know James, he's a fighter."

"I hope so. It's just so awful," Lynn said, as she picked up her cutlery and pushed the chips around her plate with little interest. "I'm not sure I'm hungry for this now."

"It would be good to have a hearty meal, Mum, to keep your strength up."

"I wonder what your Dad has eaten. Perhaps I could take a doggy bag back for him."

"Why not just try a bit?" Rachel asked, "We can always take any leftovers back."

She was aware of Lynn's mood change and knew the situation with James deeply affected her. Yet, in the last half an hour, her mother had bared her soul, and they'd both gone from antagonism to acceptance. She wanted to keep her mother on track; this had been such an eye-opening experience. Not wanting to cause any upset, she thought about how to help her mother. She decided to pull an Alice.

"When do you think it becomes acceptable to only think about yourself when you're in a relationship?"

"Oh, my," Lynn laughed. "Don't think I don't know what you're doing here."

"Ha! And there she is!" Rachel laughed, appreciating the reprieve and the return of her judgemental mother. She reached for her wine glass, clinked it in an attempt at a 'cheers!', and finished it. Lynn did the same. Just as the waitress replenished the table with two new glasses, taking the empty ones away.

"Thinking about number one is not selfish, Rachel, it's essential," she said whilst eating a chip. "If you aren't the best you can be, you're not adding value to any relationship you're in. But there's selfishness and selfishness. Putting ourselves first and understanding how we work can be the best way to know how to give back to others."

"Mum, when did you get so smart? Why did we never talk like this before?" Rachel was glad she'd restored the mood. It was still reflective and emotional, but at least they weren't talking about James.

"Years of watching you, James and Tom grow up, as you were all learning from me and your Dad, we were learning from the three of you. Jeepers, you constantly challenged us, made us doubt our judgements, question our theories and check ourselves. The three of you gave me strength; that's when I became a fighter. You all taught me that I had to overcome. As a small toddler, you made me want to try harder and have more energy, interest, and spark. You'll have this too when you have children. Although you're already a superhero, so you'll be fine."

"Honestly, Mum, thanks for the compliments, but you've said more flattering remarks in the last twenty minutes than you have ever said to me. You can stop now. You think I'm fantastic. I get it." She raised her wine glass to her mother, giving her a knowing smile. Lynn lifted her glass and smirked.

"It does feel a little alien to speak this way; I've always been so hard on you. I tried to be a better mother but ended up like my mother. I'm so sorry."

"We're in a good place, Mum. Please don't feel guilty."

"We are indeed, my sweet Rachel."

"I just wish we'd spoken like this sooner. I should've been more observant and not cruel to you."

"We've both learnt a lesson here," Lynn agreed. "However, I was trying to say that you need to think about the impact of your actions. If I did this, how would this affect that? If I didn't do that, what would that mean for them? It's a constant juggling act. Make sure you're the best you can be while not breaking any links with the people in your life."

"So why did you fight me when I said I wouldn't go for the U.S. job?" Rachel asked curiously.

Lynn sighed. Rachel could feel a change in their emotional temperature. It now felt like she was talking to Alice or Ellie; it was truthful, genuine, and honest.

"Because I was worried you'd be disappointed in yourself if you gave up on your dream. I realise now that I didn't have all the facts and should've trusted you. I'm sorry I was so negative."

"It's fine, Mum, it's all worked out for the best. We're all good." She dug into her fish and chips, and a rogue pea bounced off her plate. She caught it with her finger and put it in her mouth. "I know it lasted less than a week, but my trip to Greece was eye-opening. I learned so much about myself, and it was amazing to have time with Ellie. She's incredible. She taught me that strength comes from dealing with trouble and conflict. Strength doesn't come from things working out; it happens when things go wrong, and you work out how to overcome it. That's why Ellie is so strong. That's how she can prevail."

"She's an amazing person," Lynn agreed, digging into her food.

"She really is. I'm so lucky to have her as a friend. I love her so much. She and Gino were so sweet to me. I can't wait to take Finn out there so he can experience the magic of the place. I also learned so much about myself. I have to remember what I achieved while I was there. It was a short while but a lifetime of experiences. But I should have come and talked to you. What you've described in the last half hour has been insightful; you're a warrior, Mum, and we'll overcome this situation with James. We will prevail. I love you."

Lynn put her cutlery down, lifted her glass, and looked at Rachel. "To you," she paused. "Thank you for not pushing me away and letting me explain myself. Also, I appreciated the invitation to talk about this. I should've done that. In fact, I should've done it years ago, especially since I'm the parent here. There you go, Rachel. I don't know everything!"

"Ha! I've found you out!" Rachel laughed, "To you, too."

At that moment, Finn walked past the pub on the cool-down part of his run. He saw them through the window and knocked on the glass to get their attention. Both women, clinking each other's glasses, smiled and waved at Finn. He waved back and smiled.

"Well, look at that!" Rachel exclaimed. "Can I blame the drinking of wine at lunchtime on you?"

"Ha ha," Lynn laughed, "Of course, Sweetie. Although, if we take them all sticky toffee pudding, I think we'll be all right."

Chapter 26

Creep

Tuesday, 4th August

Rachel nipped out of the office for a spot of lunch and to get some fresh air. After all the ups and downs of the past month, being back at work was anticlimactic. Also, going to see James at the hospital every evening meant she wasn't getting home until after 10 p.m., when she'd slump into bed, exhausted.

When she returned from Greece, she'd picked up a new project with Christie, and they were working hard on it, but it wasn't very engaging. She found it creatively stifling to design a straight-laced corporate legal website. Pages of testaments and legal services in an Arial grey font made her feel wretched. Despite the naughty book name, there weren't that many shades of grey you could put on a page. She and Christie had joked that they would try to introduce a splash of blue or purple but weren't sure that the grey-haired client in the grey suit would go for it. Her trip away was becoming a distant memory.

Carrying a hot espresso coffee, she put the sandwiches and bottle of sparkling water she'd bought into her handbag and picked up her phone to text Ellie.

> I had the most unbelievable afternoon with Mum on Saturday. She told me about the troubles she'd had growing up and how she chose to bring me up differently. I had no idea.

She started walking back to the office, wanting to sip her coffee but knowing it was dangerously hot when her phone rang. It was Ellie.

"Hey TT, how's things?"

"Hey, you. I had a lovely lunch with Mum on Saturday. It was weird, as well as beautiful. She told me things about her childhood and how much she struggled. I feel terrible that I've been so mean to her in the past. She was so sweet."

"I'm glad you sorted it out. Alice will be, too. I'm sure all of the heightened emotions around James brought about her openness."

"Did she talk to you about this stuff?" Rachel asked.

"I'm not sure exactly what you mean. We discussed how I should handle boarding school. Your Mum was amazing at telling me to calm down and not fight with everyone. I was an impertinent teenager bursting with rage and anxiety. All she told me was to be strong but not an idiot."

"Did she tell you that she went to boarding school and

had a similar experience?"

"Yes. She told me how hard boarding school was for her and that her mother didn't understand her. She impressed on me that it was crucial to stay close to the people that loved me."

"Why did you not tell me this?"

"I thought you knew," Ellie answered. "I'm sorry."

"It seems so strange to learn these things about my Mum now; it changes how I see her. I've been such a bitch. I can't believe I didn't know half of what she's been through. You're right; this stuff with James has opened up the emotional floodgates. I've been having existential conversations with Finn and Tom. There've been plenty of hugs with Dad, and Mum is just being lovely. This whole situation has definitely brought us closer together."

"But that's what you do."

"No, I mean that being at James's bedside has brought us together."

"That's you, Babes. You bring people together. I bet you've organised a bedside rota and sorted everything, right?"

"Urm, yes," Rachel replied.

"Yup, that's what you do. I'm so happy that you've healed some wounds with your family. Are you feeling calmer now?"

"I am. Despite the sadness of James's condition, I'm feeling better. He's still hanging on, and the doctors are happy with his progress. I'm arguing less with Finn, which is brilliant; as I said, it's going much better with Mum. Finn and I haven't spoken about what to do next. Dealing with hospital visits has taken over all our immediate plans. Work has lost its appeal, though, but that might be post-holiday blues."

Cradling her phone into her shoulder with her chin, Rachel awkwardly swapped her coffee to the other hand as it was getting too hot to hold; she was pleased she hadn't spilt any. "I can't thank you and Gino enough for all your generosity whilst I was in Greece. I owe you big time. How about you come and see us in London soon? I mentioned it to Alice, and we could have an Alice talk-don't-talk session. I have so many things I still want to talk to her about, and after my disgraceful attempt to help you, I think you could benefit from talking to her, too. I've already texted her to ask."

"That would be lovely,' said Ellie.

"Let me organise it."

"TT, you're hilarious."

"What do you mean?"

"You're always so good at keeping in touch, you're painfully honest, you send me ridiculous animated gifs at silly times of the day, and you always ask how we're doing. Do you never stop?"

"Nope, because you're too important to me, and I miss you."

"So why do you take the piss out of me and Alice so much?"

"Ha, well, you're both too easy to wind up," Rachel laughed.

"Surely you know you're the glue that keeps us together?"

"Really?" Rachel stopped walking and sat down on a nearby bench.

"Back to my earlier comment, your Mum told me to keep the people who love me close. She meant you. She knew I needed someone like you in my life, and she was right. She knew what a comforting support you would be for me. And you are. You're the most incredible friend. You're so genuine. You're amazing. Think of all the things you've done for me over the years. There are too many to list. You continually prove to me how much integrity you have."

Ellie paused, and Rachel stayed quiet. She hadn't been expecting this conversation today. Especially after the chat with her mother. How should she deal with all these flattering remarks? It felt peculiar.

"When I was sad, you came to see me at the drop of a hat," Ellie added, "No questions. You were there."

"Well, of course I was," Rachel answered, trying not to cry.

"Most people wouldn't have. You do it automatically. You don't have to think. It's not a task or an issue for you. It's real. It's just you."

"Thanks, Ellie, that means a lot. But right back atcha Babe. What you said, right back to you. You're the most amazing friend. I don't know what I would do without you in my life."

"I was ringing because I wanted to thank you, actually," Ellie laughed. "Funny how things work out. I wanted to say thanks for showing me what it is to be a true friend when you asked me the ultimate question about losing my baby."

"Oh God, you can't thank me for that; I had no idea what I was doing. Alice is still mad at me about that!"

"Maybe, but it got me thinking, and I've been talking to Gino since you left. It did help me. It's taken the pressure off as I've realised I must forgive myself. I'm still crying myself to sleep, but I have a glimmer of hope now."

"Oh, really? I'm really sorry to hear that. But I didn't do anything, Ellie. All we did was take the time to talk. I hated to see you so sad, and I wanted to try to take the pain away. I'm so glad you guys are feeling a bit better. How is Gino?"

Rachel asked, standing up and realising she needed to return to her office. This conversation was going on longer than she'd expected, but she didn't want it to end.

"He's doing OK. He's putting all his energy into his work, which is ramping up. For now, that is how he'll cope; at least, it's a distraction for him. Our journey of acceptance will be long, but we need to move on and find some sort of normality. I think we're more accepting now. We'll get there."

"Yes, you will. When James recovers, Finn and I will visit you, and we can toast to our futures."

"Have the doctors given you an idea of how long that will be?"

"No, not yet, and I'm trying to stay positive."

"It would be great to see you both out here. You're welcome anytime. And I'm so happy to hear that you're finding some peace. I hope you realise that you don't have to prove to anyone that you've made it, right?"

"What do you mean?"

Rachel entered her office building and into an empty lift, hoping to keep her phone signal. Shifting the coffee into her other hand again and holding her head awkwardly to cradle her phone, she pressed the button for the seventh floor.

"So, after your heroic serendipitous rescue and general awesomeness, you must know that all those worries about whether you're resilient and deserving are bullshit, that you do have it all. You don't need to seek it out. You've proved yourself."

"I'm not sure about that," Rachel replied, "But I am feeling calmer. And I'm feeling the love right now. Thanks for your kind comments."

"I'm so happy to hear that, TT; you deserve it."

"We both do."

Rachel walked out of the lift and over to Christie's desk. Christie was on the phone. She put her coffee down and reached into her handbag, grabbing one of the sandwiches and the sparkling water from her bag and putting them next to Christie. She mouthed *'thank you'* as Rachel smiled at her. Lifting her coffee, Rachel moved around to her desk.

"Look, I'm going to have to go. Some of us have to work, you know."

"Ha, I know, sorry. I'm going to the beach shortly."

"Don't."

"Please give my love to your folks. Your Mum's probably feeling vulnerable right now," Ellie said. "I do feel for her."

"Of course, I'll let her know we spoke. Give my love to Gino. Bye."

"Bye."

It was day twenty-seven of James's ordeal, and Rachel was sitting on the uncomfortable, plasticky fake leather chair next to his bed, looking at her phone. During this time, she'd befriended the nurses and was on first-name terms with most of them. Every evening, she brought them in cakes that she had purchased on the way from her office. She told them that she needed to keep them sweet because she was amazed by their care and attention and loved how compassionate they were whenever they checked on James. Besides, they were always very positive when she asked, 'Is it going to be tonight that James wakes?'

Tom had returned to Southampton a week ago, so in his absence, Rachel had had several conversations with Mr Savage, the surgeon, who had given the Templeton family reassurance that the injuries that James had sustained were no longer life-threatening. What fantastic news! Rachel had taken ownership of updating the family, and her parents seemed more optimistic. James was still on a ventilator and heart monitor so that they could keep an eye on his vitals, but the superficial cuts had now healed, and James didn't look so battered, even if he still looked like a scuba diver.

"Do you want another coffee, Rachel?" a smiling nurse in a blue uniform asked as she entered the bay.

"No thanks, Becky, I've had far too many today. I'm going to have to move on to decaffeinated."

"Never do that. It just doesn't work. I could never give up caffeine; it's the only thing that keeps me going."

"Ha, you're right there," Rachel replied.

Lifting her phone, she checked Facebook and watched some YouTube videos but was bored. She hadn't been artistic enough today, making her feel restless. She wasn't going to think about work, though, until James had fully recovered. Finn and Rachel had decided not to discuss promotions, interviews, relocations, holidays or sailing into the sunset. Everything was on pause. Suddenly, her phone buzzed.

> Yo yo yo

It was Alice. How did she always know when to get in touch?

> Hey you, how's things?
>
> I'm knackered! Just finished an intense spin class and I can't feel my legs
>
> You work too hard
>
> No, I eat too much.

> Its the only way I can control it. How's James?
>
>   I'm sitting with him right now.
>
>   He can't come to the phone
>
> Oooh, that was good
>
>   He's still unconscious, but we're out of the woods
>
>   But I'm really twitchy just sitting here with him
>
> Why don't you do some sit-ups or something?
>
>   Fuck off
>
> You'd feel better for it
>
>   No, I wouldn't

Rachel stood up and started pacing. She noticed that it felt good to be moving. Alice was right. There were three other patients in intensive care, but they had no visitors, which Rachel found strange and sad. Two of them were semi-conscious, and the other was in a worse state than James. It was so difficult to watch such sick people—she wanted to block off the room. Thankfully, they were on the other side of the ward so they wouldn't get annoyed by her restlessness, and she wouldn't need to look at them.

All of a sudden, the familiar beep, beep, beep, beep of the heart monitor and the rhythmic whoosh, whoosh, whoosh, whoosh of the ventilator were now the most annoying sounds in the world. She hated it. She was so agitated.

>   Why won't he just wake up?
>
> He will. When he's ready x
>
>   I'm going to have to go, Alice. Speak soon x
>
> Later, bitch xx

It was now eight o'clock, and Rachel felt even more fidgety. Finn was coming in at ten to hand over, so she had only a few hours to kill. Usually, she would bring some work with her to pass the time, but they'd had such a rubbish meeting that afternoon with the grey lawyer that she told Christie she would give herself the night off. Rachel had taken a pee, put her hair up into a ponytail, and rearranged the wilting flowers but still couldn't settle. Becky came across a few times, but Rachel wasn't in a chatty mood.

"Can I pull the curtain across for a bit, Becky?"

"We shouldn't really, Rachel, but I can give you a few minutes until our next check in ten minutes. Is that OK?"

"That would be great, thanks."

Becky closed the curtain behind her as she left. Rachel settled into the chair, unlocking her phone to open Spotify. Swiping between playlists of rock hits, bubblegum pop, and jazz tunes, she struggled to find the perfect song to match her mood. What could help calm her down? Retrieving her AirPods from her handbag, she was surprised to find them fully charged. As she browsed through Spotify, she stumbled upon a playlist titled '007 wannabe,' and remembered it was one James had sent her last year. She couldn't remember the content, so without looking, she hit play and waited for the music to begin.

Creep by Radiohead came on. Oh my God, it was such a good song! She looked over at James and smiled fondly. She recalled listening to it one evening last summer when they'd spent the whole evening dancing with each other after drinking too much Southern Comfort. She would never drink that spirit again after that night. That bit where the guitar came in! Oh my God.

She stood up, turned up her phone to hear it better, tossed it on the bed, and started dancing around. She shook her hips and waved her arms around her head in a teenage-like frenzy. It felt so good. She couldn't hear the ventilator or the beeping heart monitor, she couldn't see the sick patients, she got lost in the song. She didn't care if Becky could hear her.

"I want you to no...tice...when I'm not around," she sang at full volume, "You're so fucking special, I wish I was special." She air-guitared her way around the room. It was so liberating! She kept dancing. She needed to release the energy, dump the angst and anxiety, and get James to wake up. She was tired of the intense concern that enveloped her every waking moment. Keep dancing, Rachel. Shake it out, like Taylor said.

"Run, run, run, run!" she yelled at the top of her voice. "Whatever makes you happy..." She kept moving until the music calmed, and Yorke said, "I don't belong here..." That was just what she needed!

Rachel walked over to the bed to check what the next song was. As she looked for her phone, she noticed that James had moved his finger to point to it.

Chapter 27

There's no place like it

Sunday 23rd August

Woken up by the sun streaming in through her bedroom window, Rachel reached for her phone. She checked the time; it was 10:15 a.m. Finn had said he was going for a run, so she wasn't surprised by the empty bed. It immediately buzzed; it was the "Bitches behave" chat.

> Are we doing this? Ax

"Oh shit!" she said, remembering that she was meant to be on a video call with Alice and Ellie.

> Can you give me 2?
>
> Sure, I'll grab a tea.
>
> Me too.

Rachel flung away her duvet and ran to the bathroom. She peed, washed her face, brushed her teeth, and changed her pyjama top to a more modest T-shirt. Returning to the bed, she picked up her phone.

> Ready when you are

Her phone immediately sprang to life with Alice's smiley face. Ellie joined simultaneously.

"Hello, bitches!" Alice exclaimed, "How the devil are you both?"

"All the better for seeing you, Alice." Ellie added, "Looking fine, Lady Logan."

"Are you kidding?" Rachel replied, pushing her hand through her dishevelled hair, "I've just woken up! Sorry, guys. It's been a mad week, and I took the opportunity to have a lie-in."

"No problem, TT. How's James?" Alice asked.

"He's amazing; he turned it around like only he could. He's off the ventilator now and breathing by himself. His voice box is still raw, so he's grunting; it's not a real conversation yet. And he is still a bit disoriented and tired. Yet, at his instruction, they've got him on a gruelling physiotherapy routine; he's still in the hospital but definitely on the mend. Tom, Lucy and the kids were up during the week, and James smiled for the first time in a long time. It's unbelievable."

"It's the best news ever," said Ellie.

"It really is. How's things with you?"

"So, me first," Alice interrupted. "I've just been commissioned to do a series of online talks about 'Empathic Understanding' for the Open University. It's an aspect of the 'Person-Centred Therapy' I've spoken to you both about. It's going to be awesome; I'm so excited."

"Don't get TT involved, she fucked me up," said Ellie.

There was a momentary silence as they all looked at each other on video.

"Yeah, I kinda did, didn't I?" Rachel admitted.

Ellie belly laughed.

"Although I don't think you started out that good," Rachel added.

Ellie continued to laugh.

"What are you two like?" Alice asked. "I left you for five minutes. Do you think you can do what took me years to study? 'Well done, Alice. You're amazing,' would've worked."

"Yeah, but wasn't it just, 'Talk and I won't answer you, but then you talk to yourself, and you'll know what you mean?'" Rachel joked. "The online talks won't be very long; make sure you get paid first."

Ellie laughed even louder.

"Fuck's sake, TT, belittle my degree into a statement like that. Not all of us have an issue with the cost of inertia."

Rachel stared at Alice through her phone. Ellie was struggling to hold it together.

"Ohhh, like your style," Rachel beamed. "You're good. You're very good."

Ellie continued to belly laugh with tears streaming down her face.

"I was thinking I could run you both through the course when Ellie comes over next month. What do you think?"

"Alice, I think that would be fantastic. I'm only jesting. That is really awesome news. Super congratulations on the commission."

"Yeah, ditto, you're such a superstar, Alice. Well done you," Ellie added. "I can't wait for us all to get together. It's going to be a blast." Then she paused, "I'm still fucked up, though."

They all burst out laughing.

Finn returned from his run and entered the bedroom covered in sweat. He stripped his clothes off and gestured to Rachel that he would take a long shower so she could carry on her call with the girls. Seeing his athletic body, Rachel quickly finished her call with Alice and Ellie, stripped out of her pyjamas and joined Finn in the bathroom.

"Can I join you?" she asked amorously.

Finn wiped the steam from the glass, looked at Rachel's tanned, naked body and smiled. "I'd like nothing better."

They made love under the steamy water, letting it wash away their worries. Finn forgot it was the same shower where he'd experienced heartache and pain. They were passionate and kissed with an intimacy they'd recently rekindled. It felt so good. After dressing, they realised they were both ravenous. Raiding the fridge to see what they could concoct, they laid most of its contents on the counter.

"Bacon, mushrooms, eggs, tomatoes, onions, brie, and spinach," Rachel detailed, "That sounds like a pretty awesome omelette to me! What do you think?"

"That sounds perfect. I'll put the coffee on. Do you want orange juice?"

"Ooh, yes, please."

Since James's condition had improved, they were in much more positive moods. The hospital visits were becoming less demanding, and they were both optimistic about their future. Rachel started preparing the food, and Finn took the ground coffee out of the fridge to make a pot of coffee. Leaning across the windowsill, he turned on the radio, and Bill Withers' *'Lovely Day'* came on.

"I swear that radio is telepathic," Rachel said after a pause.

"What do you mean?"

"It just seems to know what's going on in my head and then plays a relevant song."

"Shit! That radio is doing a better job than me," he joked.

"Oi!" Rachel laughed.

Following a massive brunch of ingredient-packed omelette and toast, they decided to slouch on the sofa for the day. Rachel quickly tidied the kitchen, and they walked into the living room with their coffee cups.

"We've had the craziest three months ever, haven't we? I'm exhausted," she said, flopping down on the sofa next to Finn and snuggling up to him. She couldn't be happier.

"It's been mad, hasn't it?" he replied, kissing her on the forehead and putting his arm around her shoulders.

"When I think back to the phone call I got from Ellie at the beginning of June to now, I can't believe what we've both been through. From arguments, disappointment, tantrums and tears to rescue missions, reconciliations, helicopter rides and intensive care, this will be one to tell the grandkids!"

Finn hugged Rachel a little harder. He loved this woman

so completely. "We sure as hell couldn't have predicted it."

She moved away from his embrace, turned towards him, and crossed her legs. "Over this short time, I've realised that no one has all the answers. All we're trying to do is play at this thing called 'life'. And what's important is understanding where we are in the moment. Right now." She wriggled a bit, getting wrapped up in her words. "It's like preparing for a sail, you've got the boat you're in, with all your resources and preparation done, but you're at the mercy of whatever the weather throws at you."

"So, like a lifeboat," he smirked.

"Ha," Rachel laughed as she lightly punched Finn's arm, "I like what you did there." She shifted in her seat again, becoming animated with her thinking. "Life is what we've been dealt, right?"

"Is that the boat in this instance?" he joked, "Or are we back to the existential sense of the word?"

"Jeez, Finn!" Rachel laughed and punched him again, "I'm trying to make sense of this. OK, so, let's say life is the boat."

"Another year blows by," Finn said, winding Rachel up and trying not to laugh.

"Stop!" Rachel stood up smiling and started walking around the lounge. "Life is what we're given, what we're dealt, and we can't change it. But we can deal with the storms, patiently wait out the doldrums, navigate the perils, and follow a course. We are the masters of our own destiny."

"Do I need a sword for that?" Finn laughed out loud.

Rachel stared at him, trying to look angry, but couldn't. She felt no negativity, stress, or animosity. She felt so good!

"Sorry, I'll stop," he said.

She laughed and sat back on the sofa with Finn. "I've

learnt so much in the last three months. Taking the time to talk openly with the important people in my life, I've realised that I can't control what others think, say or do. I can only control myself. I must stop wasting time and energy being concerned about things that I can't change and focus on things that are within my control. I'm the captain of my boat." She looked at Finn and saw he was crumbling. "Don't say it!" she said, pursing her lips.

"Aye, aye," Finn whispered, "Captain."

Rachel jumped on top of him and started play-fighting. After a few moments, they moved into a loving embrace and started passionately kissing.

The doorbell rang.

"Go away!" Rachel said, kissing Finn harder.

"I'll get it," he said, standing up, adjusting his manhood and walking to the front door.

Meanwhile, Rachel sat up on the sofa and leaned over to drink her coffee. She was ecstatically happy.

"It's for you!" Finn said, walking into the room with the biggest bunch of flowers she'd ever seen: an array of red and white roses, pink gerberas, white peonies, and red and pink sweet peas. It was beautiful!

She jumped off the sofa. "Who are they from?" she asked excitedly.

"No idea," Finn answered, "But that is some admirer. Should I be worried?"

"Don't be silly!" Rachel lifted the card and read it.

> *To the most selfless and sweet angel, Rachel,*
>
> *Thank you for rescuing our sorry asses and giving us safe passage home. We are eternally in your debt. Needless to say, we won't be chartering a boat any time soon.*
>
> *We're sorry this has taken so long to get to you. We struggled to get your address but managed to get it from a guy named Ian.*
>
> *Stay safe, and keep smiling.*
> *Love Richard, Thomas, Michael and Craig xx*

"Oh my God, it's from Serendipity! How sweet!"

"That's a very impressive bunch of flowers, Babes."

"They're gorgeous! What a lovely gesture. I'm not sure that I have a vase big enough, though," she said as she grabbed the bouquet from him and walked into the kitchen. Finn followed.

"Did you ever hear what happened to them?"

"Georgios emailed Ellie saying he'd help sort out some issues with the Port Authorities. The Coastguard wanted to impound their boat and take away their papers, citing that they were not sufficiently qualified and deliberately disregarded the safety of the charter."

"Blimey!"

"I know! Somehow, Georgios sorted it out, and they managed to fly back to Maryland a few days after I left them. I have no idea how he managed to do that."

"How does Georgios fit into this again?"

"He's an acquaintance of Gino's. Ellie said they go scuba diving together."

"It does sound all James Bond. I still can't believe you flew in a helicopter."

"If I hadn't been so concerned about getting back to the UK, I would have probably enjoyed it more."

"Do you want another coffee?"

"Oh yes, please, my last one went cold," Rachel answered as she returned to arranging her flowers.

Finn put the kettle on, came up behind her, and hugged her. "I love you, Babes, so very much. You're amazing."

She turned around and kissed him gently. She couldn't contain her joyfully happy mood. "I love you too," she said, beaming. "I can't believe how happy I am right now; it's wonderful. Thank you for being so understanding and letting me take this journey of discovery."

"I didn't let you. You kind of went of your own accord," Finn smirked, "We argued a lot before we found answers, but I'm so happy we've overcome."

"Yes, we did, and I'm sorry for all that. I can only say now that the arguments helped; it made me think."

"It made me go to Ireland," Finn nodded.

She put down the scissors and flowers she was tending and looked at Finn again. "Yes, you found some peace too. It has been helpful for us both. We've needed this. Thank you so much for helping me be happy," she smiled but then returned to her giddy mood, "And happiness is a choice, you know. It's borne out of positivity, achievement, self-worth and appreciation," she said as she adjusted the roses in the vase. "And, God, I don't want that to sound egotistical, but it's true. I'm happy because I've chosen to focus on what I have rather than what I don't; focus on who I am rather than what I'm not, and focus on the good in the world rather than the bad."

"What's changed?" Finn asked, watching his wife get all wrapped up in her speech. "Because you were searching for all of those things three months ago."

"I asked myself, 'What If?'" Rachel replied calmly. "I wanted to find answers, but I found solutions to problems that I didn't even know existed. Like I was asking the wrong questions. The whole experience with James, when I thought I might never see him again, was horrible. It made me think long and hard about how to cope with sorrow. Repeatedly arguing with you and not being there for you when you needed me was shit. I'm so sorry about that. My 'What Ifs' started to get in the way. These weren't even problems before I started my emotional journey, they appeared as a result of setting the course. Yet, once I could navigate that chaos, only then could I see the whole picture. In the search for answers, I found out who I am. I can't believe I've reconciled my differences with my mother and refreshed a relationship I never thought I'd have. I've vowed to be kinder to you and appreciate your kindness because I'm so lucky to have you in my life. I have the most amazing friends and family, and I will do my best to tell them that regularly. And I will keep asking questions because I have no idea what they will unearth. Do we want all the answers? Probably not, but we do want some answers. Shit, I'm still young; if I had all the answers, wouldn't that be boring? Questions make us feel alive. They encourage us to seek out new experiences. That's what I did. I went searching. And along the way, I found out that I'm courageous and bold. I discovered that my friendships are important and help me deal with the world. My marriage is the foundation of my happiness, and I love being a creative, free spirit. My family are the superstructure that keeps me stable, and I will always be there for them. My career does not define me but encourages me to seek challenges so that I will work hard at it." She paused and looked at Finn.

"Wow, that was quite the speech," he said, leaning against the counter, having forgotten to make coffee.

"Did I rush it?" Rachel smiled.

Printed in Great Britain
by Amazon